AMMO AND ENCHILADAS

BA TORTUGA

Ammo and Enchiladas

Copyright © 2018 by BA Tortuga

1380 Rio Rancho Blvd #1319

Rio Rancho, NM 87124

Cover illustration by AJ Corza

Published with permission

ISBN: 978-1-951532-13-0

First electronic edition published 2019

Second electronic edition published October 2019

Printed in the USA

❀ Created with Vellum

AMMO AND ENCHIL

After a night at the movies in Albuquerque, New Mexico, Brantley's best friend, Matt, is shot right in front of him during a robbery. Stunned and devastated, Brant tries to help Matt's husband, Travis, deal with the funeral details even as he struggles with his own grief and Travis's blame. When Travis's best friend arrives, Brant is both annoyed and grateful, because he is so darn tired and can use the help.

Lex Espana is ashamed to admit he hasn't seen his childhood best friend since Travis's wedding. He's even more amazed that he barely remembers Brant from that wedding, because he's sure interested now. While it's weird to fall for someone at a funeral, his feelings for Brant are real and make him long for a life he didn't realize he was missing.

Neither Lex nor Brant knows how to be part of an us, though, and they both have a lot to work through before they can settle in. To become a real couple, Brant and Lex will have to dig deep to get past the roadblocks in their relationship.

As always, to my girl. I love you. BA

THANKS

Thank you to Jodi for your support. You rock my world. BA

1

*T*he call came in at about 2:00 a.m., which was about half an hour after the swing shift coffee had worn off and Lex Espana had staggered to bed. He'd been on 7:00 a.m. to 6:00 p.m. for two weeks, barring days off, so switching to swing had him blinking and feeling brain stupid.

He groped for his phone on the nightstand and hit the button to answer just in time to keep it from going to voicemail. "'Lo?"

"L-Lex? Lex, honey?" The words dissolved into sobs on the other end of the line.

He sat up, reaching again to turn on the light. "Travis?" The voice was a bit of a blast from the past, the kind that came with calls on holidays and birthdays mostly. "What's wrong?"

"Matt. There was a shooting. Please. Please, I don't know what to do."

It took a second to put all those words together in a way that made sense. Matt was Travis's husband.

"A shooting? What? Tonight?" He hopped out of bed. "Is he okay? Is he in the hospital?"

"He's gone. He was out with a friend—a movie. I had to grade papers. They stopped for gas."

"So a gas station." Ask leading questions. They taught cops that. Let people babble and give information.

"Yeah. At the Smith's. They were getting gas, and someone tried to rob them."

"Oh God. Wait, did you say gone?" Lex went still, his whole body freezing. *Gone as in dead. Holy shit.*

"Uh-huh." There was a long, horrifying silence.

"Oh, Trav. Oh, honey, what do you need? I can come up." He'd known Travis Garcia since sixth grade. He'd been Travis's wingman. They'd been each other's experimental lovers. Confidants. And now Travis's husband was gone. Just like that.

He'd been Travis's best man at their wedding, for fuck's sake.

"Can you come? I don't know what to do next. I have no idea." Travis was so choked, Lex barely heard him.

"Of course I can. I'll be up in about three hours." This time of night, no one would be on the road, so he could fly. "I'll bring coffee and sausage biscuits. You at home?"

"Yeah, they…. He was dead from the get-go."

"Oh, hon." He tossed clothes into a bag, then his kit bag and his phone charger. "I know platitudes don't help, so I won't say them."

"Just come? I feel so lost."

"I'm on my way." God, this was…. He would call in to work on the road. He had time off coming to him, and Travis was as much family as any of the dozens of blood relatives he could pull out of the woodwork.

"Thank you. Lex, I'm freaking out."

"Okay. It's okay. I can stay on as long as you need." He would just put on the hands-free in the truck.

"No. No, I need to…. What am I going to tell his parents?"

"I don't know, but you have to call them before someone

else does." The cops might not, since Travis was the next of kin, but word got around. Someone would call to offer condolences.

"Right. Right, God. How do you do it, honey? Seriously? How do you manage?"

"I don't know, Trav. I just do. I guess it's a calling." He never questioned his need to help people.

"But how do you tell someone their... their person is gone?"

"You just do. It's the worst part of the job, even if it doesn't seem like the cop feels anything." He grabbed his bag, then looked at his one houseplant. He could ask the guys to come water it, he guessed. Dusty had given it to him, saying he needed to commit.

That was it.

He sent a text as he listened to Travis: *Nate—fam emerg. ABQ. Water plant?*

"The ones that came to the door were... nice? I guess? I don't really remember. It's an awful blur."

"I'm sure they did their job. It's too much of a shock, I think, to remember them."

"Yeah. Yeah, I... I'm scared to go upstairs. They have Brantley down at the police station for questioning, and I don't think he's going to come here."

"Who's Brantley, honey?" His natural inclination was to get all the details.

"Brant? He's Matt's best friend. You remember him from the wedding? The buff little blond. He was a soldier then. So dapper. He went to school with Matty, from kindergarten on."

"Ah, yeah." Vaguely. He'd been trying hard to hook up with the bartender at the cash bar, so he hadn't had much time to socialize. He'd bet Brant was in the pictures he had. "So, they were together?"

"Yeah. They went to the movies, remember? I was working, and I wanted to watch *Stranger Things* and get those papers done."

"Oh, honey. I hate that. Is he okay? The Brant guy? I mean, physically?"

"I think so. I haven't gotten to talk to him, but he's at the station, so he has to be okay, right?" Travis asked.

"They would have taken him to the hospital if he hadn't been." *Mental note. Check on the dapper soldier.*

"That's what I thought. He's not a suspect. Just a witness."

"That sucks for him. I know it sucks worse for you." *Poor guy, having to see his best friend gunned down.*

"You think? I mean, how… how can it be true?"

"I'm so sorry, Trav." He knew Travis just needed to babble. It happened. Matt's folks needed that call, though.

"Me too. I—" The sobs started again, hard and deep, and Lex's heart broke. *Poor baby.*

He waited out the storm, murmuring ridiculous shit like "It will be all right." Not that it would. It might take years for things to become all right for Travis.

Fuck.

"I… I'm going to call his parents. I'll be waiting for you. Thank you for coming, honey. I'm just…. I need a friend."

Lex knew Travis had a hundred friendly acquaintances— from fellow teachers to the people at their church to the mutual buddies Matt and Travis shared—but there was something about an old friend, someone who was more family than anything else.

God knew Travis could use someone who'd been his friend mainly, not the couple's. Those visits were so damn awkward and hard, when people had only known the couple and now had no idea what to do.

"I'll be there in a few hours, Trav. No worries. I'll help you out." He would get Travis through the next week or so. It was the least he could do.

"Thank you, sweetie. I'm calling Matt's people now, okay?

Call me back if you need help staying awake. I just realized what time it is."

"You know it. I love you, Travis."

"I love you."

He hung up after Travis got off the line, just shaking his head. God knew, in his line of work he was aware how fast people could die. It just never got easier when it was someone he knew personally.

His phone rang, Nate's name showing up.

"Hey, man."

"Lex, what the hell? You okay?" Nate sounded groggy but solid.

"Hey. No, I'm not. Look, can you guys take my plant for a week? My friend Travis, the one I went to the wedding in Burque? His husband was shot and killed tonight."

"Oh, shit. Shit. Man, that sucks. Is he... I mean, of course he's not okay."

"No. He's calling Matt's parents now, so I would bet I'll get another call in a bit. I'm driving up now, but you have my key."

"I do. Is there anything else you need? Anything at all?"

"Not that I can think of, but I'll call. I just got milk and eggs if you want them, huh?"

"Thanks. Keep in touch. We'll be worrying."

"Of course you will. Dorks." Dr. Dusty was a notorious worrywart. He'd give himself a stroke over keeping the damn plant alive. Nate was less OCD, but he would text every couple of hours. These days the two of them were so touchy-feely. He remembered fondly when Dusty rarely put two words together.

Of course, damn near being blown to bits had changed them all, and God knew, Dusty had been more blown than any of the rest of them.

And delivered a baby too. Lord.

"Call us if you need us," Nate repeated.

"Will do. Bye, man." Lex hung up, glad to be off the phone. He drove better with fewer distractions. He had no trouble being alone with himself.

He found the Lithium station on Sirius and put the pedal to the metal.

Travis needed him, so it looked like he was heading back home to Albuquerque. Whether he wanted to or not.

2

*B*rantley sat staring at his hands. His fingernails were filthy.

He'd cleaned his hands up, but he'd missed his nails. You'd think after all the years of scrubbing he'd never miss his nails.

"Can I get you anything, sir? Coffee? Anything?" The cop's voice was sympathetic, soft, like he was fixin' to shatter into a thousand pieces, which he reckoned he was.

Brant stared up at the detective, his vision swimming. "I.... Coffee? Please?"

"You got it. We got a K-cup thing. Coffee has been better around here." The detective moved away, and Brant wasn't sure he could remember how to breathe.

Matty. What the actual fuck? It had happened so fucking fast. The guy hadn't even given Matt a chance to give over his wallet, his keys, anything, before the motherfucker shot. The asshole panicked and ran then, or Brant had a feeling he would be dead too. Christ, how was he gonna tell Travis?

Had someone already told Travis? He closed his eyes, nausea rising up. His nails had Matt's blood under them.

As soon as the asshole had taken off, he'd been there,

trying to do triage, but the shot had gone right into Matty's temple. It was over before it had begun.

He hiccupped, and the cop handed him a paper cup.

"We'll be getting you home soon. We appreciate your patience."

"What else do you need from me?"

"Just to sign some paperwork, but that takes time to print out and get approved. I'm so sorry. I know it's been a long night."

"The longest of my life so far," he agreed. The coffee wasn't bad. Better than doctor's-office coffee.

"I can only imagine. You have my condolences."

"Thanks. I guess you see a lot of people on the longest night of their lives." He understood hard jobs; he dealt with the parents of sick kids.

"Eee-a-la, you know it. Some nights this job is all bad, huh?"

"Some nights. Tonight." He'd lost his oldest and best friend all in the matter of the same second.

"Here you go, Sarge." A uniformed officer brought in a clipboard loaded up with papers.

"Okay. I'm going to need your signature on the statement; that's all. Then we'll have an officer take you home."

"Thank you." He signed the papers, initialed all the things, and then handed back the pen. "Can they take me to my friend's house? His—his spouse is alone."

"Of course, but…. Sir. You might want to go home and change first."

"I—" He looked down at himself and almost threw up. "Oh God. Okay, yeah. Home. I can drive over."

"Yeah. Yeah, just give those back?" The papers were grabbed back, and then he was taken outside and plopped into a police cruiser. What were they going to do with Matt's car?

He guessed someone would tell Travis. He guessed. Christ.

"What address, sir?" the young cop asked. He still had pimples.

He gave them the address of his little house over off Griegos. He'd kept saying he was going to buy one day, when he decided which neighborhood to look in. Not yet, he'd said. Not quite yet.

Matty had told him life was short and he should put down roots.

He'd bought his adobe and never looked back, and his momma had cried and said he should come home to Texas. Albuquerque was too dangerous, too far away. God, she was going to lose it when he told her about Matty.

Brantley wasn't ready for that shit right now. Not at all.

No, he'd call Momma during the day, after he'd had some sleep and some food and was over his existential crisis. Which might be a few days.

Maybe a week.

It wasn't like she'd be coming out for the funeral. She was slammed with calving. Maybe he'd call Bridey, report to his brother in the morning. Bridey might be willing to talk to the folks.

Lord.

He rubbed his chin, feeling the bristles. Not much traffic this early in the morning. He needed to call in to work, give them a chance to find someone to take his shift. There was no way.

He couldn't be patient; he couldn't be calm. He just couldn't. Not after….

He shook, swallowing back bile.

"Here you go, sir. If you think of anything else at all, you have the detective's number, right?"

"I do. Y'all just catch the guy, okay? Please?"

"We'll do our best, I promise. Good night." The kid

opened the door for him, and he looked at his house, not sure what to do. The cop waited, though, so he guessed he was supposed to go inside.

He went in and locked the door, managing to make it two steps forward before pain shot up along his leg and he collapsed, right there in the foyer. The electric sensation zipped up his hip, and he groaned, grabbing at it.

"Dammit!" He sobbed softly, shaking his head as he let the pain move through him, cleanse him.

He hit the floor with the flat of his hand, furious as hell at the whole world. Matt was his goddamn friend. Had been. Whatever. How was he supposed to do this, here, Stateside where they were supposed to be safe?

He covered his face with his hands, hiding his sobs. Not that there was anyone to hide from. Oh, Lord. What a fucking mess. What a fucking, awful mess. Anything like this happened to him, he would normally call Matt....

Travis. He needed to go clean up, change clothes, and get to Travis.

He would grab some Whataburger or something. Maybe just coffee.

Maybe....

Please God, let me get up. Let me go take care of things. Let me do this. Please.

Brant grabbed the doorknob on the front door and hauled his ass up off the floor. Travis didn't need to be alone, and he could help with that. He tugged out his phone and looked at the time—4:18 a.m. Jesus.

Matt had been dead for six hours. Six hours.

He called work, left a message. "Hey, Cherie. Can you call Lena and see if she can fill in for me? There was a terrible incident tonight and a friend of mine got shot." His voice broke on the last word. "Call me if you need. I'll be at his husband's."

Stumbling over his own boots, he made his way to the

bedroom to strip off his stiff clothes. He needed to shower, just so he didn't stink of blood when he went to see Travis.

He needed to....

Wash Matt off him.

He wadded up his clothes after he took them off, then stuffed them into the bottom of the hamper so he didn't have to think about them. The water was steaming by the time he stepped in, even if he felt like he was cold and shriveled. He was afraid nothing would ever feel right again.

"I'm sorry, Matt. I swear to God. I.... There was nothing I could do. Nothing at all."

So fast. It had all happened so fast. And God knew, he'd been trained to handle armed assailants. No one could fight a point-blank headshot.

Matt was strong, but damn.

He turned his face up to the spray, letting it burn away the returning tears. He had to get his shit together before he went to see Travis. Had to.

If he was lucky, Travis would just hit him with a baseball bat, put him out of his misery.

Not that Travis had a mean bone in his body. The guy taught second grade. No, Travis would give him big, sad eyes. And Brant would deserve them.

3

*L*ex pulled up to Travis's house about five with coffees for them. His eyes burned, and he was running on caffeine and stress and grunge music. He blinked, hands on the wheel for a moment, willing the road noise to stop. His body felt as if it was still moving.

It wasn't. Hell, there had already been a dozen people at the house from what he'd heard, maybe more. Travis must have called in the whole phone tree. He'd just been the first.

He sighed. Okay. Okay, he could do this. He climbed out of the truck, his body feeling a little like frozen rope. Travis's house was lovely—a two-story McMansion in adobe with a flat roof and a balcony overlooking the East Mountains. It was always good to have a view. His place in Cruces looked out at the Organ Mountains, so he got it.

The porch light was on, so he walked up, trying to convince his heavy feet to move. He knocked on the door, then saw the doorbell. He was about to ring it when the door opened. "Can I help you?" A tired, lean man with bright blue eyes stared at him, looking bleary.

"Hey. Is Travis still awake?" Lex would go sleep in the truck if he needed to.

"He is. You are…?"

"Lex. Travis called me and asked me to come up." He was too tired for this shit.

"Of course. Sorry. I thought I recognized you. I'm Brant. Come on in. He's in the bedroom. I'll take you to him."

"Brant…. Oh, man, I'm so sorry. He said you were there." Lex reached out to the guy instinctively.

"Yeah." Brant's face tried to crumple.

Oh, poor guy. Lex put a hand on his shoulder. "Are you okay? Do you need to get some sleep?"

"I'm trying to… I'm just trying to help. Do you need a cup of coffee?"

"Oh God, no. I brought sausage biscuits." He held up the bag. "I could eat, if there's a place in the kitchen, but I want to see Trav first."

"Do you know where the master is?"

"Uh. No." He chuckled. "I'm ashamed to admit I haven't been up since they bought this house."

"Come on. I'll show you." Brant grabbed a crutch and started moving up the stairs, nice and slow.

"Hey, I can—" He cut himself off because Brant gave him this look over one shoulder. It said off-limits, so Lex let it slide.

None of his.

He was here for Travis.

"There you go." Brant jerked his chin toward the door at the end of the hall. "I'll put your food away somewhere safe or it will get gone."

"Thank you, man. I appreciate it." He handed over the bags and headed into the bedroom, feeling like he was walking a gauntlet.

"Trav? Honey? Are you asleep?" He said it softly, not wanting to wake his friend up if he was resting.

"I'm never going to sleep again, Lex." Travis sat up, lean face drawn and streaked with tears. "Matty's gone, Lex."

Lex went to sit on the bed next to Travis. "Oh. Hey. I'm so sorry, Trav."

Travis landed in his arms, the sobs hard and raw. Lex held on, giving what little comfort he could. What was he supposed to say? The man's husband was gone.

All he knew to do was make noises and hope his being there made things less awful. He stroked Travis's hair and breathed. The bedroom was totally a couple's space—two dressers, two chairs, pictures of the two of them on the walls. Jesus. He had only known Matt a little bit, phone calls at holidays, birthday presents because he had automatic shipping set up.

Now he wished he knew more so when Travis inevitably began reminiscing, he could manage more than a smile and nod. Of course, maybe that was enough. If what he knew about Matt was through Travis, then he could know just what Travis told him.

He shook his head, trying to just close his eyes and be there with Travis. If being a cop had taught him anything, it was to be any way people needed him to be in a crisis. Tough love to gentle sympathy, Lex could do them all.

It was harder when it was someone you knew, someone you loved.

When Travis was down to sniffles, Lex grabbed the box of Puffs on the closest nightstand. "Here, hon."

"Thanks. My head is killing me. I guess that's normal."

"It is. Do you have a bottle of water?" That would help.

"Brant brought a cooler up—water, pineapple juice. He's a caretaker."

"What's with his leg?" Couldn't be easy, what with the crutches.

"Brantley? He was shot in combat. Right in the hip."

"Oh, man. That sucks." Joints were the worst.

"Yeah, he was a field medic. He was rescuing someone.

He's a hero. He came out here after nursing school because of Matt. I bet he goes back to Texas now."

"Because of Matt?" Wait, had he missed something?

"Yeah. Matt loved it so much, you know? And he just talked Albuquerque up. Great weather, great people—he left out the crazy crime part."

"Yeah." He grimaced. That had gotten worse as people had gotten more desperate, but Burque had always had a reputation. New Mexico was a poor state.

"He was just getting gas."

"That sucks, honey. I'm so sorry."

"I mean, he would have given the guy anything. He didn't fight, not Matt. Matt was gentle."

"No." He tilted his head. "You don't think his friend…?"

"I don't think his friend what?" Travis looked utterly confused.

"Tried to fight back. Started a scuffle." Contrary to what a faction of the public believed, fighting back, carrying a weapon to foil criminals, usually failed miserably.

"He would have fought back, sure, but it went too fast. Brantley said the guy didn't hesitate. Either it was a hair trigger or he just shot. There wasn't a chance."

"Oh." He patted Travis's arms, which he still held. "Oh God." He'd seen it happen, and it was just pure reaction.

"Yeah. He said it was fast. He said Matt never hurt. That he never even knew."

"I imagine not. Can I get you anything?" He felt useless. Was he really helping? Jesus, he hoped so.

"No. No, I just… I'm glad you're here. There's going to be all this… stuff. Funeral and police and news cameras…."

"I'll help any way I can." That he knew how to manage. Police. Media people. Funerals he had less experience with, but how hard could it be? They walked you through it.

"Thank you. Thank you. Brantley set up the guest room for you. Made the bed up and everything."

"Oh, I'll have to thank him." And retrieve his food. "Do you want to sleep now, honey? I can buzz off for a while and get some rest too."

"I'll try. Brantley promised to hang out and deal with shit."

"Then we have a team. You want me to stay and sleep in here?" He so would if Trav needed him.

"Go have some food and coffee. I'll call you, huh? I just want… I want him to come home."

"I know." That much he did know. He'd heard it a hundred times. Maybe a thousand. He gave Travis a kiss on the cheek. "I'll be downstairs and then in the guest room. Text me for anything."

"Okay." The sobs started up again, but what could he do? At this point, Travis was going to have to mourn. Maybe he just needed to cry it out until he slept.

Lex slipped out of the room and headed downstairs to hunt up his biscuits. He found Brantley in the kitchen, sitting with his head in his hands.

"Hey, man. Do you need anything?" Lex asked, feeling bad for the guy, who was pale, his face lined.

"No. No, you need coffee? I put your biscuits in the microwave."

"Is there anything like milk? Trav always used to have some. I think I drank enough coffee to burn a hole in my stomach." Lex needed that food. "Hey, I got enough to share if you want."

"I'll get you a glass." Brant stood slowly, the man looking eighty years old.

"I can do it."

Brant gave him that same look, the one from the stairs. "I'm not helpless, buddy. I can get a damn glass."

"I was just trying to help. You look beat. And beat up."

"Just been a shit day."

Yeah, for all of them, but for this guy most of all, he'd bet.

Lex grabbed the milk out of the fridge. Okay, he would get groceries later today. Travis and Matt ate like birds, but he worked out at least an hour a day, and he ate to fuel his muscles. He needed to make a list.

He poured a glass of milk for himself, then hovered the carton over the other glass Brant had pulled out, raising his eyebrows.

"Please." Brantley went to the microwave and pulled the bag of biscuits out.

"Sure. There's enough for both of us to have two biscuits and a hash brown. It would be nice if I don't have to eat breakfast alone."

"Thank you. I'll be happy to."

"Cool." That was… well, it *was* cool. If he could make things easier for anyone involved, then he was doing his job. Or his good work, or being a friend. God, he was so tired he was losing it. He tugged a biscuit out of the bag.

"The guest room is ready for you, when you're ready for it."

"Where are you sleeping?"

"I'm just dealing with stuff down here."

"That wasn't what I asked. Look, I brought an air mattress. I have it in my truck. You can have the guest bed, and I can sack out on the floor."

"Huh?" Brant looked utterly confused, totally.

"After breakfast. You need sleep. Enough I would worry about you driving home." He didn't want the guy to cause an accident or hurt himself or something. Travis would freak out.

"I'll just sit up in the front room. People will come." And soon Mr. Brant was going to snap all in half.

"We can take turns with folks, if need be." He opened Brant's biscuit and pushed it over. "Come on, man. Trav says you're a nurse. You know how important it is to keep up your strength."

"Yeah." Brant stared at the food like it was alive and moving.

"Hey." He reached over to touch the back of Brant's hand. "One bite. That will be enough to make it start to taste good, huh?"

"You swear?"

"Yeah, man. I do. I swear. One bite."

Brant nodded and picked a bite off the biscuit. Sure enough, after Brant washed it down with some milk, he grabbed the hash brown and munched at it too. Excellent. The color came back into Brant's face, even if the heavy lines didn't fade.

They finished up in silence, and Lex's ass was dragging hard by the time he took his last bite. Brant put the glasses in the dishwasher, so he tossed the trash.

"How about that nap?"

"People...."

"There are two women in the living room, man. They can handle anything, I bet."

"I don't even remember who they are." Brantley began to shake, violently.

"Come on. Do you need the crutch?" He would just support Brant up the stairs.

"No. No, I only use it when the pain is really bad...."

Oh, man. Poor baby. This was shock. Real, genuine shock. Lex knew how to deal with that. Warm blankets and sleep. He steered Brant up the stairs, then to the guest room that had been indicated. "Bathroom?"

"That's the guest room, sir."

"Uh-huh. You're coming with me. We'll rest together." Lex took Brant's arm, leading the way. He'd get the guy settled, then go get the air mattress.

They got into the room, Lex opening up the door and finding a classy-assed, decorated in the Santa Fe–style guest room.

"I made it up for you." Brantley was barely holding on, barely with him.

"You did. Still, we can share. No one will know." Hell, there was a freaking king bed in here. They could split it, no air mattress required. He eased Brantley down on the bed.

"I need to… help. I tried to."

"You did. Now it's time to rest." He stripped off Brant's shirt before encouraging him to stretch out. "Shoes too."

Brant was covered in little bruises, looked like from the impact of Matt against him, and his hands were destroyed. Christ. He wanted to make Brant wash up, but not for any reason but comfort. It could wait.

They stretched out together, leaving a careful space between each other.

Lex thought it would be really hard to sleep next to someone, since he never did. He expected it to keep him awake, tossing and turning.

It didn't.

4

---

*C*rying woke him up, and he shot out of bed, stumbling a few steps before crashing to the ground, his leg giving out.

"Coming. Coming." He crawled toward Travis, toward the sobs. "I'm on my way."

"Wha?" That voice came from behind him, the sound utterly disorienting. He shook it off, hitting the door to find Travis sitting in the doorway to the master, face in his hands.

"Hey. Hey, honey." Brant got to him, tugged Travis into his arms. "I got you."

God. This broke his heart. He wasn't even awake enough to do this.

"I was dreaming. Oh God, what an awful dream. There were worms."

"Shh. It's okay. You're going to be okay." *Maybe. Someday.*

"I don't know." Travis was just—this wasn't fake. This was devastation.

"I'm sorry, honey. I'm so sorry."

"Why wasn't it you? Why was it him?"

Brant felt himself shrink. He didn't know. He'd been in the car for most of it. He'd been digging in his wallet for some cash for the Sonic. They'd wanted cherry limeades. He'd wrenched himself out when he heard the yelling.

"Hey." The Lex guy was there in seconds, lifting Travis up off the floor. "Let's get you back to bed, and I'll bring you something to help you sleep without the bad dreams. Huh?"

"I want him home, Lex. I need him home."

Brant headed to the stairwell, scooting on his butt to pull himself up. Travis was screaming, sobbing hysterically, and Brant worked down the stairs, then called one of the doctors at his office to explain he needed something. He needed help.

"Hey, Brant. What's up?" Naomi would have his back.

"You heard about what happened last night?"

"Yeah. It's all over the news."

"I need Xanax, something. Please." He didn't know what Travis had up there, but he knew he'd need something if things didn't ease up.

"I'll talk to Sharon. No worries. Are you okay?"

"No." No, he wasn't, but he had to be.

"I'm sorry, kiddo. You just tell us what you need."

"Just a few days off and that script, please. Pharmacy info's in my file."

"You got it." They hung up, and he winced, thinking how Travis had asked why not him.

That was a good question. Why not him? Matty was the first one out of the car. Matty was the one who was driving. Matty was the one who was going to pump the gas. He was the one with the wallet out. Matty was the one without the shattered hip and the THC candy that took the edge off.

But Travis didn't know or care about that. He'd lost a husband, and Brant was just… the husband's best friend.

"You okay?" Lex appeared in the kitchen, almost making him fall down again.

He nodded once, his voice just gone. What did he have to say? Why hadn't it been him?

"Liar." Lex said it gently, the way any stranger would when looking at him, probably.

"Yeah. Well. It was a rough night." And Travis hated him.

"I'm sorry. Travis didn't mean it, right." Lex was watching him, that expression knowing.

"Sure he did. I can't blame him. He loves Matt."

"Yes." Lex sighed. "I see it a lot. People lash out because they're hurting so bad."

"Yeah. I'm a nurse. I get that. I do." He dealt with brand-new babies, with cranky toddlers, with hysterical teenagers. And then there were the parents. Jesus.

"Yeah? I have a friend who's an ER doctor in Cruces. He gets a lot of freaked-out people."

"ER is a fast-paced job. Takes a certain type of person."

"It does. What are you in?" Lex started making coffee, the K-cup maker easy to spot, its little rack right next to it, full of coffee pods.

"Pediatrics." He sat there like a lump, a sore, aching lump.

"Oh, ow. Kids. That has to be heartbreaking." Lex made two cups. "Cream or sugar?"

"Both, please." His belly was raw, acidy as fuck.

"You got it. Would you rather have another glass of milk? Or tea? Wasn't Matt a tea drinker…?"

"He was, yeah. We teased him endlessly. The coffee will be fine."

"Okay." Lex fixed a cup before handing it to him.

"Thank you, sir." Brantley watched his hand shake, and he took a deep drink.

"You're welcome." Lex sat again. "Look, I only had two sleeping pills. I had them just in case, you know? Can we call Travis's doctor and get something for him?"

"I have a call in to my guy. I'd be happy to call his doctor, if I can figure out who that is."

"Okay. We'll find his address book. He always had one. Maybe it's on his phone now."

"Are you in Las Cruces still?" He knew he'd heard Lex's name, some, but he hadn't known much.

"I am, yeah. I drove up." Lex stifled a yawn.

"You're a good man. Thank you for letting me share your bed."

"No problem. No way were you driving home."

"I told Travis I'd stay as long as he needed. The police are going to want to talk to me again, and the news vans are out there."

"Oh, shit. I didn't even think of that. I guess this is news, huh?" Lex sighed, shaking his head. "I usually get to leave, so I miss a lot of this shit."

"Yeah. I guess." He didn't know. He didn't care.

"Anyway. I need to run out there and get my bag. I need to brush my teeth and all."

"Good luck." He'd offer to go for Lex, but there was no way.

"Thanks." A faint smile pulled at Lex's lips. "Be right back." Lex stood, then pulled a windbreaker off the hook by the back door to cover his bare chest. He tugged up the hood too, suddenly anonymous.

"Very nice." The temptation to watch him go was huge, but he was sore and tight.

Hell, as soon as Lex was out the door, Brant put his head down, trying not to cry or pass out or something. His head spun, and he thought maybe he should add more sugar to his coffee.

The door opened and closed, and he felt a touch to the back of his neck. "Let me get you a cold cloth."

"Mmm 'kay." He didn't think it would help, but if it made Lex feel better, so be it. Then the cold, wet cloth hit his skin, and goose bumps broke out, it felt so good. "Oh God."

"I know." Lex chuckled softly. "Remember to breathe."

"Right. In and out." He remembered this from school. No passing out.

"There. Let me change it out one more time." Lex put a different cloth on, the nap a little deeper. It gave him more chills, but it felt too good to say anything.

"Thank you." He was buzzing, everything just a little too much, a little too bright.

"You're welcome. Will you eat grilled cheese? I need something."

"I will. I like a good grilled cheese. Hell, I like a bad one."

"I'm on it." Lex was a machine, moving around the kitchen and tugging out bread, cheese, and butter.

"I'll go get Travis a bill of groceries today."

"We'll see what's what. I'm not sure what happened to the ladies who were here last night. They might go today."

"Yeah. The teachers from the school will start coming this afternoon. The people from Matt's work will too, I have no doubt." He wasn't sure how to help, but he was prepared to do what he needed to.

"Have you had anyone look at your hands?"

"Huh?"

Lex looked back over his shoulder. "Your hands."

He looked down at his hands, which were all scraped up and yeah, stained with blood even though he'd scrubbed. Yay. Thank God he'd gotten off work.

"Couple of those are bad enough to bandage," Lex added.

"I'll put some peroxide on them in a bit, yeah. Thanks." He guessed that was from where his hands hit the asphalt.

"If you need help, holler. I thought about changing to EMT for a bit, and I took some classes, so I know the basics." Lex just seemed way too functional after… three hours of sleep? Four?

"Yeah? That's a lot of cross-training. Good for you, man."

"I guess? Not sure my captain thinks so." Lex stacked cheese and bread.

"Why not? I don't understand."

"Oh, I think he worries I'll leave. I gotta admit, Cruces can be tough, and after the bomber thing, I got a little squirrely."

"Oh? Were you there then? Did you work that?"

"Oh hell yeah. It was ugly."

"I'm sorry to hear that." That was why he worked peds, right? Some of the stuff that went on in hospitals would curl a guy's hair. The statistics were nuts.

"Travis said you saw combat?"

"I did." He swore he felt his hip twinge.

"I'm sorry. No one should have to see a war zone." Lex put sammies into a press he hadn't even known Travis and Matt had.

"I agree." God, he didn't know what to do. He was the king of small talk, and suddenly he was dried up.

"You want some sliced tomato? There's one here on the counter that needs to get used." Lex seemed to be focused on food talk, which worked.

"Please. Uh. Do you want chips or anything?"

"I could crunch if there's something." Lex rewarded him with a smile, a real one this time, which made him blink.

Jesus—William Levy meets Diego Luna. Pretty, pretty. Lean, strong. Okay, he wasn't dead. Good to know.

Lex sliced tomatoes, so Brant got up to grab a bag of Ruffles. He needed to see if Trav needed food, but if he was sleeping….

Sleep was more important. The work ladies would start to bring casseroles. Travis's momma would come from Durango soon. Neither of Trav's people drove well at night.

God, his thoughts were just circling and doubling over on one another.

He shook his head, sitting back with his chips. Lex traded coffee for a Coke from the fridge, then joined him with the sandwiches. This time he thought he could eat without the initial nausea.

He wasn't sure if he wanted to be here when Travis's people showed up. He'd have to come when Matt's did. Maybe he needed to get them all hotel rooms. Maybe he needed to get himself a hotel room and crawl into a bottle of something.

"Do you know the plan? I mean, for the rest of today?"

He snorted, damn near choking on his sandwich. "Trav's people will be here in an hour or two. Matty's people are thirteen hours away, so... they'll be here about the same time? The police said they'd call. Matt is at the coroner's office, getting autopsied, because what if it wasn't the bullet to the brain that killed him?"

"Huh. Well, if it didn't, it was sure overkill." Lex shook his head.

"It was. Trust me. I was right there."

"I'm sorry. Cop humor sucks." Lex gave him that look, the one that he probably used as a cop too. Sympathy on demand.

"I hear you. Nurse humor is probably the same. I'm just... I'm not... I just need to find my brain." His brain was... broken. Or was that his heart?

"It will take time. Trust me, after the big bomb went off at the hospital, it took me a couple of weeks to even start thinking like myself."

"Yeah. Were you hurt?" He thought maybe he would feel better if he'd been injured somehow.

"I got whacked in the head." Lex chuckled. "That was sucky."

"Oh man. Head injuries can fuck you up for days."

"Yeah." Something grim passed over Lex's features.

"I'm sorry." He couldn't swallow all of the sudden, so he stopped, took a couple of deep, deep breaths. He needed to get the fuck out of New Mexico. Away from the crime. Away from... everything.

"Not your fault." Lex shook it off. "You want a Coke or something? The coffee just seemed super acidy."

"I think I need some Sprite or 7-Up or something."

"Yeah. I think there's some Sprite." Lex was up again in seconds, hunting. He seemed to need to move.

"That would rock." If not, he'd go get some at the corner store.

Sure enough, Lex found him a Sprite in the pantry closet and fixed it over ice for him.

"Thank you, sir. You rock." He felt about as worthless as tits on a boar hog.

"I just feel weird." Lex waved a hand. "I mean, Trav called and I came, right? What do I do now?"

"He'll need help with the funeral and all the family. You ever met Matty's people outside the wedding?"

"No." Lex plopped back down, elbows on the table. "What are they like?"

"Great big goofy rednecks—they own a diner, have for thirty years. It's wildly successful. I worked there, you know? When I was a teenager. Me and Matty both." God, they'd had fun together, and Martha and John were good, happy people.

"Oh, how cool." Lex just grinned. "They sound amazing."

"And loud and exhausting." This time Brant was the one to smile. And Matty was their only child. "I don't know how I'm going to face them. How I'm going to explain."

"You're not at fault here, Brant." Lex reached out to him again, and he let Lex touch his arm. "If they ask what happened, you tell them, but there was nothing you could do."

"No one cares about that part. They just want to know why." And it hurt to know that he hadn't been... what? Fast enough? Strong enough?

"I know. That's them, though. You were there, and you know."

"There was nothing I could do. It was over before I got out of the car."

"Then just keep telling yourself that." Lex was so serious.

"It's the truth. He was dead before he hit the ground."

"No, I mean it." Lex shook his head. "I didn't mean to sound flip."

"I just…. He was my best bud. I would have done anything. I didn't slack. I tried my best." His voice cracked, and he pushed himself up to his feet, his hip screaming. "I swear to God. I would take his place."

"Oh, son. Don't you think we know that?" John Isham was right there, grabbing him under the arms as he nearly fell. "You'd no more hurt Matty than you'd hurt a child."

"You look like hell, son." Martha hugged him from the side, letting John support him.

"I'm so sorry, Mom. I swear to you. I tried to save him. I swear to God."

"Son, you're not the Good Lord. You can't perform miracles. Have you slept at all?" Martha looked like hell on earth, like she'd aged thirty years.

"Yeah. Some."

"Good. Travis upstairs?"

"Yes, ma'am."

"Okay." She disappeared without another word.

He stared at Pop Isham. "I'm sorry. I'm so sorry."

"I know it. I do. He's your best friend." Pop was patting his upper arms. "You need to sit. Finish your sandwich, Brant. We're here." Pop glanced up, nodded to Lex. "You're Travis's best man, eh? The policeman?"

"Yes, sir." Lex held out a hand, shaking Pop's. "I'm so sorry, sir."

"Me too. Are you going to be helping to get the fucker that killed my boy?"

"I'll look into it with the locals, absolutely." Lex said it easily.

"Good. I want him off the streets. Asshole. I hope his frig-gin' heart explodes." That was Pop.

"I do too." Lex glanced at Brant. "I imagine you want something slower and more painful."

"I want to shoot him in the belly and let him go septic."

They all nodded, and Pop sighed. "Is there coffee, boys?"

"Yes, sir. I'm on it." Brant limped over to the Keurig.

"You land on your hip yesterday, son?"

"Yessir."

"Well, shit." Pop surprised a laugh out of him with that. "You got your stuff with you?"

"No, sir. I just went home and showered, then came over here."

"We'll run you back today and get some stuff together if you want to stay over here, but if you want to go on home, I understand." The way Pop said it meant he would be staying.

"I don't know what he needs, Pop. I don't know what to do. I have a guest room. I can keep folks."

"Oh, that would be a help. We'll stay with you once his momma and daddy get here. If it won't be a problem."

"No, sir. Never. I—" He squeezed his eyes closed as anxiety hit him again. *Stop it. This is Matty's daddy! This man just lost his son. This isn't about you.* "You're always welcome."

"Thank you." Pop hugged him with one arm. "Where are you staying, Lex?"

"Wherever there's room. I have an air mattress, so I can sack out in Trav's office."

"Trav's people will have their RV. They'll just hook up in the driveway."

"Oh. Right." Lex gave them a rueful look. "I've kept in touch with Travis, but his folks have always been a bit of a mystery."

"They're retired. Living the good life."

Pop snorted. "Must be nice."

"You love it," Brant accused, handing over the cup. "That diner is your life."

"Yeah. Yeah, it is. It's been…." Pop looked at him, the man's face crumbling, and Brant went to him, holding on tight.

He couldn't fix this. He couldn't, but he could cry with his adoptive parents. He could mourn and hold on.

5

*L*ex slipped out of the room, leaving Brant and Mr. Isham alone. He had no idea what to do, so he moved to the front room to look out the window. Were the press ready to give up?

Yeah, no. Christ on a pink sparkly crutch. The local news vans were lined up along the road.

Okay. He pulled the curtain back into place. He ought to go set up the air mattress in the office. That way someone else could use the guest room. Then he would start making lists. And call the local PD. He still had contacts. He wanted to speak to Brantley, find out exactly what happened, see if he remembered anything new.

The shock from last night was wearing off, so this would be a great time to sit down and go over it.

Somewhere quiet, somewhere he could take notes.

He would wait until Brant was done with Mr. Isham, though. It would be rude to push.

Mrs. Isham came down the stairs, her face haunted. "Do I know you? You're… Travis's old friend, right?"

"Yes, ma'am." His feet moved before his brain kicked in, walking him over to her. "What can I do?"

"He's sleeping. I can't believe it. And poor Brant. To have been there and not be able to help. That's so hard."

"It is." He knew how frustrating, terrifying, and downright awful it was to be helpless when someone hurt a friend. "I'm so sorry." He imagined he would say that a lot in the coming days.

"Me too. Do you know anything? I mean, anything more than it was a robbery? I didn't want to ask Travis."

"I haven't heard anything else. I still have a contact here on the force, and I was just waiting for him to be in at work before I called."

"Oh. Thank you. I just… you want a reason, right? Some reason the guy chose Matt."

"I know." He took a deep breath, not wanting to be awful but needing to say it. "You know there's usually not a good one. Reason. If the perp is caught and someone asks…."

"I just… he's a good man. No drugs, nothing like you see on the TV that's risky."

"You watch the forensics shows?" Was that weird, to try to distract her with small talk? "Would you like something to drink?"

"I watch a lot of ID. Yeah, I'll come make iced tea. How are you doing, honey?"

"Tired, but I'm here to do whatever you and Travis need me to." He walked her to the kitchen, where Brant and Mr. Isham were sitting now.

"I don't suppose you know when they'll release his body to us?"

"No, ma'am. Let me slip away for a minute and call my friend." He smiled at all and sundry, then ducked out of the room again. They needed information; they needed to be able to do for Travis. And Matt.

He was exhausted, like to the bone, but he was the one who was the farthest removed. He was the cop; he had experience and contacts.

Lex called his old buddy Juliano Apodaca, figuring he'd be settling in for coffee at his desk.

"Apodaca." Oh, he would know that gravel-and-whiskey voice anywhere.

"Hey, buddy. Alex Espana." He wanted to make sure Juliano remembered him, so the *Alex* was more likely than *Lex*.

"Espana? No shit. I haven't seen you in forever. What's up?"

"Well, you heard about the gas station shooting overnight? Matthew Isham would be the victim." Just saying Travis's husband's name made his stomach hurt.

"Yeah. Yeah, you got info on it?" The sound of Juliano's voice went from curious to interested.

"I have an in with the witness, but the family has some questions. Can we exchange?"

"Sure. We don't have much. We're looking at the video, but it looks like a robbery with a hair trigger."

"Damn. Well, I know the witness, Brant, interviewed with you guys already, but I'll sit with him today and talk turkey." He was pretty good at the interview, even if he was just at the point where he was going to take his detective exam. "Can you find out when they can release the body? Matt's folks are here."

"Sure. Sure, I'll make some inquiries."

"Thanks. I would love to take you to lunch as soon as things calm down out there a little. We've got three news vans."

"Frigging coyotes. Make sure the family tells the funeral home to call the coroners. You using Daniels?"

"I'll find out. I don't even know if the family knows." He needed paperwork. God, his head was killing him.

"It'll be tomorrow at the earliest. Trujillo and Luz will be by this afternoon late. I'll tag along."

"Thanks, man. I really appreciate it. This is.... Well, the guy's husband is my best friend from when we were kids."

"Damn. That sucks. My condolences. We'll do our best, no?"

"You always do, Juliano. Always."

"This your cell?"

"It is."

"I'll text so you have mine."

"You're a prince." He totally would take Juliano out for lunch this week. Just knowing everyone was going to push this case forward a little because he was in town and asking about it was good for Lex's soul.

"I'll text you when I know we're coming."

"Got it. I'll see you." He hung up, wanting to do a fist pump. He was doing something now, something useful, something real.

Lex headed back to the kitchen to get a drink. Maybe if he set up his bed in the office, he could snoop for papers. They needed to know what the life insurance was, the funeral wishes, all that bullshit.

He needed Tylenol and that drink, though.

The Ishams sat with Brant, two cups of coffee and a Sprite on the table, and they looked up at him.

Brantley had some blue damn eyes on him.

"I called the local PD. They'll stop by this afternoon and fill us in. Does anyone know who is doing the, uh, arrangements?"

"I want to talk to Travis about it. He says he's not ready yet."

Lex shook his head at Martha's words. The world didn't stop for mourning.

"Well, the best guys in this area are Daniels. They're great to work with. If he hasn't picked something else, I'll get the number so you can call." He could push Travis because it wasn't fair at all to put off Martha.

"Y'all know what's best. I have room in the family plot back home, but it's whatever Travis and Matt discussed. We're here to help, not be evil."

"You're good people, huh? I can tell." He smiled as gently as he could, then glanced at Brantley, not sure why he felt obligated to check in.

"He wanted to be cremated. At least that's what he told me once. I was telling him I wanted to be sprinkled in Galveston, and he wanted to stay here in New Mexico." Brant laughed, the sound soft.

"Yeah? That helps." He would leverage that on Travis.

"Yeah. We were all bullshitting one day. We'd lost a mutual friend to liver cancer, and we were having a beer in his honor."

"Oh, that's so sad." Mrs. Isham began to sniff.

"Sorry, Mom."

"No, I mean about your friend. Doesn't surprise me at all Matt wanted to stay here. The mountains, I imagine."

"Yeah, up in the Sangre de Cristo, where he went hiking all the time." Brantley smiled faintly in a remembering kind of way. "I used to think he was crazy, wandering around up there." Brant swayed a little bit. "I need a cup of coffee."

"No, you need sleep." Mr. Isham stared Brantley down when he would have argued.

"If you want that air bed in the office, man…. That way you're farther from Travis." Lex made the offer willingly. Travis looked like hell.

"It might be better on my hip to just sleep on the floor." Brantley sighed. "Yeah, please? I don't think I can wake up that way again."

"Sleep. Seriously. Take a pain pill and go rest, son."

"Okay." Brantley stood. "You'll be here?"

Martha nodded. "We will."

Brant followed Lex up the stairs, after Lex stopped to get the air bed. Lex hefted it on his shoulder like it weighed nothing and managed a watery grin. "This is a great one. Really good one. It gives great support."

"I'm sorry."

"You've been through a nightmare, Brant. Please. Rest." Lex took Brant's arm and helped him up the last few steps. "Let me just set this up." He knew there was a family room in the back of the house. Lex would sack out on the couch for a bit.

Brant watched him work, the look blank, almost dazed.

That interview was gonna have to wait. Damn. He used the tiny pump to jack up the bed. "There you go. Let's find a blanket." He hit the hall and found linens and stuff in the closet. Brant was just standing, staring, when he came back, so Lex made up the bed, then eased Brant down.

"You're with friends," he whispered.

"I don't know what to do, Lex."

"Rest. If you can, rest. Did you have pills somewhere?"

"I have them." Brant had brought up his Sprite, and he pulled out his wallet, where there was a little baggie with pills and a piece of what Lex would bet was THC candy. "Thanks."

"Holler if you need me."

"If y'all need me, call."

"You got it." Lex squared his shoulders. He would check on Travis. Still asleep, and Lex would leave him. Awake, and he would handle the funeral home thing.

He closed the door on the office before he peeked in at Travis. Travis was sitting on the edge of the bed, staring out the window toward the East Mountains.

"Hey, Trav." Lex went into the room to sink down on the bed, about two feet from Travis. "Get some sleep finally?"

"I guess? I don't remember. Did you get some rest?"

"No." He winked, because that always made Travis laugh. Today it didn't even get a smile. "I need to ask a few hard questions, and then I can get you some soup or something."

"Okay. Ask away." Travis reached out and grabbed one of his hands.

He held on, offering solid comfort, he hoped. "What funeral home do you want to use? Daniels?"

"Yeah. That's fine. He wants to be cremated. He doesn't want a big thing. I mean, we weren't hard-core church people, but everyone will need a place to cry and all."

"They will. That's perfect. The nearest one? Or did you have something arranged at a particular place?"

"Just the nearest." Travis's grip tightened.

"Okay. Is there paperwork you need me to dig out?"

"I don't know. I mean, there's insurance, there's the 401(k). Thank God we're married. That makes everything easier. Do they think they'll find the guy? Is Brantley okay?"

"He's sleeping finally. Matt's mama and papa seemed to help him relax, huh? They have the guy on video, I think. My guy on the force says it looks totally random, though, so I think it's going to depend on someone turning him in."

"It was just bad luck? Just his bad luck to need gas?" Travis shook his head. "Christ, Lex. How am I supposed to understand this?"

"Oh, honey." He pulled on that captive hand and took Travis in his arms. "I'm not sure you ever will. It will never, ever make sense. I wish I could make it better."

"I want him to come home and tell me it was all a joke. A terrible mistake, but Brantley would never do that. Are they going to let me see him? Say goodbye?"

"Well, I asked when they would release him, and they said to get the funeral home with the coroner. I think it might be better for you to see him at Daniels if you want to do that before they do what they need to do." He hated this, how flat and lifeless Travis's voice sounded, how stiff Trav was against him.

"Is he… is it… do you know how it will be?"

"Well, it will be awful, but if it's important to you to see him in person, they can make it better at Daniels before you come in. The coroner's office would be... shocking." He'd seen more than his share of DBs, and it was always jarring, even with a stranger. A loved one was weirdly disorienting.

"Okay. Thank you for coming out and helping me. My parents are coming—I may have to hide in the bathroom until they leave." That was almost a smile.

"Oh, amigo, your padres are always complicated, right?"

"Always. Good, but complicated. Mama's not doing so good, you know. She remembers a lot, but.... You know she's going to ask where Matt is."

"Oh God." He sat back and stared at Travis. "Okay, I'll run interference. Last hard question. How soon do you want the service after they release him?"

"Soon. I want his folks to be able to go home. The restaurant, you know? They can't just stay out here for days and days. That's their livelihood."

"Okay. I'll get on the horn." He could make calls now, let Travis rest some more. "You're doing great, okay?"

"I'm trying. I need to go downstairs and see the Ishams, have a cup of coffee, maybe toast. The detectives will come to see us soon, yeah?" Travis looked at him. "Do you think we have enough toilet paper for all these people?"

"Uh, I'll look." He had to chuckle a little. "As soon as the cops run off the vans, I'll go to the store too. I promise. We need more coffee and eggs and stuff."

Travis nodded. "People will start bringing food tonight. We'll have all the tamales and beans we'll ever be able to eat."

"I love tamales. You, on the other hand, like lasagna." He'd teased Travis unmercifully about that when they were teenagers. He'd even had his mom put green chile in the lasagna to make it more New Mexico.

"I love it. I bet some shows up. I work with good people."

"Good." Travis would need those people around him when everyone else left.

"Yes. Yes, my poor kids. They're going to be missing me."

"I bet." Lex hoped that helped too, having something to look forward to getting back to.

"I…. Jesus, I don't know how to just get on with it."

"Of course not, man. That's going to be one minute at a time. Then one hour."

"I guess. I don't think I can do this."

"You'll have plenty of help." He gave Travis another squeeze. "How about you get some pants on and come down like you said?" Travis needed food.

"Yeah, I'll be there in a few."

"Good deal, buddy." He hugged one last time before rising. He needed to call Daniels funeral home, make sure they knew where Matt was.

Travis moved to the dresser, his shoulders slumped.

"I'll see you there, huh?" Lex didn't want to make it weirder than it had to be.

"Yeah." Travis was crying again.

Lex slipped out of the room, feeling a lot like a coward. He just didn't know what else to do. He needed to do something useful, and he hated to see Travis so defeated.

He pulled out his phone, looked up Daniels near Trav.

That was easily done, and the funeral home would call when they received Matt's body. Now he just had to check in at the kitchen, then wait for Juliano and his guys to show up.

He needed to warn the Ishams that Travis's mom was ill.

Martha was moving around, clearly cooking, and Mr. Isham was on the phone, talking softly.

"Travis is on the way down," Lex murmured. "He says his folks are on the way. His mom is having memory problems."

"Yeah, Matty told us. She'll be in a facility in a year or so." Martha pulled a sad face.

"Oh." Oh, that sucked. He hadn't seen Travis's mom in years, but he always thought of her as thirtysomething, like she'd been when they were teens.

"Yeah. Getting old is shit."

He blinked, then grinned at her. "That's what they tell me."

"Trust me, kiddo. I know of what I speak." Martha winked, then handed him a spatula. "Travis's folks just pulled up. I'm going to go help."

"Oh, I can help…."

"No, you flip bacon." She patted his arm.

"Yes, ma'am." He knew better than to argue. Luckily, bacon he could do. Sausage. Pancakes. Anything that flipped.

Travis came down the stairs. "Hey."

"Hey, your folks are here."

"Yeah?" Travis glanced toward the front room. "Okay. Be right back. Bacon?"

"Yeah, Martha started it."

"Dad likes bacon."

"You want a plate?"

Travis looked at him like he was crazy. "God, no."

"How about some dry toast? I can manage that too."

"Uh, sure. Let me go get Mom and Dad."

Mr. Isham hung up, then started moving in more chairs. "Don't worry, Lex. Travis will recover. He needs time to mourn."

"I know. I do. I just hate to see him hurting." He got bread in the toaster oven, then found Bisquick for pancakes.

"Sure. But he has to. It's part of the deal, or so I'm told."

"That's what they say." He was saying that a lot. Man, deaths in Mexican families could be much easier. Louder. This weird silence was insane.

He wanted to start bellowing "El Rey" at the top of his lungs.

"Do you want some music, man? You're humming."

"Huh? Oh, sorry. I was thinking about when my Aunt Lorena passed away. There was this huge do with a mariachi band…."

"We'll do that back home—not a mariachi band, but a party, a celebration of his life."

"Maybe that would make Travis feel better. To have people remembering the good things." He would help make that happen.

"Maybe. We'll invite him, of course." John winked over. "He won't come."

"No?" He chuckled. "Well, we'll do it for you, then. If that's what you do."

"Yeah."

Travis's parents came in—Maria and Dan looking as familiar as he remembered.

"John. I—I have no idea what to say, man." The cracks were already beginning to show with Travis's dad, and you didn't have to look far to see that Covergirl and hard-core meds were all that spackled Maria together.

"Dan." John slapped the man on the back in a strange, uncomfortable man-hug. "Coffee?"

"No, thank you. Lex! How are you?" Dan shook his hand, not quite hiding his relief that Lex was there.

"I'm okay, considering. Bacon is on its way."

"Excellent. I'm starving. How are you? You look exhausted."

And there they went again. Honest to God, he was ready to get past day one in a huge way.

After that, things started happening.

6

*B*rant listened to everyone talk, bicker, cry. He'd talked to more detectives, told the same story he'd told last night.

Everyone was going on and on, and suddenly he couldn't do it a second longer.

He stood, nodded to no one. "I'm going to make a grocery store run."

Lex was up and standing next to him in two seconds. "I'll drive, man."

He blinked over. "Okay."

What?

"I have your list, Martha." Lex smiled. "Come on."

"Right. Okay. I'm with you." Bemused, he followed Lex out the door. The news people had backed off after the cops had made a showing a few times.

Hell, there was probably another shooting that they'd be covering anyway. That was how it worked.

They headed out to Lex's truck, which smelled vaguely like Old Spice and tacos. "Thanks for letting me come along," Lex said once they sat in the cab. "Needed to get out."

"God yes. I… yes." Yeah, he was fixin' to do something drastic, like set himself on fire or eat a bug.

"Eeee." Lex got them moving. "When do we all stop sitting around staring at each other?"

"Fuck if I know." But he was ready, and it felt good knowing that he wasn't alone.

"Yeah." Lex chuckled. The guy had been a rock, handling all sorts of shit, from the funeral home to the cops. He had this calm way about him that Brant really admired.

"You… you want to stop and grab a beer? A plate of nachos?" Please? He needed something normal.

"Oh fuck yes. Where's good? I know, like, Sadie's and El Pinto."

"El Pinto should be empty now." And it was a little bit of a drive. Way closer to his place.

"Cool. I love their nachos with tongs." Lex hummed with the radio, which was set to some vaguely cumbias thing.

"Yeah. Yeah, thank you. I just need something normal."

"I get it. I mean, this has been the weirdest few days. Travis is just totally shut down."

"It's natural, I guess."

"I guess? Maybe all the people in my family who've gone on were old, so no one was surprised."

"I lost guys in the service. I just… I don't know." His voice dropped. "I'm ready to get back to my life. That makes me a shitty person, doesn't it?"

"No. Of course not." Lex glanced over. "It's normal. You've been a trouper."

"Thanks. I'm… I've never been in this exact position before."

"Yeah." Lex sighed. "It's a strange thing to be the high school best friend. Not quite family, but not a polite stranger who can escape."

"Right? You know you'll be leaving him in decent hands. I'm… I mean, I was Matty's friend, but I'd never leave Trav in the lurch." It was weird, because he was the guy who Matty bitched to when Matt and Travis had a fight.

"No, I get that." Lex grinned. "It's been kinda cool to be back in Burque."

"Yeah? Has it changed much?"

"A lot and not at all. Cruces is dying a little, but the ABQ is the only place in the state growing."

"Yeah. I bought my house three years ago over here in Los Ranchos, and I got a great deal on it."

"Oh, I like this area." Lex grinned. "We grew up over by Wyoming and Menaul."

He nodded. "It's a good city, but the crime sucks and the police force—"

Lex nodded easily. "Oh, I know. Justice departments, shootings. It's crazy. New Mexico is crazy poor, right? People get a little wild."

"It is. Some of these babies I see...." He shook his head. They broke his heart.

"Yeah. I have a friend who works up in Farmington. She says it's a struggle to go to work some days. It's the really young and old that get her."

"Yessir." They had two traveling nurses for the clinic that he worked for, and the stories they brought home were insane.

They turned off on Alameda, which was still running fast enough. Then on Fourth, all the way out to El Pinto. Just turning into the big dirt parking lot, with its huge trees and tons of yard art, made Brant feel calmer.

"Oh damn. I haven't been here in a long time. We had a couple of precinct parties on the patio. Have you ever been here at Christmas? With the luminarias?" Lex chatted as he parked, and it was happy, natural, nothing stilted.

"I have. I like to come here for brunch."

"Cool. They have good Bloody Marys, huh?" Lex held the door for him when they got there.

"You remember. Thank you, sir."

"God love a Texan," Lex whispered.

He chuckled. Yeah, well, he couldn't help it. He was a Texan, born and bred. He did love it up here, though. The Land of Entrapment.

"Two please." Lex winked over. "You were right. Now is the time. No line."

"Yeah. We're in between lunch and supper, and it's not a weekend. What's your favorite place in town?"

"Oh, in all, not just the food?" When he nodded, Lex ducked his head. "The zoo."

"We have the best orangutans. The best."

"I hear there's otters now. I might have to go."

"I have a membership."

"Yeah?" Lex laughed. "I knew I liked something about you."

They sat and ordered beers and waters and a full nacho. That was enough to last them for well over an hour. Just… time to get back to feeling normal for a bit.

"It's okay that you get out of the house, you know? We're the friends." Lex smiled at him, the look sympathetic.

"I know. I just feel guilty for all of it. Being alive, just like Travis said."

"Has he apologized for that?" Lex asked quietly.

"I don't know that he even remembers." Hell, Brant wasn't sure Travis wouldn't say it again.

"It still hurts." Lex grabbed a chip, dipped it into the closest thing to Texas salsa Brant had tasted in New Mexico.

"Yeah. A little." A touch.

"I'm sorry. People say shitty things." Lex smiled for him, dark brown eyes kind.

"I tried to save him. It was too late."

"Nothing could have saved him." The words were firm. Yeah, Lex had seen the autopsy report, he thought.

"No. He was gone before he hit the ground."

"Exactly. I know that sucks like nothing else, but you have to know you did all you can."

"I know. I mean, my head knows. My heart will take a few days."

"Maybe more." Lex leaned on the table. "I'm not big on touchy-feely, but they made me see a counselor for a bit after the bomb thing. It might help."

"Yeah, I'll talk to the girls at work." They were like counselors in their own rights, and they understood. They were a weird, dysfunctional little family.

"Cool. When do you have to go back in?" Lex asked it casually but watched him closely.

"I'm taking this week off. I need to make sure my head's on. Those little ones don't need me distracted."

"Yeah. I told Trav I'd hang around. Maybe we could go to the zoo one day."

"Sure. Totally. I think that the Ishams are going to stay one more night and head out, since Travis isn't having any service." They were going to have one at home. He'd fly out and go. Travis didn't understand how important it was to them.

"Sure." Lex shrugged a tiny bit. "I tried to get him to understand...."

"Hey, that's not ours." He held his hands up in surrender. "Trav isn't going to deal with this any way other than he is, if that makes sense."

"It does. I know it's hard for everyone, is all." Lex sighed. "Tell me about Matt? I hardly spent any time with him."

"He was a geek. He loved all the geek stuff—*Star Wars*, *Doctor Who*, *Pokémon*, *Vampire Hunter D*. It was crazy, because we were Mutt and Jeff growing up. I was the football player, the baseball player; he was the computer nerd. Then he went to college, I enlisted, and everyone thought we'd lose touch." But they hadn't. They were buddies. Matt had flown to

Germany when he was shot, had been there online for all the classes that he never thought he'd get through.

"He sounds like a hoot." Lex munched another chip. "Travis was drama club and drama llama. I was the one getting my ass kicked standing up to bullies."

"I can see that. He's one hell of a teacher. We do connect there, you know, over the kids. We both love them."

"I bet. I feel like a bad friend, like I got busy and just wasn't around." Lex met his gaze, guilt definitely lurking in his eyes.

"We're all grown-ups, man." He shrugged. "I just didn't know where to go after school. I needed somewhere new to be."

"It grows on you." That had them laughing, and when their nachos came, it had them both staring, wide-eyed. "I forget how big they are," Lex said.

"Yeah." He wasn't even sure he was hungry, but he wasn't ready to leave, so he grabbed the tongs.

By the time he'd had one chip with guac and sour cream, Brant felt better. More human. Okay. This was proof there was a God and He loved them.

"Here, try this bite." Brant held out a chip to Lex.

Lex nipped it out of his fingers, holding his wrist to do it, and his belly went tight. *What? Stop that.*

Then he reminded himself this was normal. A reaction to stress. Like fucking at a wedding, which they hadn't done.

Not even close. And there wouldn't be a funeral to screw up, so yay.

He could just let himself relax, right? *Right.*

Lex hummed. "Perfect bite, man."

"Right? It's all good. Guacamole. Oh God."

"Yeah. I mean, I like the guac here way better than down south." Lex smacked his lips. "Did you get some beef?"

"Nope. I need that. It's good for growing boys."

"You do." Lex made him a chip, this one with beans and meat.

"Thank you." He ate it and groaned, his eyes actually closing.

"I know!" Lex laughed. "I expected more casseroles."

"Right? All their friends are hipsters. I didn't know there were hipsters in Albuquerque."

"I didn't either. Hell, I thought there weren't any between Denver and what? San Antonio?"

They got to grinning at each other.

"Austin is just expanding to fill up all the available space."

"Is it? I haven't been there in ages." Lex waved a hand. "I went for a law enforcement seminar once. It was too cool."

"Well, I'm from way farther north, but I've been there a number of times. It's a great town. Pricey, though." He wasn't quite hip enough for Austin.

"Yeah. I always say that about Santa Fe. Sweet place to visit. Too expensive to stay."

"Right? I have enough to deal with my Los Ranchos love."

"Yeah. I always wanted to live in Nob Hill when I was a kid. Or Corrales, and have a horse." Lex snorted. "I tried to ride a horse once as an adult. Bad. Bad."

"Not your thing, huh?" Oh God, he might pay to see that.

"No. It kept trying to eat my feet."

Okay, that was unexpected. "That seems… rude."

"I thought so. They kept telling me to kick it—her?—in the teeth, and I thought that was mean too." Lex rolled his eyes. "I was a mess."

"That is adorable. Seriously." He could imagine it, Lex cussing up a storm, trying not to get bit and not kick.

"I was very frustrated. My buddy was all George Strait, you know? Like his butt was attached to the horse."

"I hear that it's part nature, part nurture. I can ride, or I used to. I don't know if I could mount now."

"It takes a muscle or two," Lex agreed. "I had to hoist hard."

"I have a little damage to work around." He patted his hip.

"I bet. That can mess a guy up."

"Yeah." He'd survived it and saved three soldiers in the process, so he'd take it.

Lex got that serious face again for a moment, but he just munched away on nachos, letting it pass.

There were a lot of ills that nachos could help with.

The little cloud cleared up, Lex back to smiling in no time. See? Nachos.

He wondered what good enchiladas would do.

Maybe he'd ply the guy with them at some point. He made a fair one. Really.

"What are you thinking about?"

"Cooking." That was sort of the truth. "You cook?"

"Uh, I can make pancakes." Lex chuckled. "I was thinking the other morning I can make anything you flip."

He nodded, because okay, that was a weird question to ask a stranger.

"Can you cook?" Lex returned.

"Yeah. Yeah, I like to."

"Like what?" They were back to even keel, both of them eating.

"Ribs, steak, enchiladas…. I like to make shit up."

"Yeah? I'm not good enough to do that." Lex leaned close, lowering his voice. "I make super good cookies, though."

"Yeah? I'm not a great baker." He loved cookies.

"I make dozens at Christmas. It's like therapy, like when I'm all stressed. We should get the stuff at the store. I'll make salted caramel."

"Salted caramel…. Okay. You like enchiladas?"

"I love them." Lex spread his hands. "Born and raised old family New Mexican, hello!"

"Beef? Chicken? Red? Green?" Wait. Was he allowed to do this? Make a date? Enjoy himself?

"Oh, Christmas, man. But I love green chile chicken."

"Green chile chicken it is. Tomorrow? The Ishams are heading home in the morning…."

"Oh, yeah. I'll bring dessert." Lex smiled hugely. "I mean, am I coming to your place?"

"Yeah. You can even make cookies. I have a great kitchen. A nice backyard."

"Sounds amazing. I'm in." The way Lex stared at him made his belly warm. Happy.

"Yeah? Good. I'm… yeah. Good." He made up another good bite and offered it over.

Lex ate it, then fed him one, and he thought… yeah, this might be flirting. Crazy and fun.

At least he had a reason to smile. There was something about Lex that intrigued the hell out of him. He wanted to spend more time with the guy, and he would bet Travis had plenty of people about. To be honest, they both needed a break, a breath. Something like this. Even the trip to the grocery store today was for Travis and his folks.

Dinner would be theirs.

A part of him worried, but he squashed it quickly. It was supper. A night away from the drama.

He liked Lex, loved the look of the guy. What could it hurt?

"You're thinking hard, man. I can tell you live alone."

Brant glanced up, more than a little shocked. "Huh?"

"You disappeared in there." Lex grinned. "I mean, I live by myself, but I'm a cop. We're never really alone, and we talk everything out. Everything."

"Do you? Do you have a partner in Las Cruces?" He had other nurses, and they could coffee klatch together like mad, but mostly they bitched and talked about where to order lunch, and then they talked about *The Walking Dead* and *This Is Us*.

"I do. We've only been partners about six months. We get some turnover." Lex gave him a thoughtful kind of look. "We're all learning all over again."

"I'm sorry. That's got to be hard." He'd been working with the same doctors for five years.

"It can be. Sometimes it's good. When the unit asshole leaves."

"Oh. I know about that. The bad seed. The one that brings everyone down." They hadn't had one in the unit for a while.

"Right? We had this guy…." Lex launched into the worst motorcycle cop in history story, which had him in stitches.

He hadn't laughed so hard in months, howling with it. Lord, he'd needed that. Bad.

Even the servers walking by were smiling by the end.

He wiped his eyes. "Lord, you are a hoot."

Lex bowed a little from the waist. "Thank you. I'm here all week."

Brant rolled his eyes and applauded. "Excellent news."

Lex chuckled. "Would we suck if we got dessert?"

"Totally." He beamed. "Let's do it."

"Levante?" Lex patted his belly. "It's like tiramisu and it feeds two."

"Uhn." That was all he had. Patron, coffee, biscochitos? He was in.

Lex ordered them dessert and coffee, and the moment felt even more like a date.

His phone buzzed, Martha Isham's number popping up: *Can u pls pick up a brisket? Travis is having a service after all. Body was released.*

You got it, he sent back.

"Everything okay?" Lex asked, and Brant shrugged.

"Travis is having a service."

Lex blinked. Then blinked harder. "Huh. Okay."

"Yeah. I'm supposed to buy brisket." Assuming he could find one. It wasn't Labor Day, and it sure as shit wasn't Texas.

"Well, then, we get brisket." Lex kinda rolled his eyes. "Families."

"I know, right? Do you have a lot?"

Lex nodded slowly. "I have an enormous pool of aunts, uncles, and cousins, two sisters."

"Yeah? That's cool. I have my mom, dad, and my brother, Bridey."

"Yeah? Are you close?"

"Close enough. Bridey is a sheriff's deputy back home. The folks run a big-assed cattle operation."

"You have a brother who's a cop?" Lex started laughing again.

"I do, yeah. Why's that funny?"

"Just makes me smile. Like, I was all telling you cop stories."

"His are way more stray horses and drunk cowboys fighting in the parking lot." He grinned. He needed to go see Bridey, spend a week or two back home.

"Ah. Yeah. Well, it takes all kinds."

"It does. He's a neat guy. A real Texan."

"You're not?" Lex waggled his brows.

"I don't ride horses much, and I have cats."

"No shit?" He got a surprised little look. "Aren't you supposed to have dogs?"

"I work a lot. Cats take care of themselves." Why did he feel so defensive?

"Are they fancy cats?"

"Two Persians and a Maine coon."

"Oh, man. Good thing I'm not allergic. I want those enchiladas." Their dessert came, and Lex stared at it. "It's like the Mount Everest of tiramisu."

"I... wow." He just ogled at the sheer beauty of it. "Where should we start?"

"The edges." Lex picked up a fork.

"To dessert and best men, huh?"

"Absolutely." Lex clinked forks with him and started to steadily devour cake.

To dessert and best men.

7

*S*upper at Brant's was delayed.

Shit, by the time him and Brant got back with the brisket and twenty pounds of potatoes, there was a whole other shopping list and a huge do planned for the next day.

Travis was frantic, going up and down the stairs, on the phone with all the human beings in New Mexico, all two million of them, plus about a thousand Texans.

Lex was a little disappointed. Not that they were having a ceremony, but that they might not get another chance to do dinner. Every single time he had the opportunity to see Brant, someone was there—Travis or the Ishams or some reporter that had crept in.

So Lex put his head down. He ran errands. He cleaned bathrooms. He made beds.

Martha and John were cooking, while Travis's folks talked to the funeral home. Well, Travis's dad. His mom... floated. God, it hurt to see her that way.

It was maddening. The temptation to just get in his truck and drive was huge. He couldn't do that. Travis needed him.

A little part of him didn't wonder if Brantley didn't need him too. He sure hoped so. Lex could use some companionship of Brant's type. For real. Hell, he hadn't had an orgasm from someone else's hand in so long he'd forgotten how. He really had. Maybe Brant could remind him. He liked the big nurse, liked his laugh, liked his strength, liked the way Brant dealt with Travis and the Ishams. He was kind, but he was no pushover. Lex admired the hell out of that, and he liked the way Brant ate dessert. That was important, that a man could enjoy the simple things in life. He could spend a few hours watching Brant lick cream off a spoon.

Maybe a day.

He spent a few moments trying to decide what kinds of cookies to make for Brant as opposed to for the funeral. Those eyes had lit up when he'd mentioned salted caramel cookies, so that was on the list. Maybe peanut butter. Or gingersnaps. For the funeral he'd make some biscochitos and chocolate chip, then a couple of pies. Mr. Isham liked pecan, and Travis adored lemon meringue.

"Lex? Lex, what are you wearing to the service?" Travis was red-eyed and frantic.

"Hey." He grabbed Travis's hand, tugging him right into the office, since they'd met at the top of the stairs. "You okay?"

"Just… just stay with me? I don't want to be nice to all of those people, shake hands. What good is this going to do?"

"None at all except make the Ishams feel better." He hugged his friend hard. "I know Martha is so grateful." They wanted to remember their boy, to see that he had friends.

"She is, but I… I just want everyone to leave but you. I don't even want Brantley there. I keep thinking if he'd done something…."

"I've seen the tape, Trav. There was nothing Brant could do."

"I know." Tears spilled over again, Travis so exhausted and close to the edge.

"Then don't say it to Brant. I know the urge to take it out

on him is strong because he was there, but no one is feeling worse about that part than him."

"I'm just so mad. I want to go back to that night and tell him not to go to that movie, not to go out, not to see Brant."

"I know." He did. Anger was healthy. It was way better than staying in the denial stage too long, but focusing so much of it on Brant was just going to make things worse.

Lex wasn't blowing bullshit up Travis's skirt either. He'd seen the video, and Brantley had done everything for Matt. Brantley had been exceptional. He wouldn't press Travis on that now. "You know what? You should get a couple of hankies, put on some gray slacks and a black shirt, and go drape yourself over the recliner downstairs. Every time someone approaches, just start sobbing loudly. That will get them to leave you alone."

"Just stay with me. You can sit with me during the service. Hold my hand."

"I totally can." He would hope to God he wasn't pissing off a family member, but he would brazen it out for Trav.

That was why he was here, right? To support Travis.

God, he wanted his supper at Brant's.

Hopefully, he could still convince the man to do that when all the glad-handing was over. Things would slow down, and Travis would go out of high-alert mode. It had to be tough, having all this overwhelming stuff going on. Hell, Travis was high-alert enough, wasn't he? Just in general all the time.

Even Matt had said he was high-strung. At the wedding. In a speech.

Lex grinned, glad Travis couldn't see his face.

"Once this is done, everyone will go home and leave us here alone, right?"

"Yes. They will." The Ishams had been about to leave. They had a business to run, after all. Brantley had to go to work at some point, and frankly, so did Lex.

Not that he didn't have a breakfast meeting with his

former captain and the guys in a couple of days. He thought it was a fair bet he'd be offered a job.

He might just take it too. He loved the spring down in Las Cruces, but Dusty and Nate were really his only good friends down there, and it was a three-and-a-half-hour drive if he wanted to spend a long weekend with them. Shit, they would meet him in Ruidoso.

Travis needed him, and he liked Brant a lot. He loved the bigger group of guys up here, and to be honest, he was still…. That bomb damn near broke him. The shooting, the aftermath, the way some people were still super careful to tiptoe around him…. He needed a change. Maybe he'd see his folks more too.

Hell, he didn't know. He didn't know what he was going to do. Good thing he didn't have to worry about it right now.

He had time off, he had Travis to get through this day, at least, and he had a dinner to reschedule. Lex patted Travis's back. "Better?"

"No, but I'm going to make it. I'm going to just… stay here. Breathe."

"Sack out on my air mattress if you need to. I'll go check on stuff, shake some hands for you." He wanted to see if anyone needed him to make one more run or lift anything. Martha was wearing down.

"I think I'll just… sit and lock the door. Holler when you need me."

"I will, honey." He kissed Travis on the cheek before slipping out the door. Travis could calm down. He heard it lock before heading down the stairs. Kitchen first.

"Señora Martha? You need anything?"

"Thank you, sweetie. You've done a ton. How's Travis?"

"Hysterical. I locked him in the office upstairs for a bit." Lex gave her a one-armed hug. "It smells amazing in here. Can I grab a corner of counter and make some cookies?"

"You surely can. You just take all you need."

"Thanks." He would start with the biscochitos. The creaming of lard with sugar and the smell of anise soothed him on a cellular level. This was the scent of home and Christmas, of potlucks and Abuelita.

He found the mixer and cookie sheets. He thought maybe they'd been wedding gifts and were largely untouched. Travis and Matt had done takeout, and then, apparently, box delivery meals. They'd only cooked together under the most controlled of circumstances.

It was nice stuff. Seriously. Lex was jealous.

He chuckled, because his mama would tell him to get married and he would get all that nice stuff too. If he could just find some nice boy who wanted to fuck twice a day and share kitchens....

Lex shook it off. No thinking of fucking today. He was a dipshit, but he wasn't nasty.

"Is there any Dr Pepper?" Brantley sounded wrecked.

"Hey. Yeah, here." He dug in the fridge, pulled out a can for Brant. "You okay?"

"Yeah. Just got accosted by a reporter outside. Tired of talking to people."

"I hear you." Poor Brant. Everyone wanted a piece of him.

"Eh. I'm fine. What can I do?"

"I'm just making cookies. Martha?" He wanted Brant to sit down, actually.

"Sit and chop celery and onions, son."

"Sure." Brant plopped into a chair, so Lex got him set up with a knife and stuff.

"Thanks." Brant bent his head to business and started chopping.

Lex watched him for a moment. What the hell had that reporter said? "Do I need to call my guy at the precinct?"

"What? No. No, it was just fishing. I don't have anything to hide."

"Nope. That's true."

Martha sighed. "They're like those toothy fish."

"Piranhas?" Brant asked.

"That's it. They bite and bite until there ain't nothin' left."

"I guess it's their job." Brant shrugged. "They just don't understand that they keep opening it up over and over."

"I'm sorry, honey," Martha said. "I know how hard this is for you."

"Bah." Brant looked up at Martha, winked at her. "I'm fine."

"Hmm." She shook her head, lifting her face for a kiss from her husband as he walked in.

Lex went back to rolling out cookies. He could be quick as a bunny when he got into it. It was easy as pie. Or cookies. What have you. He cut out some plain rounds, then found a star cutter. That was better. He didn't imagine either Travis or Matt would care, but he would know.

Once the first batch was in the oven, he cleaned out the mixer bowl and started on the chocolate chip.

"You're a machine, Lex. You want to come bake for us in Texas?"

"I'd be happy to. How much do you pay?" He winked at Martha.

"We can pay in brisket…." John waggled his eyebrows at Lex, playing even as tired as he was.

"I love that." He added two more batches to his list. He'd send them home with the Texans.

"Excellent. We'll pack you up and take you home with us in the pickup."

"I require Mexican food weekly, at least. Otherwise I can survive on greasy burgers and fries."

"Burgers and fries are one of our specialties." Martha was all grins.

"They're better than Whataburger," Brant said.

"Yeah, but are they better than Blake's?"

"Mmm. Well, the green chile is better here." Brant grinned over at Martha. "The guacamole is too."

"Is it? Maybe we'll leave closer to lunch tomorrow so we can stop and have some." Martha lit up a little. Someone liked guac.

"You should run to Garcia's if you get a chance."

Oh, good one. "Nice," Lex said. "Anywhere but Garduño's."

Brant cracked up, the laughter ringing out, filling the air.

Martha just smiled, but Lex was so damn happy to see Brant laugh. They all needed it, but Brant had been looking used up.

"What's funny?" Travis asked as he walked in.

"The guys were telling us where to avoid, foodwise," Martha said.

"Garduño's," Travis intoned, which set them off again. Travis actually smiled. "What smells so good?"

"Brisket," Brant said.

"Biscochitos." That was Martha.

Lex went with "Potato salad."

"I think it all smells yummy." Travis was trying really hard. "I would love a cookie when they come out, huh?"

"Sure. Absolutely. You want a Coke?"

"Is there tea?"

"Of course there is," Martha said. "In the fridge."

"Thank you. I'm not looking for the burn." Travis headed for the fridge. "Are we all ready for this?"

"We're getting there," Lex murmured. "We can do it."

Brant nodded. "It'll be fast."

Travis looked at Brant, lips tight, and Brant looked away.

Lex fought not to roll his eyes or slap Travis on the back of the head. *Seriously.*

"You know I didn't shoot him, right?" Brant's voice was full of ice. Pure fucking ice.

Oh fuck.

Martha closed her eyes, her hands stilling.

"I know that," Travis snapped.

"Then quit treating me like I'm to blame. I was his best friend for his whole life. I miss him too."

"I'm sorry! I just know you were with him. I can't help it."

"Now, Travis, you stop it," Martha snapped. "Matty would never want you to treat Brant bad, and he did all he could."

"Cut me some slack! I'm just trying to get through this. Can't you just go home, Brant? Just leave me the fuck alone for a second? You're acting like you lost your husband."

John Isham lifted his head, fury written as clear as a signature in black ink, but Brantley just held up one hand, shook his head.

Brant took a deep breath, and Lex could see it, how Travis was about to get his head torn all off. Once the blood started flowing there, it was going to suck so hard. It didn't happen, though. Brantley just stood up and left out the kitchen slider without a word.

"Damn, man." Lex tossed a glare at Travis before following Brant out.

Brant was already in his car, the engine revving up, Brantley's cheeks a bright, dark red.

Lex waved at him, hoping to get him to rethink.

Brantley rolled down his window, shook his head. "I'm going home, bud. I'm not welcome here."

"You're not just here for Travis." Martha and John liked Brantley there. "Will you at least come to the service? You have a right to be there."

"I'll do my best. I can stand in the back." Well, that was a no. *Goddamn.* He got that Travis was losing his mind, but....

"Travis wants me up front. I—I can come back after." He wanted to help Brant, who had to be hurting, and Travis was his best friend. Christ. Why wasn't everything as easy as cookies?

Brant shrugged. "You're here for him. It's cool. Seriously. I'm good."

One of the land-shark reporters noticed them and started toward Brant's SUV. He rolled his eyes and started to warn Brant, but Brant followed his gaze.

"Damn. They don't have something else to talk about? Surely we've had another murder or two for them to chew on."

"Easy. I'll get rid of them." Fuck, he wished he had his badge on him.

"I'm leaving anyway. I'm not welcome here. Call me when you can. I'll make you enchiladas. Maybe when you get back to town. Rumor is you come in once every ten years."

"Sure. Maybe even sooner than that." He wanted that date night kind of intensely.

"Soon. Go save your cookies." Brant waved, then pulled out, damn near hitting the reporter on the way.

Lex headed back inside, walk turning into a run when he heard screaming.

"...selfish little bastard! Matt loved Brant to death! They've been friends since they were babies, and you're going to drive him away!"

To his utter shock, it wasn't Matt's mother who was screaming. No. No, it was Travis's.

"Mom!" Travis held his hands up, backing away from her. "He could have saved him. He should have!"

"Lex. You saw the tape." John Isham stared at Travis, then turned to Lex. "Is that true? Was there anything Brantley could have done?"

"No." Lex said it flatly. "And that's my expert opinion as a cop. Brant had no time to intercede, and Matt died instantly." Time for some tough love from him too. "You're being unreasonable, Travis. Not gonna lie."

"You're here for me. Not him. I need you. I'm allowed to be unreasonable right now! I loved him."

"So did I." Martha stared Travis down, pinned him like a bug on a board, the pain in her voice so vast there was no way to describe it. "He was my baby. I held him under my heart for thirty-nine weeks. You talk about loving him? I am his *momma*. I lived for him. So did John. So did Brantley. We were all here first."

"Martha." John caught her, just as she collapsed under the weight of her agony.

Well, fuck.

Lex helped haul Martha into the closest chair.

Travis crumpled. "I can't do this."

His mom went to take his hands, suddenly calm and collected in the middle of this emotion windstorm like she'd never lost her shit. "You will. Now, let's go get dressed. You can't go like this."

She eased him out of the kitchen, toward the stairs, and Lex just watched him go.

"Save your cookies, Lex." Martha sighed and stood slowly. "Lex, forgive me. John, I want to go home right after the service, okay?"

"Anything you want."

"I'll stay," Lex offered. He grabbed an oven mitt. "Travis is not good in emotionally charged situations, and he and Matt were a tiny bit codependent."

"You're a good boy. I bet Matt adored you."

"I liked him a lot." He really hadn't known him all this time. Not really. Lex felt bad about that. He probably would have liked Matt a lot, so that wasn't a lie. He loved Travis dearly, like you loved your bitchy brother. Matt and Brantley had been best friends. Ever after all the years.

Sighing, he changed out cookies, getting the chocolate chip in the oven.

8

*B*rantley went to the store and bought beer, Velveeta, Ro-Tel, and tortilla chips.

He was going to celebrate Matt in his own way. He had *The Mummy*, *The Matrix*, and the entire *Lord of the Rings* series. He intended to eat and drink and watch their favorite movies.

Fuck services. Fuck Travis. Fuck everyone.

He sighed, resting his head on the steering wheel. He wasn't responsible for Matt's death. He wasn't.

Maybe he'd have a nap first, something long and helped by the Xanax in his pocket.

He headed inside, his house smelling a little like pizza. He'd indulged with Matt's folks day before last. He opened up the windows and turned on the fans.

Okay. Okay, couch. Then queso. He needed some rest.

After the last few days, he needed a goddamn nap.

Brant sat down, but before he could even stretch out, his phone buzzed. *Jesus fuck.* He grabbed it, looked.

Hope ur ok. That was from Lex.

Yeah. Thx. U?

Ok. All dressed. Lex sent him a selfie. White shirt, black tie. He looked a little like a door-to-door religious guy.

V. nice. He settled in the cushions. *Gonna have my own memorial.*

Sounds more fun than mine.

What was he supposed to say to that? Fuck yeah? *Beer. Queso. Movies.*

Have some for me.

Will do. I hope it goes well. Because he did. He loved Travis. That was why he was staying home.

See you soon I hope. Lex was a sweetheart. He really was.

Anytime.

He dropped his phone on the ottoman, laughing as Mouse pounced him from the top of the hutch. "Oof! You heavy bastard! Where are Peaches and Cream?"

Mouse yawned, showing those super sharp teeth.

"Yeah, yeah. If you scared them, I'll let the girls eat you." He imagined that the twins were still sound asleep on his pillows. They only woke for food and evil.

Mouse was his buddy, weighing him down on the couch.

That was all right. Matty approved of naps.

Lex sat in the guest room, which was his now, staring at the wall.

He felt… kinda run over by a truck. Both sets of parents had left right after the ceremony, after Travis had wailed and ranted and tossed a couple of floral arrangements….

Christ on a sparkly crutch.

He eased off his dress shoes. At least he wasn't on the floor. When he checked his phone, hoping for Brant, he saw Dusty. So he called.

"How's it going, honey?" Dusty's voice was soft, gentle, like a breath of fresh air.

"Oh, man, it's been intense. Travis, my friend? He's losing his shit."

"Yeah? Not handling it well?"

His snort was shockingly loud. "There was no casket to toss himself over and pound on, but that's about all he didn't do."

"You sure he isn't Southern?"

"He's a drama llama, but at this point, he's family. Lord. Should I order food? There are surprisingly few leftovers. None of his friends brought much, and Matt's mama's brisket is all gone."

"That's... weird. That's really weird, Lex. Aren't Travis's friends teachers?"

"Yeah. I mean, they're all hipsters, Dusty. Like, younger than us by ten years. The two older ladies brought desserts, and Travis isn't huge on anything but cookies and pie, so I sent one home each with the parents since the pans were disposable." He'd been organizing like a general, and he wanted to call his old sergeant to thank the man for instilling organization in him.

"Tell me someone brought avocado toast or craft beer." Dusty hooted like an old owl. "What about the other guy? The friend?"

"Brant? Travis ran him off. Stone-cold looked him in the eye and said he didn't want Brant here." That had made him ashamed of Travis, and he was going to have to say it.

"Oh, ouch. He didn't have anything to do with it, right? We all saw the TV footage. Looked like he was in the car until the very end."

"He was. And Matt died instantly. I just... I love Trav, I do. But God knows, bad shit happens. I'm not as patient as I used to be." He undid his pants. Maybe he would take a shower.

"No, and we've all seen a lot. We understand that we lose sometimes, you know?"

"I think that's a good part of it. Travis hasn't lost anything but grandparents, and he was super young when they died. His mom...." Lex had been happy to see lucidity in flashes, but she was definitely forgetful and easily confused.

"Well, that sucks, doesn't it? You heading home soon?"

"I don't know. We'll have a beer when I do."

"Fair enough. Is there anything we can do for you, buddy?"

"Just keep my plant alive." He chuckled. His plant. Lord.

"Will do. You call whenever you need."

"Thanks, Dusty." Lex really appreciated everything the guys did for him.

"Anytime, buddy. Anytime."

God, he didn't want to open the door. He so didn't want to face Travis.

He stripped off his clothes, then pulled on some sweats. Shower. Then he would see what Trav wanted for supper. One thing at a time. First, he'd just creep down the hall, nice and slow.

Travis wouldn't even hear him. Good thing there was no dog.

Brantley had cats.

Cats.

That thought made him grin. Persians, with the smooshy faces. Maine coon he wasn't sure about. That didn't sound like a New Mexico kitty, but who knew.

He wanted to see Brant's house, wanted to get to know the man a little more.

He would hang out a few more days if he could get Brant to let him come over…. He jumped about a mile when he heard Travis's bedroom door open.

"I thought that was you. You want a beer?"

"I do." That was the first good thing Travis had said all day.

"Cool." Travis looked like he was almost calm. Lex was ninety-nine percent sure it was a lie.

But he would have a beer. He could always storm off and

take a shower if things went bad. "Better now it's quieter?" Lex asked.

"Yeah. It was a little intense in here."

"Must have been." He dared to tease gently, softening it with a smile.

"Yeah. You know, I didn't go with Matt that night because I wanted some time to myself. I mean, the guys went to the movies a lot."

"I know." He'd overheard Travis telling Martha about it. "You guys were okay, right?"

"We were. I had papers to grade, and Matt had gotten free passes to the movies. He and Brantley saw each other at least once a week—a quick lunch, a movie, a Bloody Mary, something. I told him to go. I wanted our weekend free."

"Well, frankly I'm glad you didn't have to be there to see it." Lex knew, as he'd said over and over, that no one could have done anything, and Matt had seemed the type to get gas, not make Travis do it.

"Yeah. Yeah, I guess. I wouldn't have known what to do."

"Not a lot of people would." Lex sat across from Travis at the kitchen table. "You want me to order something?"

"No. No, I think I just want tea and toast." Travis sighed, reached out and took his hands. "I lost my shit, Lex. I just…. I hurt so much that I don't know what to do now."

"Well, part of the battle is knowing you lost it. Everyone has their way of dealing, but there are some folks you'll need to talk to when you're ready."

"I know. I just… I wish it had been him. I know that's evil. I understand, but I wish it had been Matt that came home." Travis wouldn't meet his eyes.

He let go of Travis's hand. "It's human. But it is mean as hell, and you need to talk yourself out of it every time you think it." Not least because Lex wanted to see Brant again and it would hurt Travis's feelings, but he just couldn't care.

"Yeah, I know. Hell, sometimes I think Matt liked Brant

more than me. Good thing they had zero chemistry. Like zero. They were brothers in everything but blood."

"Matt loved you so much, man." He did smile now, a real one. "He was so sappy at the wedding."

"He was. He never once made me feel like he didn't want me around. Or like I was too high-strung. Or that I was in his way." Travis teared up, but there was a bittersweet smile.

"See? I think he liked you too. He just got different things from Brant, like you do from Dahlia." He'd just met Travis's incredibly pregnant best work friend at the service.

"I know that. I do. I just… I need to be angry at someone. I can't be angry at Matt."

"Sure. I just hate to see you lose someone like Brant. He'll be there to help remember Matt, you know?" Lex reached back over to squeeze Travis's hand before he got up to make toast and tea instead of grabbing a beer. "I wish I'd known him better, but I'm here when you need me."

"I know. I appreciate it. I think my head's going to explode, just go all boom, right?"

"I bet. I'll have some tea with you, and then I think you ought to just go lie down. I can totally fend for myself."

"Yeah. I might take a pill and just crash for a few. See if I can't dream about him."

"Oh, honey, I'm sorry." Lex just figured that was the best way to go.

"Me too. I loved him. I really, really thought we were going to grow old together. Be crusty old queens with martinis, talking about the good old days."

"That sounds amazing." He managed not to grimace. Lex wanted something easier than that. Someone who would still spoon at sixty. Hell, he just wanted a mutual blowjob and a laugh.

That brought his thoughts back to Brantley, sitting alone, watching movies and drinking beer and mourning his best friend.

He bit his lip. Okay, toast and tea, and then maybe he'd call Brant. Might as well have pizza with someone.

If nothing else, he could assure himself Brant was okay. That was good, right? Lex hated that wanting to see Brant made him feel selfish enough to have to make excuses. Screw that. If there was one lesson he'd learned in the past few years, it was that life was too short to be sorry for normal urges.

And Brantley gave him all the urges—normal and otherwise.

He chuckled, and Trav looked at him. "You okay?"

"Just thinking how weird life is." He buttered toast, then laid out tea, toast, and cookies. "Ta-da."

"Isn't this adorable. I'm impressed. Seriously. Thank you."

"What can I say? I am one of us deep down." Lex winked, because it made Travis laugh when he tried for any gay stereotype. Trav always said he was this weirdo exception....

"You're only gay because—"

"I like dick?"

They both cracked up at the old, stupid joke.

Travis finished off his toast. "I think I will go sleep. I'll take a pill, so if you decide to go out for food, could you make sure I'm locked up?"

"You bet. I'll even leave a note."

"Cool. Love you, Lex." Travis came to him, hugged him tight. "Thank you for coming."

"I love you too, honey. We'll watch some movies tomorrow, huh? Something sappy."

"Yeah. *The Matrix*."

"I like it. It's kinda sappy, with the whole 'I love the chosen one' thing...."

Travis snorted, then kissed his cheek. "I'll see you in the morning, probably. Take the rest of the day and do something fun, huh?"

"Uh-huh. Post-funeral happy." He rolled his eyes and

bussed Travis's cheek right back. "If I go, I'm a phone call away."

"Thank you. I'll be fine. You know I like the quiet."

"That's because you're with kids all week long." He walked Trav to the stairs.

"Yeah. Yeah, I miss them. Really. A lot. They offered to give me next week off. I might just go back."

"It would keep you busy." What else was he supposed to say? Trav would know that first day if he was capable of going back to work.

"Yeah. And they're good kids. Really. All of them."

"Not one bad apple? You remember how awful we were to Señora Gonzales?" They'd put tacks in her chair, stolen her chalk, and superglued her pen to her desk.

"Oh, she was evil. You know she was still teaching when I started?"

"No shit? Did she remember you?" That would be cosmic vengeance.

"You know it. I was her goddamn student teacher, man!"

"Oh, fuck." That tickled him so much he got laughing, clutching at the post on the stairs.

"Mr. Garcia," Travis intoned. "Please remember to mark the children's papers clearly."

"Oh, God." He slapped his leg with his free hand.

"Mr. Garcia, if you don't mind, we ought to wear a tie, don't you think?"

"No. Stop." He was just wheezing. Travis was a wicked mimic.

Travis grinned at him, just beaming. "Breathe, man. Breathe."

"I know! I just hadn't thought of her in… years, I guess. Dios mío."

"She retired about five years ago. I actually go see her every now and again."

"Does she like you now?" he asked. He had retired cops who adored him now they didn't work together.

"Weirdly, I think so. She's relaxed, a lot. I never realized how tense she was."

"Good for her. She got grandbabies?"

Trav nodded. "Oh, yeah. Four. She loves that."

"Well, next time you see her, say hi for me. She'll look like she sucked a lemon."

"I have no doubt. I'll tell her Deputy Dawg says hi."

"Thanks, hon." He let Travis disappear upstairs before trotting up to the guest room. Shower. Clothes.

Text Brant. *Want me to bring WisePies?*

OMG. Spicy Capo? I have queso and beer.

Be there in about an hour?

Brant's answer was to text his address. Well, okay, then. He pumped his fist. Then he took the fastest shower in history. He would call for the pizza before he left Taylor Ranch and pick it up on the way.

Brant was down off near the Griegos drain in a nice little adobe that was decades older than Travis and Matt's McMansion. The doors were bright turquoise, the wrought-iron window guards and front gate purple. The front yard was filled with huge rose bushes and deer tongue. *Damn. Nice.* There was even a big lilac bush. That was gorgeous, all blooms and aroma.

He headed up to the door and knocked. Brant was wearing a pair of pajama pants and an ancient T-shirt with Taste the Rainbow on it.

"I like it." He jerked his chin at the shirt. "I got a Big Meat-Up, the Spicy Capo salad, and some wings. I also brought some cookies."

"I have beer and chips and queso. Come on in." The house was warm on the inside—a huge leather sectional, coffee tables, the biggest fucking cat he'd ever seen.

"Holy shit. Is that a domestic cat or a bobcat?"

"Mouse?" The huge gray beast with yellow eyes like a demon just glared at him.

"Mouse? He looks like a mouse eater. Is he friendly?" Lex stared at the cat, who turned his head to stare at the pizza boxes.

"He's an angel. It's Peaches and Cream that you have to watch for. They're drama queens." Brant tapped Mouse's nose. "That is not for you."

Mouse seemed to harrumph, then turned his back, ears twitching. *Hilarious.* "I like him already."

"They're all pretty good company. The girls will take a little while to come out."

"Shy, huh? This guy knows he's the apex predator." He put the pizza and salad on the table. "Is that the queso I smell?"

"It is. Let me grab it. The plates are in that cabinet beside you."

"Got it." He pulled out plates, then hunted silverware for the salad. Brantley had a bunch of great mismatched plates and silverware and glasses. Not messy, but just every one different, separate.

His dishes had come from Big Lots. One of those box sets that came with four of everything. Lex did have a great collection of beer glasses, though.

"I like the stuff."

"Thanks. I like garage sales. I go on Saturday mornings."

"Yeah? My mom does that. Dad never wanted me to go. I think he knew." Lex laid out plates.

"Knew?" Two bottles of Shiner appeared on the table.

"Yeah, that I was gay. Like when I was little. He tried to discourage me from anything he thought was girly." He and his papa, they were… strained a little.

"Ah. I didn't come out for a while. I mean, I knew, but it was right after Basic."

"Yeah? I came out in high school to my family. It caused

some stuff." He tended not to think about it now. Most of his family had decided he was the same as he ever was.

"It always does. I mean, my people were fine. There was the 'are you sure' and the 'you know this won't be easy, right,' but that was about it. Now we're at the 'when are you going to meet someone and adopt babies?' part."

"Oh, God. Your brother? Can't he do it?"

"Uh. I'm sure he can, but, uh…. Well, he's sort of playing for our team too. He's not out and proud, not at all, but Mom knows. Bridey's just… sensitive."

"Oops." He grinned. "So she figures you're her best bet. You like kids, obviously."

"I do, but I work with them all day. I sort of… like my cats." Brantley turned pink. "I know that's selfish, but… I'm just not all that paternal."

"Hey, trust me, my mom doesn't even ask. Like, she knows it never even crosses my mind." Lex wasn't exactly a player or anything, but he wasn't the white-picket-fence kind either.

"No? Well, we're on the same page. Ready to eat?"

"God, yes. Martha made enough food for an army, but I was dealing with sorting the flowers and I got maybe a mouthful of potato salad. I've had cookies." Lex thought maybe he was drooling.

"I fell asleep and just crashed. I feel like I might be a functional human being again. Maybe."

"I hope to get that way. Did you manage to say goodbye to Matt's folks?"

They settled at the table, but Brant popped back up to grab salad tongs.

"They stopped by to collect their stuff. Apparently it was rough. If I was Travis, I'd sort of leave them be awhile. They need some time."

"He doesn't think any of Matt's family likes him." He

glanced at Brant sideways. "Hell, he thinks Matt liked you more than him. Like on a daily basis."

"He's kind of a jealous butthead." Brant shrugged, the words matter-of-fact. "Matty loved him to distraction."

"That I think he knows." Lex had gotten that impression.

"That's all that matters. The Ishams worried that Travis didn't feel Matty was good enough. It wasn't true. Travis loved Matty to death. They were happy together. Really, truly happy."

"Man, relationships are complicated." He grabbed a couple of slices. "Smells good, huh? Pizza and salad and queso. Who would've thought." Lex hooted. "You know here queso is just cheese."

"Yes. Yes, I do." Brantley kicked him under the table. "I tell you what, when I first moved here, I asked for a breakfast burrito with queso? What came out, it was not what I asked for."

"And you learned to ask for chile con queso, huh?" Lex remembered Dusty telling him that. "I have a Texas buddy in Cruces. He ordered a side of queso, and the server was all, 'it comes with cheese on it.'"

"Yeah. Do y'all have Tex-Mex down there?"

"In some places. Especially over in El Paso. Dusty assures me you have to get to San Antonio before it resembles real Tex-Mex, though in his part of the world, they have gringo Mexican, I swear. He does this thing where he layers Wolf Brand Chili and flour tortillas and cheese and calls them enchiladas." They were good, but everyone knew that stuff was more burrito casserole than enchilada.

"Uhn. I would eat that. Is that bad?"

"No, I eat it all the time. But it's not enchiladas." The pizza was good tonight. Meaty. Saucy but not wet.

Brantley took a huge serving of salad, making him cackle. The Texan noshing on the lettuce.

"Hush, you." Brant grinned. "It's not like it's all that healthy. I just love the crunch."

"Uh-huh. Do you smoke? I know a bunch of nurses that smoke."

"Cigarettes? Nope. We get a bonus at work for not."

"So do we. They want us to be able to run." Lex only had a beer once in a while, and usually ate better than he had recently, thanks to Lean Cuisine.

"Yeah? I'm a runner too. Three nights a week at the gym."

"Cool. I gotta admit, I like the treadmill. The road is hard on the knees, but I get out a couple times a week because that's my work landscape." *Cheese. Uhn.* "You make good queso."

"I'm a Texan. It's a thing."

"It must be. Too many people here try to use a roux." The key was obviously Velveeta and Ro-Tel. That was how Dusty made it too.

"I know, and I've tried a bunch of fancy-assed recipes, but I come back to this, again and again."

"I see why." He smacked his lips. Then he ate some more. He was gonna be running for hours, but it was so worth it, and he was so damn hungry.

Brantley didn't waffle about eating. He was eager, chatty, and not prissy at all.

Lex thought that was a good sign. He'd had dates with people who'd eaten less than a bird, and he'd been with guys who were so picky he was embarrassed to be seen with them. Brant was just a dude.

A hot dude.

A hot gay dude.

Lex nodded, which caused Brant to squint at him. "Sorry, I was just discussing another piece of pizza with myself."

"Go for it. You've been starving."

"I know it's silly." Not like he was wasting away to nothing.

"Stress." Brant got it.

"Yeah. I deal with it in weird ways. And Travis, well, he stops eating when he's wigged out."

"Yeah. That's why he's tee-tiny. Me? Not so much."

"Hey, you look amazing." Lex's cheeks heated, but he didn't backtrack.

"Thanks. I work at it."

Lex bet Brant did. "So the running doesn't bother your hip?"

"Every damn time."

"Ouch. Have you thought of aqua running? Lane walking in a pool? Easier on the joints." He did have some EMT training, after all.

"One of the nurses in my unit does water Zumba, but no. No, I hadn't."

"It's way easier on the joints. So is elliptical." He tried the salad. *Oh, spicy. Nice.*

"Good, isn't it?" Brant dipped another chip. "I like my spice."

"One thing New Mexicans and Texicans have in common." Lex winked broadly.

Brantley hooted, the laugh lines around his eyes attractive as fuck.

He liked this guy. A lot. Like more than anyone he'd met in years.

"So, why'd you become a cop?" Brantley finished his beer and leaned back in his chair.

"Well, I could recite all the stuff from the academy, but really, I wasn't sure I was smart enough to go to college, and I wanted benefits." Lex paused. "You know, I grew up watching how bad the cops here were on TV. I wanted to be the good one."

"Good on you. You must like it; you've been doing it a while."

"I do. Some parts suck." Lex thought shooting someone,

killing them even if it was necessary, left a stain on a guy's soul. "What about you? Why a nurse?"

"I went into the service after high school. Trained as a medic. Got shot. All I knew was medicine, so I got my RN license."

"You like it, though. Right?" God knew Dusty was in for life. So was Dusty's man, Nate, who was an EMT.

"I do. I don't want to be a doctor. I want to help the patients. I need to interact."

"That's awesome. Nurses are the best." They really were the meat and potatoes of medical.

"Thanks." Brant grinned at him, like he'd just said the most wonderful thing.

"'Tis true." He blinked at his empty plate.

"You want to come sit, man?"

"Sure. I would love that." Lex put his plate in the sink, following Brant's example.

The Mummy was already playing when Brant turned on the TV. "This cool?"

"I love this shit." He even liked the one with The Rock. The only one he didn't love was the last one with the different Evie.

"Yeah, me too. Matty and me, we saw it at the theater."

Lex loved how Brant said "thee-A-ter."

"I saw it with Travis! That's funny." He moaned when he sank into the couch. Oh, God. That was good.

"Nice, huh?" Brantley stretched out on the lounge end, wiggling his toes.

"It so is. My couch is a hand-me-down. I really need to look at a new one if it feels like this." He rested his head back.

"Big Lots. I love it."

"I was just thinking how my dishes came from there."

"Yeah? They have some great goofy shit."

"A bunch of us go every year at Halloween and Christmas." He didn't really decorate, but they did the precinct up.

"Right? The unit goes all out for holidays, and we spend a lot of time hunting goofy costumes and decorations."

"I love it. I bet the kids do too." He sank deeper into the cushions.

"Mm-hmm. It's really fun." Brantley blinked at the movie, relaxed and easy.

Lex took a sip of his beer before setting it aside on his coaster. "It is. I love Halloween best, but Mama does Easter in a big way."

"What did you dress up like last year?"

"A cop," he deadpanned. "I was on duty on Halloween, but I did go to a party the weekend before dressed as Gru from *Despicable Me*."

"Oh, that must have been something…."

"I had minions. It was great. What did you do?" Man, his eyelids were heavy.

"At work I was the tooth fairy. For trick or treating, a vampire. For the party? I was Zorro."

"The fox. No one is as something something as the fox…." The words escaped him, but Papa had loved the reruns of the old black-and-white show.

"Uh-huh. I love a cape." Brant rested back into the cushions.

"I can see that. Did you have a sword?" Buckling a swash was a good thing.

"I did, and the mask, the hat."

"Nice." That gave him a happy little fantasy for a bit.

"It was. It was an epic party, but somehow I came home alone."

"Bummer, man." That sucked. Lex knew exactly how that felt.

"Yeah. The best action is in Santa Fe, I hear."

"Santa Gay, huh? I'm just not that… cruisey." He liked dating and sex a lot but not clubbing and game playing. He kept thinking it would work better with Nate as his wing-man, but no.

"Obviously I'm not either."

"Yeah. I get it."

"Well, we'll figure it out, right?"

"Sooner or later, yeah. By that time your mama will give up," Lex teased.

"She'll never give up. Never!" Brantley slapped his fore-head playfully.

"I guess mamas have to be tough." Lex chortled. "Mine doesn't want me to be a cop anymore, but she keeps losing the argument."

"No? New Mexico is a tough place to be a police officer."

"It's tough all over, I guess. I mean, maybe Beverly Hills." He only knew that from movies. He was a cop, and that was all he was ever going to be. "I've heard guys at conferences. Like Detroit, or even LA. Cruces is smaller, at least."

"Yeah. I deal with the kiddos. I've been lucky, up 'til…. Well, you know."

"Yeah." Lex wanted to reach over, but Brant was far away. So he grabbed his beer instead. "You know I never had a Shiner until I met that friend I was telling you about? Dusty."

"Really? It's my favorite. What do you like to drink?"

"Bud Light. Uh, Corona." He liked a Corona with lime now and again.

"Corona with lime is always a good choice. There's some in the fridge, if you'd rather."

"Nah, this is good stuff. I might switch to Coke if you have any." Just in case. Who knew when Brant would kick his ass out?

"Sure. There's a bunch in there. What do you want?"

"Uh. Just Coke, if you have it. Or Sprite. Are you a Dr Pepper Texan?"

"I'm a Diet Cherry Dr Pepper guy, but I have a Coke. Hold

up." Brantley sat up, so slowly, then headed into the kitchen, the crutch leaning against the wall.

Damn. Now Lex felt bad. He kept forgetting about that sore hip. "Are you…?"

"I'm fine. Don't stress it."

"Do you have some Tylenol?" He had to stress it. He cared. "Muscle relaxants?"

"Before bed. A while after the beer." Brant handed him a Coke when he came back, then eased down toward the couch.

"I could have gone." He reached out, the motion instinctive. His hand connected with Brant's hip, and he swore he felt electricity between them. Brant glanced at him, eyes wide. Lex licked his lips, but he had to let go. He wasn't wanting to push, not if Brant was hurting that bad.

Brant's lips quirked, twisted just so. "It's not weird, right? To be all… interested?"

"I sure hope not. Because I am." Lex wanted that plain out in the open. Brant made him look, and Brant made him smile. So there.

"Cool. I am too." Brant turned halfway, met his eyes. "Hey."

"Hey." He held that gaze, just—his cheeks heated, his heartbeat kicking up. *Wow.*

They watched each other, and when Brant reached out and stroked his cheek, he gasped. Lex grabbed Brant's wrist, holding on. Then he turned his head to kiss Brant's hand, just below the palm, which was protected by Brant's curled fingers.

"Oh…." That sound was pure sex, and Lex wanted to make Brant give it again.

So he pressed his mouth to Brant's wrist, opening up room by shifting his grip. He felt Brant's pulse thundering against his lips. Oh damn, he could smell Brant—soap and spice and something musky and rich. He breathed deep, then dared to scoot across the couch cushion to get nearer. He wanted more.

He wanted a kiss direct from the source. Brantley wrapped one hand around his arm and encouraged him to move closer.

Lex leaned right in, wanting to taste. He pressed his lips to Brant's, asking for the man to be right there with him. Brant sighed softly, one kiss becoming two, then three. They sat there, resting together at the knees, kissing like fools. Long, slow, happy kisses. Exploring.

God, he was making out. Not humping in a corner of a bar. Not just finding a friendly hand. They were making out like teenagers.

He loved it.

Lex smiled against Brant's skin. Then he went in for more kisses. He needed this, the slight tang of beer and the hint of spice.

Brant was tactile—hands sliding over his arms, cupping his shoulders, touching his hair. Lex kept his hands busy too, pushing them along Brant's back, careful not to push too hard at the hips. Brant was lean but strong, and solid as an ox. That whole working-out thing was working for Brant. Come to think of it, it was doing great things for Lex too. He moved one hand up to cover Brant's left pec, feeling the heartbeat there.

Oh. Hard little nipple. Bingo. Very nice.

Pulling back a tiny bit, he plucked at it, wondering if Brant was a yes-nipple or no-way kinda guy. Lex was a hell-yes type, but some men didn't like nipple play at all. Brantley's bright eyes went wide, and the soft gasp proved that maybe he wasn't a no-way type.

Damn. Okay. Lex turned a little more and scooted so they were pressed together even more. He was pushing it. Screw the waiting game.

"Hey there." Brant let him straddle that strong body, and when their cocks slid together, Lex figured he was in the best possible place.

"Hey. Is this okay? Am I too heavy?" Supporting part of his weight on his knees seemed fair, a good way to keep Brant from hurting.

"More than okay. You feel good." Brantley cupped his ass and drew him in tighter. That move gave him some friction, and Lex took another kiss while he rocked gently. The noises Brant made spurred him on, sending his cock to greater heights.

He decided to explore that hard little nipple again, stroke and pull and twist, just to see what would happen.

Brant gasped against his mouth, gripping his ass tight. "Damn. Gave me goose bumps."

"Yeah? I like how hard that little nip is, man."

"You… you want to see?"

Hallelujah.

"God, yes. Let's get this off." He reached to tug at the hem of Brant's T-shirt, which was a treasure, so Lex was gentle.

Brant's chest was covered in fine blond hairs, a tree of life inked on one pec. He stared from close up, then traced the lines of the tattoo, thinking it was a great, hopeful symbol.

"Looks good, doesn't it?"

"It does. Really smooth work." Not gang tattoo at all, which Lex saw a lot of, unfortunately.

"I got it a while ago." Brant arched and brought his nipple in reach of his fingers.

"It looks amazing." Lex abandoned the tattoo and pinched Brant's nipple, loving how it throbbed and swelled. More than that, he loved how Brant swallowed, stared at him.

A smile stretched his cheeks. "Again?"

"Y-yeah. Again."

Okay, that counted as hot.

He chose the other nipple, rubbing it gently before tweaking. Brant hummed for him, sliding one hand down to pull at his shirt.

"Mmm. Here." Not that Lex wanted to let go. He didn't. Naked with Brant, though, was a goal.

He stripped his shirt off, and Brantley moaned for him, hands both dragging up over his abs, then his chest.

That kinda made him want to flex. He worked hard on his body because he had to, but Lex was glad Brant liked what he saw.

"Jesus... you're fucking inspirational." Brant rolled up, lips finding his chest, tongue moving over his skin, his dark chest hair.

"Oh." One hand just flew up to cradle Brant's head, holding him right there. Brant moaned happily, keeping himself upright with his hands on Lex's back as he explored. Lex tightened his muscles to help, wanting to be a solid support.

Brant licked and nuzzled, and Lex hadn't ever done this—been explored like he was necessary. A lot of his experience was hurried. Not furtive, just a means to get off. This was sweet and heady, and he wanted more.

"Love how you smell, man. Pure sex." Brant's voice was gravel and honey, rough and so fucking sweet enough that Lex's whole soul responded.

"You make me feel that way. Is this nuts or what?" *Please say no.*

"Stress and proximity. We'll use that as our excuse today."

"Okay. We'll find a new one tomorrow." Lex wanted to have a tomorrow, which was a new thing for him too.

"Fair enough." Brant wrapped his lips around one nipple, pulling hard enough to ache.

Lex arched, then pushed back upright, not wanting to unsettle Brant. They needed room to stretch out, but he didn't want to lose the mood.

"I—is it weird to ask you to come to bed? The couch is nice, but...."

"I was just thinking it would be nice to stretch out. I bet you have an amazing bed." *Same page. Score.*

"Come and see."

They managed to get off the couch and move deeper into the house. There was an office, a guest room, a bathroom, and then a lovely huge master.

"This has to be half the house, man. Hot as hell."

"That's why I bought it. Huge master, huge kitchen, huge backyard."

Two fuzzy cats were in a puffy purple bed at the end of Brant's king. They both looked at Lex, blinking, then disappeared under the bed.

"Oops. Is that going to be weird?"

"Nah. They'll leave the room as soon as you're up there with me."

"Cool." Pet TV he wasn't.

"Now Mouse, he's evil. He'll pounce in the middle of the night."

"Good to know. I bet you wear jammie pants to bed." They sat, but Lex stood right back up. Bye-bye, jeans.

"Sometimes. Sometimes I just risk it." Brant's eyes were fastened on his belly.

"Yeah?" He opened the button and zipper of his jeans, then shoved them down along with the underwear. His cock had lost no hardness in transit.

"Uhn." Brant licked his lips and reached out for him.

Lex moved closer, meeting Brant's hand halfway with his dick. Oh, Jesus, it had been too long since someone not him had touched him. Brant hummed for him, stroking him from base to tip.

"Fuck." Lex thrust gently, wanting more of that, just that way.

"Mmm…." Brantley kept hold of him as he leaned forward, nose sliding on his side.

"Damn." Lex wasn't sure what to do with his hands, but

he wanted to touch, so he petted Brantley's hair, then his neck.

Brant's hair was thick, a little coarse, and he found himself fascinated by it. He threaded his fingers through it, then rubbed. Massaging.

Brant moaned, the sound brushing the tip of his cock. He huffed out a breath, his mind going immediately to mouth, dick, sucking....

The hot swipe of tongue over the tip made his eyes cross.

"Brant. I want you too."

"Mm-hmm. Soon." Another lick threatened to dry his mouth out.

He stroked one bristly cheek. "Fuck. Oh God."

"Mmm...." Brant opened up, tongue dragging along Lex's shaft as he went down.

All he could do was close his eyes and let Brant have his way. His belly pulled in, his breath coming hard. Brant hummed softly, head bobbing as he swallowed.

"Brantley! Making me crazy." That mouth was a work of art.

He felt Brant grin all around him. Oh, pushy butthead. Beautiful man. Lex spread his stance and thrust, balls swinging. Brant took him, every inch, swallowing carefully on each push in. The man was a wonder. That hot, wet mouth was more perfect than anything sexual Lex had ever felt. No exaggeration.

"Don't stop," he whispered, and Brant nudged his balls with his chin.

No, he thought Brant was taking some pride in his work. Holy hell. Also, praise God, because he was going to remember this forever.

He laughed, but Brant didn't seem to mind. In fact, it seemed to inspire even better efforts, if that was possible.

Brant wrapped one hand around his backside, easing him in, over and over.

His body went tight as a bow, and his balls drew up. "Gonna, Brant. Can't hold it." He was just gonna go off like a rocket in seconds.

Brant dragged one finger along his perineum, the touch firm, maddening.

His mouth fell open, and he grunted, his body jerking when he came. Brant was blowing his mind. So to speak.

His mind. His soul. His cock.

Staggering a little when Brant released him, Lex tried to find something steady. His knees felt like jelly. "Wow."

"Thank you. Come here before you tumble."

"Yeah." Not so gracefully, he made it to the bed so he could flop. "You're amazing."

"You taste good, man." Brant leaned back, stretching out alongside him.

"Do I?" He slid one hand behind Brant's head to take a kiss, tasting himself on Brant's mouth. He liked Brant's heat, his scent, more than his own come, but it wasn't gross or anything. More bitter and salty.

Brant was warm and relaxed, easing into his arms like this was the most natural thing ever. Maybe it was. Lex loved the feel of it. He took another kiss, then another, urging Brant to rub against him. Brant's hunger began to push up to the fore, tongue pressing his lips open.

Lex moaned, opening up with all he had to let Brant in. He wanted to give as good as he'd gotten, wanted to please his lover. Brant was ready to go, he could tell. He reached down, stroking Brant's cock, going from the very base to the tip.

Arching against him, Brant nodded, his chin dipping twice. "Like that. You have the best calluses, man. Like the best."

He grinned, working his fingertips over the tip, then around the flared part of the head of that dick. Letting Brant feel his calluses all over.

Brant's lips dropped open, a needy gasp filling the air. Then Brant began to move, hips rocking as he worked to meet Lex's touch.

Lex gave a firmer grip, knowing what Brant needed now was more friction. He bent to kiss that open mouth, taking advantage and he knew it. It was worth it, making it easy to push in and taste every bit of Brant's mouth.

"Jesus. Please. So fucking good." Oh, that was a lovely sound—Brant's begging for him.

He nodded. "What do you want? My hands? You want me to suck you?"

"Uhn." Brant took his hand and started moving their fingers faster.

That was all the answer he needed. Yes. He stroked and pulled and tugged, watching Brant's face. Jesus, he was a little stupid about the expression in Brant's eyes, how he was focused on Lex, watching hard in return.

He licked at Brant's mouth again, leaning close to really press down, giving Brant an incredibly firm touch. Brant cried out, spreading wide and humping up toward his hand with a wild nod.

Boom, Lex felt fifty feet tall, because he'd found just the right touch. He pushed and pulled, almost too hard, but Brant took it and begged for more, so he gave all he could. Hungry bastard. He wanted to know what Brant smelled like, wanted to know everything.

He pressed the tip with his thumb on the next upstroke, really letting Brant have it.

"Lex!"

That was special—his name, yelled in passion. Goddamn.

Then Brant shot, seed spraying over his hands.

The scent was perfect, the heat wet and good. He rubbed what he could into Brant's skin, stopping only when Brant groaned and curled around his hand.

"You good?" Lex asked, low and hopeful.

"Uh-huh." Brant moaned for him, blinking and dazed.

"Oh, good." He smiled, this bizarre feeling opening up in his chest, expanding his worldview a little. "Me too."

"Can you stay, man?"

Oh. Oh, could he? Would Travis be okay? Hell, Travis had told him if he spent the night out to lock up. He had, right? So yeah, he would text and then settle in. "I can. I want to."

"Cool. We got all the streaming in here. Midnight snacks if we wake up."

"I like it." Better, he liked Brant, liked his house, loved that tight body. "Wanna wash up, or do you just want a warm washcloth?" His phone was in his pants. "I need to text Trav so he sees it when he wakes up."

"I'll wash up a little. You want a glass of water or anything?"

"Mmm. Water would be great. Hey." He took a kiss. "You're amazing. Did I say that?"

"Thank you. You… this was… so fucking good, Lex."

"Yeah." Okay, he could tell Brant meant it. On the same page again. He was falling hard.

"Cool. Two waters. I'll put a new toothbrush out for you. I buy them in four packs at the Costco."

"Smart move." Nurses. He didn't even worry that Brant meant he had a lot of guys over. Medical people were germ phobic. They really liked to have single-use things for hygiene.

"How long can they stay clean, right?" Brant sat up, and he got to see that hip as he walked by. It was, at once, horrifying and not that bad. There were scars from the surgery, but the actual bullet hole was clean. He knew from seeing too damn many examples that it was the exit wound that caused the big holes. This bullet had to have lodged against a bone. Lex let his fingers slide over it as Brant passed, then got up to follow Brant to the bathroom. Of course, he turned right around to grab his phone, then texted Trav.

Staying out overnight. See you tmrrw.

Brant had pulled out towels, washcloth, and a toothbrush for him, and even stole a kiss on the way out of the en suite.

He danced a moment, hands up like little pistols. He felt like a frickin' king. Washing up and brushing his teeth took only moments, and he was tickled to see Brant used Crest Whitening too.

God, it was amazing how mutual orgasms made life better.

By the time he made it back to bed, Brant had locked up and procured water. All they had to do was slip into bed together.

That huge beast of a cat was at Brant's feet, a giant fuzzy lump. As long as he stayed there and didn't try to claw Lex to bits, that was okay. He was a gorgeous animal.

Brant turned on the television, the sound of the *Lord of the Rings* movie starting up. "This is a perfect movie to sleep to."

"I used to use *The Thirteenth Warrior*."

"Oh, I love that one. Tons of eye candy."

"Totally." Lex loved younger Antonio Banderas. The guy was kinda... wrinkly now. Lex guessed that happened to everyone sooner or later.

Brant's hand landed on his hip, solid, sure. So Lex scooted closer, pressing a kiss to Brant's shoulder. "Thanks."

"Glad you came by, huh? We needed this."

"We did." Lex might be damn sad if he never got it again, in fact.

He got a long, lazy kiss, and then Brant settled next to him with a soft little sigh.

Time to let everything go for the night and just sleep. Tomorrow would be tomorrow.

9

*B*rantley's phone rang at six thirty, and he grabbed for it. "Yeah?"

"Is Lex there? His phone is going direct to voicemail."

"Trav, it's six thirty in the morning."

"Oh. Oh! I'm sorry. I didn't look." Travis sounded more… normal. Brantley hoped he'd gotten some rest.

"No worries. He is here. He's asleep. You need me to wake him?"

"Um. Well, I would love to take him to breakfast."

"How about I have him call when he wakes up?" *After a morning quickie.*

"Sure. Thanks. Is he okay? He didn't get all drunk and sloppy, did he?"

"He's fine, Trav." He slipped from the bed and went to feed the cats. "We watched movies and ate pizza."

"Oh." Now Travis sounded a little baffled. "Well, thanks, Brant. Just have him holler."

"I will. Are you…?" *Not okay, of course he's not okay.* "Did you get some sleep?"

"I did. Look, Brant, I'm sorry."

"I know. It's okay." What else was he supposed to say? Fuck off and die? He poured out kitty kibbles.

"No, it really isn't. I was an asshole. Like a giant, spoiled, gold-plated one."

God, he needed coffee. "It's understandable."

"That's really kind, but God knows I know when I'm bitchy. Anyway, thanks."

"I'm your friend too, Trav. I'm not going to disappear on you." He made himself a mocha with the Keurig.

"I might push it sometimes. I'm bitchy." Travis laughed, the sound far less tired. "Later, hon."

"I'll have Lex call. Bye." He went to the backyard and sat. It was cool this early, before the sun was really awake.

It didn't take Lex ten minutes before he peeked outside. "Hey."

"Hey, you. How goes? Did I wake you?"

"Nah. The cat did."

"Ah. I fed them. Travis is trying to get hold of you. Coffee?"

"Please. What did Travis want? I didn't have a charger on me, so my phone is out of juice."

"Oh. I have one." He stood up and offered Lex the K-cup carafe deal. "He wants to take you to breakfast."

"Mmm." Lex chuckled. "I'm a Cinnamon Toast Crunch kind of guy. Maybe a late lunch."

"I'm a coffee and orgasm kind of guy."

"I like the sound of that too." Lex hummed, grabbing him to take a quick kiss.

Oh good. It wasn't too much. He wrapped one hand around Lex's waist and held on, and the kiss went a little deeper, Lex moaning.

"Mmm...." They could share his coffee. He walked them to a chair so they didn't fall down.

"Good idea. Good morning." Lex grinned at him, smiled against his lips.

"Morning." He liked Lex on the chair, him on top better.

He took one kiss, another, then another. Brant really wanted to taste Lex. To feel him.

"I like how you wake up, Brant."

"Do you? I would have woke you up in bed if I'd've known."

Maybe they could try it tomorrow. Was that too much? He didn't know. Lex made him feel new things. Different from anything things.

Lex laughed for him, hands sliding down along his arms, warming him up. He hadn't realized he'd had a chill, but Lex was like a furnace. "You're cold, babe. You ought to come snuggle with me, in bed."

"I could. It's early." He stood, then took Lex's hand. "No one will care."

"Maybe the cats." Lex moved with him, climbing the steps with him side by side.

"They'll live. They're used to having me to themselves."

"I guess so. I saw one of the Persians when I was in the bathroom. I think she was judging me."

"She didn't run. That's amazing. She's a fraidy cat."

"Well, I was kinda stuck." Lex winked over at him when they crawled into opposite sides of the bed. They pushed under the covers and into each other's arms. Lex kissed his jaw, then his chin just under his lips, warm and easy. He was shivering—least of all from being cold. He was mostly just jonesing on being with a hot cop in his bed. And Lex was hot. Like physically as well as in charisma. He really revved Brant's motor. Lex seemed to agree. Or feel the same way. About Brant.

Lex dragged him in and rocked them together in a slow, steady rhythm. That big hand on his good hip made him smile, because Lex was hyperaware of his sore spots already. One kiss became two, then three, and suddenly he was dazed, trapped in their embrace. His breath came hard, his cock stiff. Damn. Orgasm was on the way.

"Mmm." Lex draped one leg over his, bringing their cocks together, wrapping them in one of Lex's hands.

Electricity shot up Brant's spine, surprising him with its strength. He wasn't a virgin by any means, but this was taking things up a level.

"Mmm. You like this."

"What's not to like, honey? Seriously." Orgasms were a good thing.

"I'm just glad, is all. I was afraid you'd be all, see ya. Not that you gave me reason to believe you would. I just don't want to be weird and pushy." Uncertain Lex was downright cute.

"Not weird. Not pushy. You're welcome back, anytime. I still owe you enchiladas."

"You so do. I might be pushy and ask when." Lex moved his hand, reminding them both there was hardness going on.

"Sup—oh God. That's good. Please, honey." His leg drew up, and he pressed it against Lex's balls, careful as could be.

"I know." Lex panted a little bit, rocking with him. Their bodies slid easily against each other, both of them doing their dead level best to keep things moving. Lex's thumb worked their tips, every single upstroke, and he found himself just holding on, clinging. His breath sounded so loud in his ears, and Lex was talking, hot, filthy little sex words strung together in no particular order. It liked to light him on fire, and he did his best to encourage.

Finally he needed more, though. Brant didn't think of himself as particularly demanding, but he rolled Lex to his back, wanting to press all along that muscled body.

"Oh baby. Yeah. Look at you." Lex grabbed his ass with the one free hand, jacking him and pushing him all at once. God, the man's hands…. Those calluses were inspiring.

"Want all of you." Solid, strong—Lex was like a jungle gym, just for him to explore.

"Oh God. I want that. I mean, this is perfect, but maybe soon…." Lex's eyes glinted with pure need.

"Yes. Yes. Please." He approved. He'd go buy good lube and rubbers.

"Oh." Now those eyes went wide, almost black. "Okay. Oh, fuck." Lex moved faster, bucking beneath him.

"Uh-huh. Over and over." He leaned down and fastened their mouths together before he said something else. Lex made him babble, made him do all sorts of things that were firsts. Like offer to let Lex fuck him on the first date.

Although, if they had another meal before supper, it would be the third date and that wasn't too slutty. Yeah. So there.

Lex bit his lower lip. "Why are you laughing?" Lex asked breathlessly.

"Happy. Horny. Trying to rationalize how bad I want you."

"I hear you." Lex drove up, cock sliding against his, then slapping against Brant's balls when he overbalanced. "Whoa. I got you."

Oh. Lex did. Those hands were sure, holding him tight, keeping him from going ass over teakettle, which was good. He didn't want to forfeit his orgasm one bit. No, he was on track for a spine-tingler.

"Good catch. God, I need you," he murmured, moaning against Lex's lips, the stubble there enough to make his eyes cross.

"Thanks. I have a vested interest." Lex chuckled but got him resettled so they could rub and bump and get cooking with oil again. Lex slid that hand down between them again, and they were roaring toward the finish in no time.

Brant cried out, digging his fingers into Lex's shoulders so he didn't lose his place again. He gritted his teeth, trying to hold on this time so he could see Lex's face when Lex came. He'd missed it last night because he'd been very busy sucking that fat, heavy cock.

Which he'd just promised to ride like a prized pony.

"Close, baby. So close."

Fuck, he loved a man who called him baby. He was a Texan, after all. That was hardwired into his DNA.

"Yeah. Now, Lex. Now." He couldn't hold back. He shot so hard he thought his head might fly right off. Hell, the first rush of it made him dizzy.

"Uhn!" Lex's shout rang out, bouncing off the walls of his bedroom. Christ, the man was gorgeous. Brant watched every moment, keeping his eyes open by sheer force of will.

Then he slumped down on Lex's chest. "Whoa."

"Mmm." Lex helped him ease off to one side, one hand lingering on his hip, rubbing away any stiffness. "Whoa indeed."

"Did you want to call Travis?"

Lex drew back to stare incredulously at him. "What? No. Why? To brag?"

Brant burst out laughing. "No, to tell him about lunch."

"It's still only sevenish. I'll call him after we snuggle and have coffee and something like carbs."

"My charger is over here...." Brant trailed off because he felt a huge yawn coming on.

"Later." Lex pulled him close, and even though they were gonna stick together when they woke up, it felt too good to argue. There was nothing a nap or two couldn't fix. That was his professional opinion as well as his personal one.

Phone calls could come later.

10

*L*ex hung out with Travis for a whole day—helping with paperwork and cleaning up. Travis had been calm, apologetic, almost dear when Lex had shown up, which was good, because he was done with the drama. They'd managed to do some of the hard work, and then they ordered the hottest Thai food in history and cussed and sweated their way through it.

"Jesus, Trav. You eat this shit every week?"

"Uh. Uh-huh. I love it." Travis was sweating like a whore in church.

"You're insane." Still he kept eating, didn't he? "You mind if I head over to see a friend tonight?"

"A friend? Another cop?"

His cheeks started burning, but he let himself blame the food. "I'm going to go see Brant."

"Brantley? Really? Are you sure?"

"What?" Lex grinned, not taking that obvious shock personally.

"He's so… staid."

Staid. Oh, so not his Brant. "He's got his moments, honey." He thought Brant was pretty damn exciting.

"Huh. Are you and him…? Uh…." Trav flapped his hands in the universal idiot sign for "together."

"Yeah." His face heated again, but Lex wasn't one to lie.

Travis gaped at him, looking amazingly like a landed trout. "You horndog!"

"I know." He shrugged. What could he say? "Brant does it for me, man."

Travis stared at him like he'd grown another head. "So… what's the plan, then?"

"What do you mean?" Surely Travis wasn't asking what he thought the man was asking.

Travis rolled his eyes. "Are you going out? Staying in?"

"He's making enchiladas." Lex was so all over that. Food. Sweat. Spicy kisses.

Oh.

Spicy blowjobs.

Uhn.

"Oh… you must be special. He's cooking for you. He's a good cook, really. We keep telling him to start a restaurant."

"Yeah?" Hoo, boy. Excelente. Lex rubbed his hands together.

"Yeah, so… what are you going to wear?"

"Um. Do I need to dress?" He'd been planning on jeans.

Travis rolled his eyes, lips gone prissy, and suddenly they were back in high school, the two of them about to go cruising. "Hon, maybe a little? A nice shirt, at least. He's cooking for you."

"Okay. A nice shirt and dark jeans." He would make Travis happy.

Travis looked him up and down before giving him a nod. "Very nice. You do clean up well."

"Thanks." He hugged Travis. "You'll be okay?"

"A couple of the teachers from school are coming by. We'll be fine."

"Cool. Call me if you need me." He winked. "Just not too late."

"Or too early, apparently...."

"Right. I mean, who calls someone at six thirty, Trav?" He'd been teasing Travis all day.

"Shut up," Trav shot back. "Who has a booty call with someone at a funeral?"

"I didn't do it at the funeral!" He cracked up, not able to keep the outrage.

Travis leaned against him, laughing too, and if the sound was a little bit wild... well.... Travis needed time. His emotions were on a roller coaster that was running off the tracks.

"Might as well have, huh?" Travis rested their shoulders together. "It's going to be a week soon. A whole week."

"The milestones are hard." He leaned in, creating a little pressure, something they did so much when they were kids. "I can come up whenever. Like holidays."

"Thanks. Thanks. I think I'm going to go back to work Monday. Get on the horse."

"Cool." Damn. That meant he had to stop waffling and go home. He needed to make that lunch date with the guys here too.

"Yeah. You want me to iron a shirt for you?"

"I—do you think Brant will want me all ironed?"

Travis blinked. "No. But your shirt, maybe. I do. Pick a shirt."

He laughed. "Okay, fine."

"Thank you."

Now Lex wiped his hands on his jeans, his palms ridiculously damp as he stood at Brantley's door. Enchiladas were probably not formal enough for what he was wearing—the dark denim and dress shirt over-the-top. Still, this was his date with Brant, right?

Right.

He knocked on Brant's door, sure he was already drooling at the scent of roasted chile.

"It's open, Officer. Come on in."

"Thanks." Travis had sent him with a bottle of wine, but he'd stopped to get beer as well. "Corona and limes."

"Oh, my hero! I have chips and guac on the counter here." Brant turned, wearing a T-shirt and a pair of loose shorts. "Oh, look at you! You dressed up! God, that's a great look on you."

"Travis made me." He held out the wine too. "He even ironed my shirt." This was hysterical. Really. Maybe he had workout gear in his truck.

"It's gorgeous. You want something more casual? We're going to be eating in the backyard."

"I think I'd better. You've seen how sloppy I am." Lex flexed. "Admire while you can."

"Mmm." Oh, he did enjoy the drag of Brant's eyes on his body. "I tell you what, I'll grab you something and watch you strip down. Fair enough?"

"As long as nothing will burn when I get to kissing you." He waggled his brows because he wanted those kisses.

"I was in the chopping stage, not the heating." Brantley grinned at him as they headed back toward the bedroom. He got a soft Lucky Charms T-shirt and a pair of shorts.

"Thanks." Feeling a little silly, Lex still gave Brant a tiny striptease, unbuttoning the shirt slowly. He popped each one open, then pulled the edges apart to show more and more skin.

"God, honey. You make my mouth dry." Brantley reached out and drew a single finger down along his chest.

"Mmm. Not the desert air?" His nipples hardened.

"I'm pretty sure. I've been here long enough to acclimate."

"Well, I'm pretty happy with that." He wanted to make Brantley crazy. Also happy, which was kind of a new one for him. It wasn't just about the sex.

Brantley leaned in, one hand wrapping around his hip. "Kiss me?"

"Yes." He bent his head to kiss that mouth, loving the way Brant moaned into his lips, leaned into his touches. Brantley tasted like salt and lime, like spice.

So yummy. Mixed with Brant's unique flavor, it was heady and wondrous.

"Mmm." They pulled back to breathe, grinning madly at each other.

"Here's comfy clothes. You like music?"

"Love it. What's your favorite?" He tugged his clothes the rest of the way off, then dressed in the soft stuff.

"I like country, nineties stuff, the Eagles."

"I like all those and Tejano too." Mexican three-step dancing was his jam.

"Oh, I love Tejano." Brant got a Tejano Hits Pandora radio station going.

"Woo." He grabbed Brant in the kitchen, dancing him about a little. It was fabulous, because Brant followed his lead like a dream. They stepped out smartly, ending in a dip, which made Brant hoot and holler. "What can I do?" Lex finally asked.

"You want to pull the chicken? I did it in the pressure cooker with the green chile in."

"Smells so good too. Your neighbors must be hoping you're making enough for them." Brant's house was little and cute, so the neighbors were pretty close. Not annoyingly so, but these old houses came in little pods.

"Señora Garces is in the hospital. She broke her hip, and Steve next door... well, you're probably right. He probably is hoping I'll bring some."

"Is he nice?" He found a big bowl, then started transferring chicken to it, pulling out the bones before scratching at it with two forks. Lex yodeled along with "Ay! Papacito"— which was one of his favorite songs ever—shaking his booty. He could do mariachi too, from "El Rey" to more modern Freddy Fender mash-ups. His mom had put him in a ballet folklorico when he was a kid.

"He is. Owns a clay studio on Fourth. Works a lot."

"Neat." He had no idea who his neighbors were. He'd bet Travis didn't know his either.

"Yeah. He's got a pit bull named Lilo that is in love with Mouse. They have playdates."

"Playdates. A cat and a pibble?" He paused, forks poised. "That sounds like a movie." Really, and he would pay to go see it.

"It's adorable. The other two won't have anything to do with her, but Mouse waits for her in the front window."

"Oh, that's cute." He hadn't seen any of the cats today, but only Mouse had been brave enough to attack his feet by the time he left yesterday, so….

They started rolling enchiladas, working together like they'd done it for years. It was weird, because he'd cooked with his mama, but not a lover. In fact, he'd eaten out on dates, but he couldn't ever remember having a guy over to his place. He always went to theirs. Would Brant come down and see him?

They got the enchiladas in the oven, and then they took beer, chips, and guac to the outside table. The air was redolent of the flowers and roasted chile from the grill, and the shade cover was perfect, making the small backyard into an oasis. Lex really admired it, and he told Brant so.

"Thank you. It's taken forever to get it cleaned up like I wanted it."

"You did all this, huh?" Lex didn't have a black thumb, but he had the one plant. His mom, now, she had wisteria and lilacs and bell bushes and butterfly bushes… anything that bloomed.

"I did. I wanted a place to sit and drink a beer. I have a patio heater and a fire pit too." Brantley looked so pleased.

"Neat! I always wanted one of those chimineas." He loved toasting marshmallows. "I took a vacation up in Durango once, and they had the best fire pit at the lodge."

"Yeah? I'd love to go. Matty invited me a lot, but they hiked and did rock climbing. I can take long walks just fine, but long hikes can be hard."

"I bet. I don't hike as much, but I love to snowboard. I grew up skiing, but boarding is cool. I don't get the chance near as much now." He didn't do a lot but work. He hung out with Dusty and Nate, watched movies, worked out….

"I bet I couldn't do that either, but damn it looks fun."

"Did you know they do five-man inner tubes in Ruidoso? Like with seats. You can slide." Lex had bounced down the mountain with four other cops as a team-building thing. What he'd found out was cops were vicious.

"Yeah? I could do that. I need to start exploring more places."

"I bet you let Matt set up a lot." He could see that. He let Nate do all sorts of stuff for him, picking places to go to eat for the three of them. He had a few guys at work too, who recommended burritos and tacos and dry cleaning.

"Right? He was so in love with New Mexico that it was easy to just let him choose."

"Yeah." He sipped his beer, and the mouth of the bottle had enough lime on it to draw his mouth up. "Hoo. That was all sour, huh?"

"Oh, let me taste." Brant leaned over and took a kiss.

Lex opened right up to share the lime and beer flavor, and to get his happy little jollies. Those kisses were amazing. Long and slow and sweet.

They were lost in the contact until Brant grunted and eased back, rubbing his hip. "Sorry."

"Do you ever get massage therapy for that?"

"I have, but not for a long time."

"I can offer a good pair of hands. I took classes, but I never got my license. Just lost the time."

"Oh… that sounds like…. Are you real, man? Married? Closeted axe murderer? Have an army of man-eating rats?"

"Uh… I live three and a half hours away? I snore. And I work a lot." Lex wanted to be up front.

"I hear you. I am obsessed with cookbooks, I love my cats, and I try to leave my work at work."

"Cookbooks. Trav says you're like chef material."

Oh, that pleased Brant. Look at that blush. "I just like to cook. A lot. Good thing I like to eat."

"Me too. I mean, I will totally be a guinea pig."

"Yeah? You're not picky?"

"Not really, no. I mean, I am about biscochitos and tamales. Christmas food. Otherwise, well, I'm a cop." He'd put some truly awful things in his mouth.

"What's your favorite type of tamale?"

"Pork with red chile. Like super classic."

"I love goat cheese and black bean, to be honest. Green chile chicken too. I've also made apple pie tamales." Brant grinned at him, the look almost sheepish. "But I know how to make Christmas tamales."

"Apple pie?" He tilted his head. "With cinnamon and butter?"

"Yeah—I put a little sugar and cinnamon in the masa, fill with apple pie filling."

"Oh my God." Lex blinked, because that sounded life changing.

"They're great with ice cream. Cinnamon ice cream."

Lex was going to fall to his knees and beg. He'd had a

cheesecake chimichanga once. This sounded so much better. "Someday? For me?"

"Sure, honey. I'd love to cook for you."

"Well, you are. But those tamales sound ah-mazing."

"They go good with chili for supper." Brantley touched his knee. "Or pork belly and polenta."

"You're making me drool." Lex liked how Brant talked about food. There was passion there.

"Matty used to tell me when he made his fortune, he'd buy me a restaurant. I just like to cook for people I love, though."

His cheeks heated, but Lex didn't comment on that last part. "Not everyone is in it to make a living. My mom sews, but she only did alterations for, like, a month. It put her off sewing for a year."

"Right? I don't know that I want to deal with food costs and overhead and stuff."

"Nah. And you like nursing." He got that. Dusty was committed to medicine. That was why Lex had stayed a cop instead of going on to be an EMT. He helped people in his own way with less puke.

"Eighty-five percent of the time, yeah. Everyone has their days, huh?"

"Shit, yes. When I'm on some damn disturbance call because some asshole wants me to solve his problem with his neighbor or when someone makes pig noises when I walk by…." There were worse things, but he didn't want Brant to have trauma.

"Mine normally involves shots. I hate when they scream when they see me."

"Oh, man. Do you feel like a villain?" He would. Like when kids in some neighborhoods were worried he was ICE, or that he would shoot them.

"Yes. God, I'm the fucking boogeyman with a syringe. Somehow to them I have an ice pick instead of a tiny needle."

Brant shrugged. "We try to switch off, so I inject Dr. Montoya's patients and Lacey does Dr. Nunez's."

"That's smart." That way the kids saw their nurse as the hero and only saw the other one for shots. "I like to do school visits early and let kids know we're not the enemy."

"Is it as bad down there as up here? The news makes the cops sound like... villains."

"It's not, because we're so much smaller. Better run. We have more border stuff." More drugs.

"Ah. I'll have to visit Las Cruces one day. I've never been." A timer went off, and Brant stood. "Enchiladas ho!"

"Oh, yum. No? There are some good events. The Ren faire is great. A juried art show and all."

"That sounds like fun. I loved the big Scarborough faire deal in Waxahachie." Brantley pulled the big red pan from the oven. "You want to plate up in here or bring the casserole out?"

"Oh, I don't stand on ceremony. We can dish up in here."

"Well, come on, honey. Let's eat."

"Woot." He loaded up a plate with the spoon Brantley handed him. Okay, that looked like green chile heaven. He wanted Christmas next. Who was he kidding? He wanted everything.

They settled back outside, the lights coming on as the sun sank. God, it was like magic. Lex loved this whole moment.

Brant lifted his beer. "Cheers, honey."

"Cheers." He clinked his bottle against Brant's and then dug in, moaning softly. This was the real thing. Good shit. Something about this moment seemed... oddly profound.

Strange for beer and chicken. Strange but wonderful.

Lex let go of all the pressure and stress of the last week and kinda... basked.

Brant had music playing, and they chatted and ate, laughing at each other. They traded more work stories and family stories and just sat together. The sun went away, and the heat faded quickly. It felt good for a bit, but then they had to head in. Lex helped with the dishes, and then they stared at each other.

"You want to go to the bedroom?" Brant finally asked. "We can watch TV for a bit. Maybe take a shower?"

He took Brant's hand. "I do, yeah."

"Me too." Brant squeezed his fingers. "Thank you."

"Hey, it's been an amazing night, baby." He grinned over, his heart thudding.

"You know it. Easy, fun, delicious, and not over yet."

"Nope. Not even close." It was only about nine.

They had hours to explore each other. Hours. Lex was over the moon, because there was no rush, and they could stretch out the anticipation all they wanted.

Magic.

Pure fucking magic.

BRANT WOKE up with Lex in his arms, the man snuggly and warm, wrapped around him like an octopus.

He kissed Lex's temple, being careful, gentle. He wasn't trying to wake his new lover, just enjoy him. The early morning sun was just peeking in through the slats of the blinds, and this was one of his favorite times of day. The birds were out there going crazy, the world was fresh, and he didn't have to be up because he was off until Monday.

He wiggled his toes because stretching would disturb Lex, and Brant was jonesing on the way Lex was breathing against him. They had a wonderful time last night—they'd laughed, showered, watched bad TV, made love. Lex was funny. Hot. He did a mean dish. Told a great story. Of course, he lived hours away and got shot at for a living.

Brantley shook his head. That was borrowing trouble. Lex might leave and never be seen again.

Not that Matt hadn't disappeared. Hell, it wasn't like he was drowning in lovers, so why was he worrying?

Hell, he knew the answer to that. He'd had his two long-time guys. Two—one guy hadn't come home from overseas, the other had driven his SUV off a bridge outside of Dallas after coming after him with a knife. He wasn't Mr. Lucky.

He stroked Lex's back, trying to relax and let his mind wander. Even the cats weren't up yet. How often did that happen? Seriously?

Mouse would be there soon, he was sure. The silly beast could tell when his breathing changed. Either that or he was psychic. Maybe an alien kitty. Oh, this was New Mexico, after all. There it was. Alien.

He should have named the cat Mulder.

"Why are you laughing?" Lex murmured.

"I was maligning my cat in my brain."

"Which one?" Lex lifted his head, looking about cautiously.

"The evil one. The girls are just pseudo-evil."

"Eventually they might warm up, huh?"

"They might. It took them almost a year to pretend to like me." They'd been rescues from a hoarder in Chama.

"Ah. Persians are like that, right? I read up on the internet."

"These two are. And since they have each other…."

"Right. Who needs the hooman? Good morning."

"Good morning." *When are you planning on going? Why do I care so much?*

"Mmm. Kiss me?" Lex lifted his face, smiling.

"I can so do that." He leaned down and took a long, slow good-morning kiss, one hand tangling in Lex's heavy shock of hair.

Lex moaned, just arching and giving it up for him. Oh, he did love another morning person.

They grinned at each other, and he thought maybe Lex felt the same way.

A wild screech sounded and Mouse landed between them, looking incredibly pleased with himself.

"Oof." Lex pulled back a little. "Heavy."

"Rowl."

That was a clear answer. He wasn't sure what Mouse meant, but the answer was clear.

"He's hungry," Brant said.

"You mean he can't feed himself?"

"Well, if he had thumbs…." He leaned his forehead against Lex's, both of them chuckling. Lex reached out to scratch Mouse's back gently. Brant held his breath, waiting to see….

Mouse slowly eased himself into Lex's lap, the purr like the Latvian chainsaw drill team. *Oh wow. Look at that. Good enough, huh?*

Lex blinked up, obviously stunned.

"I know, right?" He said it softly, not wanting Mouse to know he was stunned.

"Yeah. I guess I'm okay."

"I guess you are, honey."

Lex just beamed. "Wow."

"I guess we'll have to keep you, then."

"Yeah?" That made Lex blink and flush. "Well, then."

He began to heat, and he ducked his head. "You want some coffee?"

"I do, but I want another kiss first." Lex grabbed him, and they shared a long, slow embrace, his tongue sliding against Lex's. How could he be self-conscious when Lex kissed him like that? Lex made him believe. That was probably dangerous as all get-out, seeing how little they knew each other, but he couldn't help it.

He was a stupid optimist.

Meowing loudly, Mouse dropped back to the floor and walked to the door.

Right. Food.

"I'm going to feed the beasts and start coffee. You think about what we should do for breakfast."

"I can help feed them. If you want."

"Perfect. The girls will be tickled." He found the two cans, the three bowls.

"Cool. I mean, I figure they might like me more. Then again, they might starve rather than eat food that smells like me."

"No. They slept on your feet last night." They were just shy and a little goofy.

"Did they?" Talk about goofy. Lex's smile was utterly happy and free.

"Yeah, I woke up for a second, and they were snuggling. It was too cute."

"That's cool. I never see them. Except in the bathroom."

"Girls! Come on. Get your breakfast."

Lex was being mauled by his hungry boy, Mouse rubbing Lex's ankles, then sinking in heavy claws. "Dammit! Mouse! I'm hurrying!"

Don't laugh. Don't laugh. Lex was getting trained already.

He fed the girls and started the coffee.

Mouse and Lex ended up on the floor, Mouse sitting in Lex's lap, head in the food bowl, so he fixed Lex a cup of coffee and handed it down.

"Thanks. He's, uh, firm about what he wants."

"He's a beast. Is it weird that I adore him?" He leaned against the wall with his own coffee.

"No." Lex dared to touch that fluffy butt.

Mouse arched up, rowling softly.

"Are we buds now? Huh?" Lex scritched carefully, but well.

Mouse flipped himself over, dancing on Lex's lap.

"Oh, now you've done it." Brantley snorted. "You're owned, man. Owned."

"I love it." Lex was laughing with him, just rubbing that furry belly.

Mouse rolled dough, huge claws moving in and out.

"Man, he's got some muscles." Lex grunted the words, rubbing hard.

"He's a monster." Miss Cream snuck up, barely brushing Lex's elbow. "I think they like me," Lex murmured.

"Wow," he whispered and settled down on the floor too.

"Yeah?" Lex winked. "My animal magnetism."

"Yeah, it's amazing."

Peaches watched for a long second before curling up in Brantley's lap. "Bet this isn't how you imagined spending your morning."

"Nope, but that's okay. I like not having to have an agenda." Lex pulled a bit of a face. "I hate to think of us both having to go back to work, but I know we'll have to." Then Lex brightened. "But not today."

"Not today. When will you leave, do you know?" Was that needy?

"I don't. I need to call in before Monday, see if I still have a job." Lex winked.

"Ah. Well, you're welcome to hang out with me, you know…." That was totally needy. "And I'm sure with Travis too."

"He seemed better yesterday, but I'm loving being with you. And I feel so bad for him and want to help."

"I don't know how else to help. Honest." He stroked Peaches's long, soft fur. "But whatever I can do."

"I know you will. What he'll need from here is to be remembered on holidays and such, and to have someone to remember Matt with."

"Yeah. One day maybe he'll forgive me for living. That'll take a while."

"I think it will, yeah. He's a butthead." Lex said it without malice.

"He's a queen. I love him a lot. Matty adored him." And that had been enough for him.

"Yeah. He'll be better about it now, I think, but people react to grief differently."

"Sure they do. I'm not mad." *Much.*

"Uh-huh." Lex chuckled but shrugged. "I would be, because Trav can say the most hurtful things."

"Yeah. Yeah, he can. I tried, you know?"

"I know." Lex reached over to grab his hand, then squeezed. Peaches leaned in and bit Lex's thumb. "Ow!" Lex blinked at the cat. "So much for friends."

"I don't think she's made her mind up yet. Cream, though, she's got you."

"Yeah." Lex shook his head. "Breakfast?"

"Weck's?"

"Hell, yeah." Lex eased up off the floor, grinning wide.

"Rock on." He let Lex help him up.

"What's your favorite?" Lex asked. "I like the ultimate papas."

"Uhn. I like the veggie papas with extra veg. Oh my God."

"Yum. We'll have to split a cinnamon roll at some point too." Lex rubbed his belly, looking pretty lascivious.

"Oh. Oh, a man after my own heart." He was all over a grilled roll.

"Good deal. What do we need to do before we go?" Lex was surprisingly domestic.

"Not a thing. I'll just close up after we're ready to go."

"Cool." Lex bounced a little, kind of like a boxer, from foot to foot. God, that was cute.

He reached out, cupped one buttcheek. "Come on, honey. Let me feed you."

"Yes, please." They headed back to dress, moving around

like two people far more used to each other than they ought to be.

"You want to hit the Fruit Basket and grab stuff for supper on our way home?"

"I do. We'll make some kind of pasta, huh?" Lex bumped hips with him on his good side.

"Oh, hell yeah. With garlic bread, hmm?" He was all in.

"Yep. I love me some garlic bread." They both found clothes, tugging them on and going through the teeth-brushing, hair-combing thing. The best part was the random touching, the kisses.

He could get so used to this very fast.

Lord, he was in so much trouble.

11

"*H*ey, boss." Lex kinda held his breath, knowing he was probably about to get a tongue-lashing.

"Do I know you?"

"Ha. Yeah, I've been evaluating my life choices."

"What the hell does that mean? Are you going to become a belly dancer?"

"No. It just means I might be asking for a leave of absence. I'm looking into moving back up here." He believed in being honest. He needed to see his folks, needed to find out what was going on with him and Brant....

"No shit? You know that force is having... issues." *Issues.* That was like calling World War II a skirmish.

"I do. And I love you guys. You know that." He did. The men and women he worked with were amazing.

"So? What's up, Espana? Seriously."

"I met someone." Hell, he told this guy everything. "I don't want to rush things, but I want to leave my options open."

A short, sharp bark sounded. "At a funeral? That's damn impressive, Espana. Damn impressive."

"I know, right? What's even weirder is I met him at the wedding and didn't even remember."

"You're not serious."

"He was the other best man."

"Wow." Gutierrez paused. "Okay, I can probably swing it, but I need you to come work a few days of shifts so I can move things around."

"Sure. Of course. I won't leave you hanging." He needed the recommendation. Hell, he needed the friends.

"Cool. I can live with that. I need you by Wednesday."

Well, that was better than Monday.

"I'll be there. I just…."

"Don't waffle, man." God, he respected the fuck out of the son of a bitch.

"Okay. I'll be in Wednesday. What shift?" *Right, no waffling.*

"Be in at seven. We'll talk."

"Got it." He couldn't believe he did that. He'd just told his boss he was going to…. To what? What the actual fuck?

He shook his head. Christ. Now he needed to call the guys up here and see if they were even interested in him transferring. And then there was Brant. What if this was a fling?

He had no idea. Maybe it was Matt dying. He'd not known the man well, but… well, after the bombing, he didn't need a huge reminder that life was short. He wanted to try. He wanted to cook with Brant, laugh, play checkers, and watch stupid movies. He'd never once wanted to go on more than just a few dates. Now he wanted to… see what happened.

"You okay, honey? Everything all right?" Travis popped his head in. "I was going to make popcorn."

"I would love some." He smiled at Travis. "I just asked for a leave of absence."

"At your job? For me?"

"Yeah." He pushed back guilt. It was partly for Travis, to reconnect with his old friend, with his family.

"Honey, are you sure? I mean, you know you're welcome here, for as long as you want, but...."

"Oh, hon, if you don't want me here, I get it, but I'm thinking it might be time for a change."

"Really? It might be nice to have a roommate."

Yeah, and it would be nicer to be Brant's. Lex just made a noncommittal noise. He would start at Trav's and work his way over, come to that.

"I'm going to have to head back for a few weeks. You know, this is going to take time. It's a process."

"Sure. Of course." Travis watched him carefully. "What does Brant think?"

"I have no idea." None. Well, that wasn't true. Brant seemed to like him in that big bed just fine. But did Brant have an opinion on him moving up? Lex hadn't been brave enough to ask.

"Maybe you... I mean, you've spent the night there...."

"I'm not sure, Trav, not of anything." Lex spread his hands, not wanting to lie, but not wanting to make himself promises.

"No. None of us are, right?" Travis came to him and held him. Tight. Lex held on in return, knowing Travis had to be freaking out over everything. Every single thing. Lex couldn't even begin to comprehend all this, and Matt hadn't been his husband.

"We'll be okay, buddy." He kissed Travis on the cheek. "Want to go to lunch? I'll take you."

"I—sure. Where?"

"You pick, honey. You want the Flying Star?"

"Oh, fancy! I'd love that."

"Well, get dressed." Lex felt like he was neglecting Travis a little.

"Yeah, yeah. I'm not naked."

"You stink," he teased.

"Oh ho! Asshole. At least I brushed my teeth."

"Thank God for that. Dragon man." Lex loved the hint of the former Travis.

"I'll be right back." Travis looked him over. "You could comb your hair." Trav grabbed his hair, tugging. "You need to do your roots."

"Do I?" He hadn't even looked. "I'm all gray."

"Silver, but yeah. Old fucker."

"Am not!" Just early to gray. Lex pinched Trav's ass. "Go on. We'll have an outing."

"An outing. Christ." Trav grabbed him again. "Thanks, honey. Seriously."

"You're welcome. You know I love you more than my luggage."

"I know. I know. Penal queen."

"Go." He pushed gently, then flapped his hands. It was weird, and it was going to be hard, but Lex thought Trav was going to be all right. He would help any way he could too. He texted Brant, just to let him know what was up, then wondered if that was oversharing.

Cool. Coming for supper tonite?

Totes. What do I bring?

Thinking steaks and potatoes?

Sounds good. Send me a list and I can stop on the way.

K. Looking forward to it.

Me too.

He sent a smiley with a heart and got a picture of Mouse sitting on the vacuum for his trouble.

He headed upstairs to make sure his hair was okay and that *he'd* brushed his teeth. Maybe he did need to do his roots. Yikes. What was that stuff? Brylcreem or something?

Travis would know. He probably had, like, a guy. A stylist. Lex had a barber who did fades and mohawks. Brant had… Supercuts. He knew it. Supercuts on his lunch hour. He chuckled. That was so practical. Like all medical folks he knew, except the ones who had wild colors in their hair. He could see Brant doing that for Halloween. Maybe... maybe he'd be able to see Brant's costume this year. Oh....

He liked that idea a lot. A hell of a lot. Grinning, he trotted down the stairs to meet Travis.

"You driving or am I?" Travis asked.

"I can, no problem." He'd just gotten gas, and Travis hadn't been out in days.

"Thanks. I.... It doesn't seem like it should be the same place, you know? Like it's disrespectful for life to go on."

"I know, honey. I swear, you'll figure it out."

"Maybe. I don't know yet. Right now, I'm going to have lunch."

"Yep." He took Travis's hand. "I might have a burger."

"Yeah? I'm going for the quinoa salad."

"Skinny minny," he teased, leading Trav out before he changed his mind.

"Only because I want dessert."

"Ah, now we see. Good choice." Flying Star was known for its baked goods. "Chocolate?"

"God yes. Something that's ten thousand calories with ice cream."

"I'm with you, man." He so was. With two forks. "You want to go to that one on Rio Grande?"

"I do. That's better than Corrales."

"Cool." If they could find a parking space, they'd be golden. He knew there was parking out back, which a lot of folks forgot.

"Hey, Lex." Travis reached over, patted his leg. "I love you, huh?"

"I love you too, hon. I really do." They were going to make a good day out of it.

Then he was going home to Brant.

12

*S*orry, man. Not feeling great. Breakfast instead?
    Brant had taken a tumble in the driveway moving out the trash cans, and more than his pride was hurt. He wasn't even sure he was going to be able to get off the couch.

Ever.

What happened? Lex's text was gratifyingly fast.

Fell sorry huh

I'll be over in a few

He didn't know what to say. No, don't? He wanted Lex there. He didn't want to look like a wuss. And he couldn't cook. No way.

See you soon.

He sighed, putting his head back on the couch. Maybe a tiny nap. Lex had a key, and Brant had muscle relaxants. Both important things.

He dozed, or at least he thought he must have, because he woke up to the amazing smell of baking bread.

"Lex?" *Come on. Come on, sit up.*

"Yep. Don't move, baby. It's okay. Do you need anything

right now?" Lex came out of the kitchen to peck a kiss on his lips.

"I'm sorry. I didn't mean to."

"Right, because I would think that." Lex stroked his cheek. "What happened?"

"I went ass over teakettle, moving the trash cans." He wasn't sure what he'd slipped on, to be honest.

"Do I need to go look, make sure there's nothing to trip over? I put rolls in the oven but haven't started steaks. I wanted to make sure you hadn't hurt your face."

His knees, his hands, his hip—yeah. Face? No.

"So, I have the stuff for soup or steak and potatoes."

"Sounds great. I'll come help." If he could stand. *Come on. Come on, up.*

"No. You sit. Seriously. Do you need Tylenol or something? Did you clean up any scrapes?"

"I took a muscle relaxant." Brant's cheeks were burning. He hadn't tripped like that in a while.

"Okay. I'll have a thorough inspection later." Lex gave him a cheeky wink.

"Yeah, yeah, yeah." He levered himself up on his butt. "Did you have a decent day?"

"I did. Travis was in a good mood."

"Good. Is he ready to get back to school?" He was going back Monday—at least assuming he could walk.

"I think so, yeah. He talked to the admin folks, and they're giving him a classroom assistant for a few weeks, just to see how he does."

"He'll be fine. He's a great teacher." *Okay. Up to help in the kitchen.*

"Hey. Sit. I got this. I'll holler if I need you." Lex came back over to ease him down on the couch again. "Seriously."

"I feel like an idiot."

"Trust me, we all do when we go down. Happens,

though." Lex flapped a hand. "Be right back. I'll just put the potatoes in."

"Yeah. We all have our moments, I guess." Some more than others.

"We do." Lex laughed. "You should have seen me last year. I was pursuing a suspect on foot during monsoon season. I busted my ass in the middle of West Picacho, just slid like a runner going into third, legs up and spread."

"Oh man. Did you get road rash on your jewels?"

"I got it on the jewels, on my ass, on my thighs. I looked like a motorcycle cop."

"Mmm...." Lex would look hot on a motorcycle. "Do you ride?"

"I know how." Lex's voice floated from the kitchen. "I'm not good at it. Lack of practice."

"I do too. I mean, I did when I was a kid. I thought I was a stud."

"You were. You still are." Lex sounded very sure.

He laughed, but he appreciated it. "You know, I do pretty good for a guy who was told he'd never walk again."

"See?" Lex wandered back into the front room. "Will it hurt if I sit?"

"Not a bit." He slid his legs around. "Come sit with me."

"Cool. No sense starting the steaks until the rolls and spuds are done." Lex moved in beside him, but let him decide how close. Fuck that shit, he wanted access. Lex was here; he was taking advantage.

"Hey, you." He took a gentle kiss.

"Hey. I'm sorry you're feeling bad, baby. That sucks."

"I'm sorry to have almost wasted part of our time together. I'm guarding it."

"So am I." Lex chuckled, then leaned to kiss him again. "But I'm stubborn."

"You? No." He let himself press in, hard. "Never say so."

He felt like a flirt, like he was trying to lure Lex in, which was weird.

"Mm-hmm. I really am. I want to be in homicide some-time soon. They say those are the most stubborn cops."

"Yeah? Detective Espana, huh? Nice ring." It was a little scary, thinking about that, about Lex hunting murderers.

"You know it. I would love a desk more than a car."

"Yeah? How does it work? I mean, I don't know anything about it." He held Lex's hand, tracing the strong fingers.

"Well, we're all overworked, but I would be on a better shift, a better team. Less face time with the street."

"Do you like it? Being an officer?"

"I do. I mean, I thought about becoming an EMT, but that's way more bodily fluid."

Brant began to laugh, because his life was all bodily fluids, all the time. Babies didn't care.

"I know, right? My doctor friend, Dusty, laughs at me. So does his partner, Nate."

"Yeah. They're watching your house?" He needed to remember that he had a life here too, one that wasn't lonely. He had a support group outside of Lex.

"My plant. That's really all I worry about."

That was sort of sad. "I bet Mouse would find you a friend."

"I bet he would. I can always come see Mouse. Right?" Lex looked right into his eyes.

"Always. Mouse and the girls adore you. They're going to miss you when you go home."

"I know. Me too." Lex cleared his throat, and then the strangest look crossed the man's face. "I asked for a leave of absence. I have to go back Wednesday so shifts can be rearranged."

"A…. You're going to come up here?" Seriously? A thou-sand questions crossed his mind, but behind that was a quiet, hysterical little voice cheering.

"I want to look into it, yeah. I think I could have a job, no problem. I need to see my folks, maybe." Lex grinned a little sheepishly. "Warn them."

"Are they local?" *Are you staying with them?*

"Uh, mostly. Placitas now. Not too far."

"Oh, that's nice. Neat art."

"Yeah. Mom's people had some land out there. They used to be down off Menaul."

"Oh yeah? There are some nice houses out there." Brantley didn't know what to say, dammit. He had ten thousand questions. Ten thousand and one. The big one was, *does this have anything to do with me?*

"Is this okay? I mean, I told Trav it was partly for him, but I want—" Lex took a deep breath. "I think we need to see where this is going?"

"Oh." He felt like all the air went out of the room. "I was too much of a coward to ask. I should have."

"You should." Lex grabbed his hand. "I feel like this is different."

"I was dreading you going back forever. I was already considering a trip down." Was that silly as all get-out or what?

"Well, I think you should totally come down and meet Nate and Dusty, but I'll only be gone about a week this time." Now Lex was beaming.

"Yeah? I could come see over a weekend or something." He could drive down and let Lex show him around.

"That sounds amazing. We can go to Mesilla and see all the cheesy fun. Billy the Kid and stuff."

"Sure, just tell me when." He would head south Friday after work, be there for a late, late supper.

"I would love to see you this coming weekend. It's not a bad drive on 25."

"Okay. I could come Friday night, stay 'til Sunday…."

"That would be awesome. I can't promise I won't be on

shift a bit of it, but I'll have plenty of time to show you around." Lex kissed him gently. "If you're up to it."

"I'll manage. I'll be ready to get out of town after work."

"Sounds great, baby." Lex kissed him one more time before rising. "Steak time."

"Steak time." Had they just…? Were they having a thing?

Lex winked and headed to the kitchen. Yeah. Yeah, he thought this was a thing.

He made it to the bathroom, and he washed up, trying to put this whole thing—this whole damn near two weeks, Matty, Travis, Lex, even falling—into perspective. The whole world felt a little topsy-turvy, like he'd gone down the rabbit hole. A little.

Shit. A lot. Was this normal? Even for him?

He grinned, then splashed some water on his face. The muscle relaxants made him goofy.

"You okay, baby? No falling."

"No. No falling." Though he'd done that. Hard. For Lex and in the driveway. He headed back out into the house. "It smells amazing."

"Yeah? I do the potatoes in the mic, but crisp the skin in the oven. I'll finish the steaks in there too." Lex was moving around his kitchen easily.

"I love that."

"What?" Lex looked over at him.

"That you cook too. That we can make things together."

"Me too." Lex nodded and slid steaks on a sheet pan to put in the oven. "I love your kitchen, man. It's well-equipped."

"Thank you. I bought the house for the big master and the way the kitchen and outdoor space works together."

"It seems way smaller from the front, for sure, but back here it's roomy."

"Exactly. It sort of balloons. It's… it's home." And he

couldn't help that. Somehow, the Land of Entrapment had caught him too.

"It's too cool. Do you need to sit?" Lex came to put big, warm hands on his hip, and the touch made him cry out in ease, his knees wanting to buckle.

"Oh, baby." Lex knelt on the floor, rubbing at him just enough so he got heat and not pressure.

"Lex." This was better than sex. This was fucking magic.

"I got you. I learned this a while back. It's almost like Reiki."

He'd heard of that, but had no idea really. All he could do was stand there and breathe, in and out, and feel. Lex warmed him, then eased him down, massaging gently. His muscles let go, and he almost cried.

"Oh, baby. I have you. That's better. Now you can eat supper."

"I can." He felt dizzy but good. "Thank you, honey. God. That was magic."

"You're welcome. You looked so sore."

He hadn't known it could feel so good. "Yeah, I think I was. Seriously."

"Well, hopefully this helps. Steaks are tough on the couch." Lex winked.

"Let's sit at the table. You want a beer?"

"I do, if you don't mind."

"Shiner or Corona?" He was going to have tea. If he had a beer, he'd fall asleep in a second. In his steak.

"Shiner for beef, I think." Lex plated up, and dinner looked glorious.

"On it." Soon they were sitting and eating, like they were meant to be there together at his little square dining table. The A.1. sauce sat between them, and Brant had the strangest urge to laugh. So normal.

"What's funny, babe?"

"How fast this has become easy. You. Me. Together."

"I know." Lex dipped his chin. "I feel weird sometimes, but I want it too."

He dared to reach out, take Lex's square hand. They sat there like that for a long while, grinning at each other. The food was pretty much gone, so it was no big deal to take their time.

"You want to sit and watch something terrible on Netflix?"

"God, yes. Do you need a heating pad or a hot water bottle? You have to have one." Lex let go to stand up and clear dishes.

"I'll grab the pad. There are cupcakes in the fridge for later."

"You're amazing." Lex dropped a kiss on his mouth when he passed by.

No. No, he was just a little in love.

13

"*D*amn it, Espana, get your head in the game."

"Huh?" Lex glanced at Sergeant Gutierrez. "What did I miss, Ben?"

Wednesday had gone tough. Thursday wasn't shaping up to be better. Lex just couldn't seem to concentrate on a cruiser or on reports. He just wanted to be home. In Albuquerque. With Brant.

"Well, we have work to do." Ben smiled. "How's your buddy?"

"Devastated." He sighed. "Freaking out." Travis had melted down on him when he left. Christ.

"It's a shit situation. They have any leads?"

"No. I mean, he's on camera, but they assume he wasn't local." Lex wasn't sure he bought that, but the I-25 corridor was a vast thing, and Albuquerque was the biggest metro in New Mexico. The guy could be anywhere in Albuquerque, even, and not get found.

"That sucks, man. Seriously."

"Yeah. I feel bad for him. His folks can't help much. His mom is pretty sick." Travis's school friends were finally kicking in some, but they were all just so damn young. They didn't know what to do with loss.

"Fucking sick bastards, just shooting guys." Gutierrez shook his head. "You really got a honey up there?"

"I do. I gotta admit, he's on my mind." He sat back from even pretending to try to type.

"He a cop?" Was that a spark of interest?

"Nurse. Nothing dangerous, thank God. I worry enough about me." Lex winked.

"Nurse, huh? Damn."

"I know." He never knew what the hell Gutierrez meant by those statements. "He's a good guy. Veteran. Good cook. Has his own house."

"Sounds like a great situation. We're underserved down here. I bet he could get a job, instead of you going up."

"Yeah." Somehow he didn't see it. Brantley was happy up north, was fascinated by the mountains, loved his house. "He's coming down this weekend to visit."

"Well, good. Keep me posted."

Lex nodded, but he knew he was already gone. He wanted to sit on the comfy sofa with Mouse and the girls, *Sherlock* playing on the big TV while Brant rested against his shoulder.

Mouse had begun bringing him gifts when he stayed over. Toys. Beef jerky. Big spiders....

Lex was going to get a laser light to see if he'd play. Hell, maybe the girls would, but they were pretty dainty.

"...going to bring him to meet us?"

"Huh? Sorry, I did it again. Uh, maybe not this trip." He winked, not wanting to be ugly.

"Man, you are in deep, aren't you?"

"Yeah, well, I'm going to take him to meet some of my buds, you know?"

"So, we'll all meet somewhere. Have a beer. Eat. Chips and salsa for everyone."

"Okay." That would be way less scary than the police department. "Sounds good, actually."

"Cool. I'll make a reservation for a dozen at Sí Señor for Saturday lunch. Work for you?"

"I'll text Nate and Dusty, make sure." God knew what the guys' schedules were.

"Sure. Just holler at me." Gutierrez winked. "I'm off."

"Asshole."

"Yeah, yeah. You might as well be off yourself."

"Huh?" He blinked. "Are you serious or just teasing me again?" Lex was really, really never sure.

"Espana. Fucking focus, man. Pay attention."

"I am now. I might as well be off myself…." He waited.

"You're not focused, man. You're not here. I need officers that aren't going to be killed."

"I know. I can ride the desk, do everyone's paperwork…."

"Go clean your house. I'll rubber-stamp your leave of absence now."

He stood, stunned a little. Had that just happened? Just like that? "Thanks, Sarge. I mean it. I'll call."

"We have a date for Saturday. I expect to meet the nurse."

"You got it." He shook hands with his sergeant and hit the road before someone changed their minds. Damn.

He headed to his apartment, intending to take a long shower, maybe a long nap, when Nate called.

"Hello?" He hoped nothing else had happened.

"Hey, man. How goes?"

"Surprisingly good. In fact, I'm a free man."

"What?"

"I don't have a job." He hadn't had to say that in a long, long time.

"Whoa."

Lex laughed. "Well, I'm on a leave of absence, but I really think I'm just gone."

"Huh. Want to meet for a beer? I'm off."

"I do." He could nap later. A beer sounded great.

"Fucking A. Where?"

"Uh. Down at the Game?" That was a decent sports bar.

"I'll be there in fifteen. Order munchies."

"You got it." He switched directions, going toward the bar. They had brisket and queso nachos. God. He was... unemployed. He was unemployed, and his lover was coming tomorrow to visit. Lex shook his head. He needed to call the guys in Albuquerque about that job they hinted at....

Hell, he needed to call Travis and tell him... shit, was it wrong that he didn't want to call Trav? That he wanted to ask Brant if he could come and stay? Would Travis be super hurt if he didn't at least pretend to be a roomie for a bit? Maybe he'd ask Nate and Dusty. Well, Nate. He had no idea if Dr. D could come too.

God. He pulled into the parking lot and sucked air. Okay. No panic. He could do this. He'd picked up and moved before. He'd come here, hadn't he? Knowing no one. Just down to Cruces and hop into work. He'd made friends; he'd gotten commendations. Now he could build a life back in Burque.

The tap to his window shocked the hell out of him, Nate standing there with his goofy grin. "You look like you're about to puke, dude."

"I totally am. I'm out of work and about to be homeless." He got out of the truck, so Nate hugged him, which felt good.

"Well, shit. You can come couch surf with us, Wingman." The old nickname made him grin.

"Thanks. Travis says I can room with him." He took a deep breath. "I have a guy coming down. Someone I want you guys to meet."

"No shit. Come on. Beer. Food. Tell me everything. Dr. Dusty gets off shift at seven. He can drive us home if we're fucked-up."

"Cool!" He could so get toasted a little. Not slaughtered.

Just happy. "He'll be pleased to know I've developed a taste for Shiner."

Nate's eyes lit up. "You got yourself a Texan, did you? What type? Central? East? West?"

"Central." He grinned. "Very. Pediatric nurse."

"Ooooh, way to go, man!" Nate fist-bumped him.

He snorted, but his mood immediately rose. Yeah. He was out of a job because he had no real doubt they'd let him come back home to APD, and Brant was so worth it.

They settled and ordered, got their beers, and then Nate leaned forward. "So, I need to know everything. Start with the good stuff. Is he good in bed?"

"Nate! What would you say if I asked that about Dr. Dusty?" He was stalling, of course. Brant was amazing.

"You did. A lot. Do not try to bullshit me, man." Oh, Nate did have his number, didn't he? Lex wasn't a dog, but he liked sex and sex talk. He was a dude. What could he say?

"Yeah, okay. My reluctance to kiss and tell should say something."

"Okay, so he's a medical guy. Pediatrics, you say?"

"Yep. Works in a doctor's office. He was military."

"Rock on. Texan. Medical. Cute?"

"Yeah. Blond, blue eyes, lean. A little scarred. Totally hot." He found himself leaning forward, eager to share. God, he wanted Brant to be there now, but he knew better. The guy had just gotten back to work and needed to wait until Friday to come down.

"And you met him at the funeral? I think that makes you a dog."

"No! I met him at the wedding." Lex hooted with laughter at the look on Nate's face. "I just didn't want to get with him until I met him again."

"Wow, that's kind of cool. So, now the shitty part. How's your friend?"

"He's hysterical. But functioning. I'm actually really proud of him."

"That's so hard. And your new guy? He was there at the shooting?"

"Yeah. They stopped the car to get gas, Matt gets out, and boom. Perp shot Matt. Blood and brains everywhere." He'd seen the crime scene photos.

"Jesus. Not a chance, but there's a shit-ton of guilt, no matter what. We're all trained to save lives."

"Right?" He shook his head. "Brant is the one who hasn't lost his shit yet. And I know he will. I know that from experience." A guy could only stiff upper lip it for so long.

"Well, I hope you're there for him when it happens. Are you really moving? Are you moving in with him?" Nate ate a pile of nachos. "Man, it took me and Dusty ten years to get together, and you? Ten fucking days. I'm jealous."

"Hey, I can't help y'all are slow." He grabbed a chip. "I want to move in. Travis wants me to stay with him a bit, at least. Take it slower. Says we're not lesbians." That was an old joke, but he was allowed, according to Diane in Records. She said he was an honorary dyke.

"What does your guy want?" God, Nate was asking the hard questions.

"Well, he wants me to come up there, for sure. But we haven't talked about me moving in." He needed to talk to Brant this weekend, feel the man out.

"Okay. But you will."

"I will. He's coming down this weekend. Gutierrez wants us all to have food on Saturday."

"I'm off at three, Dusty's off duty. We can do it."

"Awesome. Sí Señor."

Nate put up his hand to slap. "Good deal. Have you tried their new creamy green sauce?"

"Nope." Huh. He'd give it a shot.

"Yeah, even Dusty likes it."

"Well, he's a Texan. Those guys do that suiza sauce." He shook his head. He'd never even heard of that until Dusty fed it to him. It was good, but he wasn't sure it counted as Mexican.

"Texans. Can't live with them, can't beat them."

"You know it. They're everywhere." Lex might make a long-suffering face, but his Texan made him happy.

"Yeah, and they are so much fucking fun, dude."

"They are." Brant was… well, he made Lex want to settle down. Have a real home. "He has cats."

"What?" Nate blinked at him like he was speaking Swahili.

"He has cats. Brantley. He has three." Lex wanted Nate to know that.

"Wow. Three? Huh. Dusty wants a dog, but there's no way."

"No? No one you can trade day care with?" Dusty's hours were crazy, but Nate was home off and on.

"I'm not ready. Maybe when I'm a supervisor? Then I'll just have a regular shift."

"That what you're going for?" He wasn't sure what Nate's five-year plan was.

"Yeah. I mean, I like working on the bus, but the money's better, and I like the idea of being able to see Dusty more often."

"Are you sure? You might kill each other." He could so see Dusty and Nate with a big old lab, though. A golden. Something.

"Oh, Dusty's easy. He needs naps, guacamole, and the periodic road trip to Ruidoso."

"He does like the mountains." They all did. Why else did people live in New Mexico? You had to love the land.

"Yeah. They're an addiction." Nate grinned at him, rolled his eyes. "Still… I can't believe you're leaving. It'll be nice to have friends up in Burque."

"You guys can come up anytime." Really. No matter where he was living, he would find them a place.

"Yeah? Cool. Man, I can't wait to meet this guy. I never thought you'd be settling down."

Was he that much of a horndog? In his mind, he was just a dude, but Nate and Travis had said the same thing in the same tone. "I'm no virgin, but I'm not a fuck, man."

"Hey, I know that. You just got your first plant, though. That's all."

"I promise not to let Mouse eat it."

"Mouse? Who names a cat Mouse?" Nate teased.

Lex just pulled out his phone and showed him a picture.

Nate's eyes went wide. "That's not a cat. No way."

"It is. A Maine coon, he says." He was as proud as if Mouse was his.

"Damn, man. That's a big goddamn pussycat."

"Yeah. The girls are good size, but Mouse is a monster. When he wants attention, he tells you." He tucked his phone away in favor of more nachos.

"Wow. It's like a wild animal. Pretty, but wild."

"God, yes. Especially in the morning." Mouse was vicious when he wanted his breakfast.

Nate grinned at him, the look fond and weird.

"What?"

"You really are into him, aren't you?"

"I am. You can tell, huh?" He kinda hoped so, because he wanted Brant to believe it.

"I can totally tell. I love it. Does he feel the same?"

"I hope so. He seems to." He wanted it to be true. Shit, he wanted Brantley down here, at this bar, having a beer and eating nachos.

Dusty showed up about ten minutes later, so Lex braced himself to have the discussion all over again.

What he got was a hug and a kiss on the cheek. "Nachos!"

"Yep. We just ordered some boneless wings for you too." Nate patted the seat of the chair next to him.

"Thanks. Good day, y'all?"

"It could have been way worse," Lex admitted. "I mean, I'm out of a job."

He would never tire of seeing someone's face when he said it.

"On purpose or on accident?"

"Well, officially I'm on leave of absence. But voluntarily."

"Congratulations, man." Just like that. Congratulations. Damn.

"Thanks. I'm feeling like I need a life change."

Dusty nodded, shrugged at him. "Happens to all of us."

Nate stared at Dusty. "It does?"

"We got married, didn't we? Bought a house? Built a shed? Life changes."

"Yeah." Lex grinned over. "I hear you want a dog, Doc."

"Shiner, please," Dusty told the server. "I do."

Nate put on what everyone who knew him called stubborn face. "We're not ready for a dog."

"I'm not talking about adopting a baby, Nate."

"Yeah, but you're not home enough." Nate stared, and Lex knew he'd hit a spot. Oops.

Eee-a-la. No getting in the middle of married folks.

"Lex's man has cats," Nate stated, ending the discussion. "Big ones."

"Cats? That might work. Are they very smelly?"

"Uh, no. I mean, if you have ammonia issues, don't be the one to clean the cat box." Brant had a fancy-assed cat box deal and a cat door into the garage.

"Right. I can do cat boxes. We only ever had ones in the barn."

Nate was glaring. At him.

"What?" Man, he needed to call Brantley.

"We'll talk about it," Nate finally said.

"I've just got a text to call. Be right back." He stepped away and headed toward the patio, dialing Travis, who was at least off work.

"Hey, honey. You okay? Did something happen at work?"

"No, no. I'm okay. I was checking on you." Travis made him grin. Everyone worried when the cop called.

"I'm… I'm glad to be back to work. The kids have been so nice."

"Good. That's good, man." He leaned against the wall, soaking up the sunshine.

"What's going on?"

"Nate and Dusty are spatting. I ran."

"Oh?" Trav's voice trailed off before the light bulb came on. "Your friends?"

He nodded, even though he knew full well Trav couldn't see him. "Yeah. They're having a bitch about dogs, cats, or kids."

"Ah. Umbers, no?" Travis chuckled, and Lex cackled at the sound of the old cry. He wasn't sure where the saying came from, but it fit here. Two kids just about to get themselves into trouble. "Don't give them too long."

"Right? I'm glad to hear you laugh, man."

"Thank you. It's been hard, but I'm feeling more… even-keeled."

"It'll come and go, I bet." It had been that way for him, after he'd shot the bomber.

"Yep. What about you?"

"I started my leave of absence today." If he kept saying it, it would get real.

"Oh? When are you coming home?" It felt nice, the excitement in Travis's voice.

"I'm down here for the weekend, but then I'll start bringing stuff up."

Travis took a deep breath. "Let me know when to start emptying the guest room."

Oh, he was sort of quietly hoping that wouldn't be necessary. "I'll see what's what soon."

"Fair enough. Just holler. You talked to Brant?"

"He's coming down tomorrow." He bit his lip, waiting for Trav's reaction.

"Oh? Good deal. You do know he's... he's really looking for a long-term partner, right?"

"Uh-huh." Did he know that? "I'm not a dog, Trav."

"I know. I just thought I'd warn you. He has long-term relationships. Sort of."

What the hell did that mean?

He didn't want to ask Travis. He'd check it out with Brantley instead. "I know I've never really had one, but I think I want to try." *With Brant. Soon.*

"Huh. Neat. I think you could do better, and I like Brant."

"Wait. You like him, but I can do better?" He was confused as hell now.

"Well, you are my best friend. I want a wealthy Italian lord for you or something."

"Oh." He chuckled. "I thought Matt was perfect for you."

"He was." Travis chuckled. "Holler at me when you know what's going on. You always have a place here."

"Thanks, honey. I'll call you later this weekend."

"Bye!"

Okay, that was done, now.... *Hey babe.*

Hey. Miss u. Can't wait for tomorrow.

Me too. Miss you. He peeked inside to see if Dusty and Nate were relaxed any. Yeah, that seemed to be over, the two men laughing together, head to head.

I'll be there around 8. You need me to bring anything?

Just you and maybe something for dessert. He would provide supper.

K. Will do. Can I call tonite?

Yes. I'll text when I get back from supper. He wanted to hear Brant's voice.

Good deal.

He loved the goofy smile of Brant's selfie.

Soon. Time to rejoin the guys.

"That was a hell of a text," Dusty said.

"I called Travis too. Just because." He slid into his seat, grinning. "All domestic action done?"

"Shut up," Nate murmured.

"Shutting up." The last thing he wanted was drama. Seriously.

Dusty chuckled. "Yeah, yeah. We ordered more food."

"Yeah?"

"Uh-huh. More nachos, and you missed the wings, so…."

"Wow. You guys were fast, huh?"

"I was hungry," Dusty admitted. "It was a long shift."

"That sucks, man. I'm sorry."

"Yeah. I won't tell you."

Lex frowned. "Yeah, you will. You hold too much in. I've been lounging around. I need my vicarious stress."

Dusty hooted, and then they started swapping war stories —everything from traffic stops to hedge trimmer accidents to births in the bus. They ate and had some beers, and Lex felt better, trying to forget what Travis had said about Brant. He didn't need to start asking stupid questions as soon as they set eyes on each other. Travis could really say the very worst things when he was trying to be helpful.

When Dusty started nodding off about nine, Lex slapped Nate on the shoulder, smiling. "Take him to bed, man."

"Yeah. Yeah, that's a plan. You going to call your guy? You got your car keys?"

"I do. I switched to Coke about an hour ago." He was good to go. "And yeah, I'm ready to call."

"See you Saturday for lunch. Three, right?"

"Yeah. Sounds good." Somehow he'd gotten all scheduled up. Everyone wanted to meet his new squeeze.

He headed to his apartment, tromping up to the second

floor and getting in and settled with a beer before he finally, blessedly, got to call Brant.

"Hey, honey. How was dinner with the couple?"

"Good. They made up. It was great." He chuckled. "I swear, they're amazing, but they're fighting over dogs and cats."

"Dogs and cats? Like literally?" He heard a can opening. "Mouse misses you, by the way. He ate one of your socks."

"Oh, yay. Yeah, Dusty wants a dog, and Nate thinks Dusty works too much." He popped open his beer.

"Ah. Cats are a good compromise. How was your day, honey?"

"Weird but good. I was having trouble focusing at work, so I just started my leave early."

"Oh, honey. I'm sorry." There was a long pause. "Do you still want me to come?"

"Hell, yes! Uh, I ought to warn you. The guys all want to do lunch." With his new guy. God, didn't that make him smile.

"Yeah?" Brantley chuckled softly. "That sounds fun. Is it? I mean, is that bad?"

"No. I just thought I would warn you now. A bunch of cops, some EMTs, and a doc."

"Sounds right up my alley. I happen to be stupidly fond of a cop, and I have met a doctor or three in my day."

"Good deal." He chuckled. "I just worry about everything we do that's new."

"Well, my shift ends at three tomorrow, so I'll be there in the evening." Brant sighed softly. "Have I mentioned that it's already weird sleeping alone?"

"No, but you can say it all you want. Who's watching Mouse and the girls?"

"My friend Lisa. She works internal medicine in my building. I watch her guys when she goes to Denver to visit her folks."

"That's cool. I worry about them, you know?" *Mouse, especially.*

"Mouse is still sleeping with what's left of your sock."

"Aw, that makes me happy." It really did. He looked around his apartment, thinking about how different it was to Brant's place. He was living like a bachelor, like a teenager. He had a couple of posters framed on the wall—Abbey Road, a Day of the Dead skull—a comfy couch, a collection of fancy beer glasses, his gun case.

This was just a place to stick his shit.

"Yeah, I'm thinking about making a cat jungle gym for him."

"I can help with that. I'm pretty handy." Was that too much? He always felt a little pushy.

"Yeah? Cool. I'd love that. I could just buy one, but making one sounds fun."

"It does." Doing anything with Brant sounded fun. "How was your day, baby?"

"Spate of impetigo. Stomach flu. One baby I had to send to the ER."

"Oh, man. Respiratory?" His wince was purely instinctive. How many calls had he been on where he'd had to help with that? Babies were hard.

"Yeah, she needed immediate help. I hate when they're really sick. Breaks my heart."

"I bet. That sucks, huh? She'll be all right, though."

"Yeah. They end up okay, for the most part." There was a pause, then a soft chuckle. "Tell me not to just get in the car and come see you."

"Oh, baby, you need to rest, huh?" He didn't want Brant falling asleep at the wheel. "Besides, you have work tomorrow. I'm going to…." Start packing. He was going to start packing his shit and hoping Brant or Travis wanted him.

"Yeah. Yeah, but I can get off at three and leave before the rush, and I'll bring goodies." Brant took a deep breath. "I feel a little like a teenager, you know?"

"I do too. Of course I was just thinking how I was living like a college guy. My place is clean but kind of… embarrassing."

"Yeah, I'm curious to see it. See more of you."

"I want that, baby. I'll cook for you."

"I can't wait. Okay, I'm going to go before this dissolves into 'you say goodbye.'"

"Okay, baby. I—love you." He did, so he would say it.

"Yeah? I love you too. See you tomorrow." *Click.*

Oh God. The L word. Or A word, if he was going in Spanish….

He'd said it, and Brant had accepted it and given it back.

Now what the hell did he do to top that?

Nachos. That would do it. Texas-style nachos. That was what he would cook tomorrow. Hell, yeah.

A plan. That was what a man needed.

A plan and some tortillas.

14

*B*rantley had the Eagles on the radio, a Route 44 Cherry Dr Pepper in the cup holder, and a green chile apple pie ready to deliver to his lover.

The drive down had been nice, really. He'd left from Kaseman and missed the worst of the traffic, and just headed south.

It was actually... fun. He was looking forward to seeing Lex, the desert was alive, and the Sirius was being damn good to him.

He hummed along with "Take It Easy," tapping his fingers on the steering wheel.

Las Cruces loomed up in the late spring dusk, all the lights sparkling away. He drove into town, following the GPS. Lex lived up near a mall, which was kinda cool. *Ooh, Ruby Tuesday. Uhn. Salad bar. Maybe tomorrow for supper....*

He thought he was meeting everyone at a lunch. So maybe for lunch the next day if not supper. Something. He'd get Lex to take him.

He pulled into an apartment complex that looked like every other apartment complex on earth, and he started looking for number six. It was a first-floor apartment, and Lex's truck sat outside. *Boom.*

Okay. Okay. Little duffel bag of stuff, Coke, keys, pie.

He hoisted his ass out of the SUV, his hip twinging. *Lord.*

He locked up and headed down the sidewalk to the little bright red door. Lex answered right after he knocked, beaming at him.

"Brant. Hey, baby. Come on in."

"I found you." He stepped in, the scent of hamburger and cumin and onion hitting him. "Oh yum. I brought pie."

"Cool. I'm making nachos. Is that okay?" Lex took the outstretched pie and his drink and set them aside before kissing him.

Oh. Oh, he was stupid over this man. He stepped right in, wrapped his hands around Lex's waist, and opened up, his tongue sliding in to taste his lover.

"Mmm." Lex took the kiss deep and hard, which just made him moan. His bag dropped to the floor, and he reached up, his hands sliding into Lex's heavy shock of hair. He did love that springy mass of curls, the way it twined around his fingers. The kiss went on and on, making him dizzy, weak at the knees.

They finally had to break to breathe, and he was impressed that Lex still stood there, on his own two feet, because he was considering just falling down. "Hey. I made it."

"You did." Lex chuckled. "Come, uh… well, do you want to sit? You've been on the road."

"I want to see. It was a good drive. Not too long at all." Not quite four hours. Doable.

"I like it okay. It's got some pretty to it. Not as much as, say, the old road to Santa Fe or anything."

"You were at the end of the drive, though." That made it something to look forward to.

"I am. Was. Are." Lex hooted. "Need the bathroom or a drink?"

"Yeah, I could totally pee. I have about half a drink left. Maybe."

"Cool. I'll meet you back at the couch. We have some necking to do while the beef finishes cooking."

"Oh, I do love how you think." He found the bathroom, did his business, and washed his face. Necking, huh? That sounded like a lovely way to wait for something to cook.

Whatever it was, it smelled amazing. Lex, cooking for him. He hoped there would be more cooking together soon.

He wandered into the front room, noting the posters on the wall, the huge television, the comfy couch. Lex was right —it was like a grad student's place. Better that than an under-grad, he guessed, and it was meticulously clean.

Overall, he liked it. He smiled at Lex and went to sit. "Hey, you."

"Hey. Come here." Lex hauled him closer. "You're okay? You have a better day?"

"It was a Friday. All the doctors disappeared, and I answered a thousand phone calls." He leaned in, letting his hand slide around Lex's knee. "What did you do today?"

"I slept a little. I cleaned the bathroom. The rest was clean. Uh, I got groceries."

"Sounds nice and lazy. I love it." He kissed the corner of Lex's mouth.

"It was. I'm really not used to being so relaxed." Lex kissed him back.

Brant wanted to ask so much. Seriously. He wanted to ask Lex if he wanted a place to stay. He wanted Lex there, even though it was fast, even though Travis probably needed him, even though Lex was obviously used to living alone. Honestly, he just dove into the kiss because that was easy and hot and good. Lex loved on him, hands sliding up and down his back, and they were, indeed, making out. He thought Lex was keeping it sweet and easy because dinner was smelling so good. They didn't say a word; they just shared long, gentle kisses that went on and on, dragging. Not in a bad way, not at all. And he got to touch, stroking that broad chest.

Lex chuckled at him, and the laugh went husky when Brant traced one nipple, making it hard.

"Such good hands." Lex put a hand over his, pressing his palm over the hard bit of flesh.

"I try. I like making out with you, hmm?" He felt Lex's strong, steady heartbeat under his palm.

"I do too. With you." Lex laughed and shook his head. "You make me goofy. Come on and help me crisp up the tortillas so I can load them in the oven."

"Sounds great. You're making me flat nachos?" That was... hell, that made him want to suck Lex off and beg him to move in.

"Yep. And I made your salsa to go with them." Lex winked. "I have high hopes for what that will get me."

"I have a few ideas, honey. I surely do."

"Yeah? Well, the nachos had better live up, huh?"

"I'm not worried." The kitchen was clean, simple—just another galley, and Brant couldn't help but think that it didn't seem like Lex belonged here. He thought Lex needed Saltillo tile and a pizza oven. Hell, they could totally build a pizza oven. It would be amazing in the backyard. Something tiled and adobe. They'd have a ball building it....

"You're grinning. It looks happy." Lex slid a pan in the oven to heat it up.

"I am. I really am. It's good to see you."

"It is." Lex came back to kiss him again. "So, halves?"

"Halves?" He didn't follow.

"The tortillas. Want halves or quarters?"

"Oh. Quarters. I was thinking about asking you to move in with me and I lost track of things."

"You were?" Lex paused, knife hovering over the defense-less tortillas. "For real?"

"I was. For real. Is it too soon?"

"No. I was about to ask how you felt about it. I mean, Trav will let me stay if need be, but I would love to give it a go."

"Well, we can fit you in. I think you'll be comfortable." His heart was beating a million miles a minute.

"Okay." Lex stared at him, lips curving into a smile. Oh, that expression was amazing.

"Okay." He grinned right back and stepped in for a kiss.

The nachos waited about ten minutes for that one. Brant figured it was worth it.

15

$\mathcal{L}$ex couldn't stop grinning, and he knew Sarge and the boys would give him no end of hell about it. He was moving in with Brant.

They'd actually spent the morning packing, discussing where this and that could go. They were going to put some of his stuff in storage, because Brant had a bigger bed, but his dresser was coming, his nightstand, his comfy couch from the spare room. His dishes and cast iron were coming, his television was coming for the front room, and they were going to move Brant's to the bedroom.

Brant had a fit over his comal, and now there would be room for his tools in a real workshop.

He grinned some more.

Brant touched his arm. "You okay?"

"I am more than okay. I feel a little giddy, as a matter of fact."

Brant bumped their shoulders together. "A little giddy?"

"Just a bit." Was that weird?

"Good. We're in it together, right?"

And that was it, wasn't it? They totally were. "We are."

Lex felt like that was too true. He pulled into the restaurant parking lot and stopped the truck. "Ready for this?"

"Sure. They're not going to eat me, are they?"

"No, no. They're way more likely to josh me." Lex shook his head, grinning.

"Well, then...." Brantley hopped out of the truck. "I'm all over that."

"Good deal." Lex climbed out too, then took a deep breath. "Come on. Sí Señor awaits."

"Chips and salsa?"

"God, yes." Lex did love his Mexican food. Which, you know, stood to reason. Because, as he called it, food! His dad's old joke made him cackle, and he laughed all the way inside.

Lex touched Brant's hand, steering him toward a table where two men already sat. One was a burly, salt-and-pepper Hispanic man, the other a twentysomething kid who still had freckles. And pimples.

"Sarge. Andrew. Good to see you guys. This is Brant. Brant Dime, Sergeant Ben Gutierrez and Corporal Andrew Nye."

"Hey, y'all. How goes it?" Brant shook and grinned, just all smiles.

"Good to meet you," Gutierrez said. "We ordered chips and queso and salsa, so we're just waiting on the rest."

"Dusty and Nate," Lex agreed. "Who else?"

"Towa. Richards. I think Pecina and Henry."

"Cool." Lex nodded; no one he hated had come along.

They sat, all of them staring at each other for a little bit.

"So." The sergeant smiled. "Albuquerque, huh?"

"Delicate, Sarge. Yeah. You guys know I was there for a while. My folks are up there." *Brantley is up there.*

"Sure. We'll miss your stupid jokes."

"And your ugly socks."

Lex grinned at Andrew. "I'll have to send you guys some."

"Great, we'll be all wearing flamingos and pit bulls."

Brant grinned. "Socks, huh?"

"I brought serious ones up for the funeral," Lex said.

Everyone went a little grim, a little quiet.

"Looks like we got here in time to cheer everyone up." Two more guys showed up, and Lex shook hands with Pecina and Henry.

"Thank God for that. How's it going?" Lex hadn't been back long enough to see anyone and get the gossip.

"Marnie is pregnant." Henry shook his head mournfully.

"What's that? Four?"

"Yeah. Four. God. That woman catches pregnant if she walks through a room with a hard-on in it."

"Lord." Gutierrez blinked. "You didn't tell me."

"I knew you'd put me on desk duty."

"You...."

"I like being in the cruiser, Sarge."

Gutierrez rolled his eyes. "You're a freak."

"Yeah, yeah, yeah. So you're the boyfriend?" Henry asked. "The one he's leaving us for?"

"I'm the boyfriend, yeah." Brant didn't hesitate a bit.

Lex beamed. He couldn't help it.

"Don't suppose you'd be willing to move here, man?" That was Sarge.

"Um. Well, it's pretty, but I like the higher elevation...." Brant touched his thigh under the table, just giving him a little pressure, so he tried to stop it.

"Sarge, quit it."

"You can't blame me for trying, Espana."

"No, you said you would."

Brantley pinked, head ducked, but there was a grin there.

"Still not going to work. I'm throwing my lot in with his." Lex couldn't stop grinning.

"And I have a house," Brant added.

"Just don't tell him about the cats."

The phrase fell like a turd in a punchbowl.

"Hey, Nate." Lex rolled his eyes. He was about to get it now.

"Cats? Cats?" Andrew's eyes were wide, his hands flapping.

"Yes. I am a gay nurse with three cats. I'm also a retired vet who can kick your asses, in case that didn't come up." Brant's smile was almost friendly.

"Army?" Nate asked quietly. "Dusty and I both were."

"Yeah. Took live fire pulling Marines out of a Jeep that was hit by an IED."

"Ouch."

The guys all nodded, giving Brant the respect that deserved.

"Also, his cat is gigantic. Huge. Monster kitty." Lex needed to make sure Brant knew he wasn't ashamed.

"He's not lying," Nate said. "Show them the evidence."

Brantley, to Lex's pure joy, pulled out his phone and started showing off "baby" pictures.

"Holy shit," Pecina murmured. "That's the biggest cat I've ever seen."

"He's a Maine coon. They're gorgeous. The other two are rescues."

"Wow. See, that's like you're a lion tamer or something," Henry said.

"That's me. Lion tamer, ho."

Lex burst out with laughter. "Who you calling a ho?"

Everyone else cracked up. Then the other guys showed, and they all got serious about food. Lex was so damn pleased at how Brant rolled with it. Cops could be hard. Brant couldn't be grossed-out, the man just matching them, story for story, joke for joke. In fact, since Brant worked with kids, a couple of his bodily fluid stories made everyone but Nate and Dusty *ewwww* out loud.

At the end of the meal, they were rolling, the entire group, and Lex was busting his buttons.

"I gotta head out," Gutierrez said. "I like your guy, Espana. Nice to meet you, Brant."

"Very nice to meet you, sir." Brant stood and shook hands. "If you're up in Burque, you have a place to stay."

"No shit? Thanks." Gutierrez grinned, then waved. Most of the guys rose and shook hands and stuff, leaving them with Nate and Dusty.

"Good job, man. You handled those guys like a charm." Dusty shook Brant's hand. "Seriously. Good job."

"Thanks. It wasn't hard work. I like people."

"Yeah, but you start at a deficit," Dusty said with a grin. "You did great."

Nate nodded. "I like you."

Lex was never going to stop grinning. He hadn't realized how important it was for his friends to like his new lover, but Brantley was... shit, the man was easy to like. He was easy-going, smart, and generally decent. Funny too. And hot.

"Lex, pay attention."

"What?"

"I was asking you a question," Dusty said.

"Were you?" He was busy being in love.

Brantley began to laugh, the sound soft, fond.

"I was. I was asking if you needed any help moving. Nate and I can swing a few days...."

"Oh. Oh, seriously?" He knew how precious that offer was. Their time off together was sacrosanct.

"Yeah. I mean, we're nosy too."

"I—we have a great guest room. Y'all are welcome." Brant sounded a little stunned.

"Awesome." Nate gave a thumbs-up. "We'll bring up a load, then."

"We can have a cookout. Steaks on the grill."

"That sounds amazing," Dusty said. "You text us what you need."

"Can you believe it's happening so fast?" Nate asked. "I mean, no judgment, just wow."

Lex nodded. "Mama always said it was that way."

"I've never asked someone to move in, but he's been staying, and it feels… right." Brant pinked but held Lex's eyes.

"Then we're happy for both of you." Nate and Dusty exchanged glances, smiling. "Sometimes it just takes something to nudge you into going after what you want."

"And sometimes you just have to know what you're looking at." Lex reached out and took Brant's hand, feeling all daring, right there in the restaurant.

Brant gave him this look, one that just burned his socks.

"Damn, y'all. Damn. Go home. Have quiet times."

Nate hooted. "Yeah. Yeah, go get alone."

Brant nodded. "I could handle that, honey. Wanna?"

"I do." Lex so, so did. "Thanks for coming, guys. I'll holler tomorrow?"

"Late tomorrow, hmm?"

"You know it." Lex winked, then reached for the bill. Which was gone.

"Your sergeant got it, man. Sweet."

"That is. Wow." He would call Gutierrez tomorrow. "Okay, guys. We're going on." Lex rose, then grabbed hugs before dragging Brant out to the parking lot.

"Hungry, hungry," Brant teased, but he was laughing all the way.

"I am. You just—I…." He had no words.

"Uh-huh. Come on, dork. I have you. Take me to your leader, I mean, your bed."

"I can totally do that." Back in the truck and back to his soon-to-be-not-his place. "I'm going to move in with you."

"You are. We're going to make house."

"Is that a Texanism?" Lex loved that.

"I guess? Is it? I never know. I know that sometimes the ladies at work cackle."

"Well, it must be." They were moving in together. Officially. The house was big enough for them, the cats liked them, and…. Was there an *and*? He guessed they would see. Lex wasn't an idiot. He knew live-in relationships took work.

"Hey, we can work things out, huh? We will." Brant squeezed his fingers.

"We will. I'm actually kind of looking forward to it." He'd never been serious, so everything would be a first.

"Me too. I've never had a live-in lover. Someone to share a life with."

"No? Me either. Travis would probably tell you I've never had a lover…."

"I had one in the service, and I've had a couple buddies and one disaster."

"Yeah?" Lex reached over to touch Brant's hand. "Want to tell me?"

"He was a party animal, and I thought it was going to be exciting. Then I found out party animal meant he was an alcoholic. And I discovered that alcoholic meant drugs, and that? Meant he stole my TV and my laptop."

"Jesus. The worst I've had was a guy who stiffed me for drinks." Lex chewed his lip. "I—I'll warn you, Travis seems to think I'm some kind of player."

"Are you?"

"I've never thought so. I mean, I've never been serious until now, but I'm not out every weekend with someone new."

"So long as you're with me now, that's all I care about. I want long-term. I want… what Matty and Travis had."

"Yeah. I think that about Dusty and Nate. You'll see."

They started toward the apartment, and Brant reached out, hand finding his thigh again. "We have a lot in common. We have a lot to talk about. Hell, we have a shit ton of chemistry. It's going to be okay."

"I think so too." Lex was stupidly optimistic, in fact.

"Good. Is it bad to come on to you while you're driving?"

"Gently. I did take police driving, but you distract me."

"Fair enough. I'm sort of enjoying this, though. Wanting you so bad." Brant's voice was husky, low. Wanton. "Usually I don't walk around half-hard."

"Neither do I." He didn't drive that way either. Not usually.

"I am looking forward to late night blowjobs with you," Brant murmured. "And long Sunday morning showers."

"Oh, God." Yes, please, to all of it.

"Right? I mean, the normal stuff is cool, but I've never been taken over the dining room table."

"Brant." Did he even have a dining room table? "Maybe the back of the couch?"

"Sounds like a great start."

"I think so too!" Look at them. On the same page.

"We have a plan. You. Me. Couch. Orgasms."

"Uhn." He wasn't going to speed. No getting pulled over for an off-duty cop. That would be damned embarrassing. That did mean it took forever to get back to his apartment, and he was… ready.

He was aching.

He was going to take Brant inside and make his lover scream.

They ran the last few steps, and Lex had to fumble with the keys, because his hands shook. Brant wasn't helping, not at all. Those hands were dragging over his ass, squeezing it tight. He wiggled, dancing in place, then finally got the door open.

Okay, what first? Condoms and lube? Foreplay? Nakedness?

Couch. Which meant condoms and lube first.

"Stay, babe. Please. Be right back."

Brant stripped his shirt off, nodding. "Staying."

"Yep." Lex ran to the bedroom, glad he didn't have stairs

and shit like Travis. *Oh, no thinking about Trav. Grossness. Not now. No.* He grabbed lube and condoms out of the bathroom. Lex tended to masturbate in the shower and put condoms in his pocket when he was dressing for a night out. He'd have to start leaving them in the night table.

Damn. Life was changing. Quick. He liked it.

How could he not? This was the best thing that had ever happened to him.

Brant was waiting for him, bare naked, bent over the couch, and Lex tripped, staggering the last few feet and banging into Brant. "Oops."

Brant and the sofa moved a few inches, the feet scraping across the carpet.

"Sorry, baby." He wasn't about to get the giggles now.

"Trying to scrape my dick!" Brant cracked up, and then it was all over, both of them howling away.

"I promise I'll kiss it and make it better." *With glee.*

That didn't help the laughter at all.

He covered Brant with his body, holding on tight. They both laughed until his cock poked hard at Brant's balls, and then they trailed off.

Right. He needed to rev his lover back up, remind him what they were up to. He slid back and forth, getting a nice bit of friction, and Brant began to rock toward him. That fine ass was tight, round and muscled, and Lex traced the scars leading from that injured hip.

"You don't mind them, right?"

"I think they mean you're a survivor." He touched them again, refusing to act like they weren't there.

"I think so, yes."

"I'm so damn glad you are." He knew how fast things could go horribly wrong.

"Me too. I want you to make me come, Lex. I want you to drive me crazy."

"Good." He got his hand unclenched, glad the lube and

condom seemed intact. He kept touching, stroking Brant's ass, his thighs.

He wanted more of that skin. Lex was addicted. Brant spread a little, balls exposed, swinging. Laying the lube and rubber on the back of the couch, Lex paused then to strip down. Brant would feel so good against him. He hummed as the cool air hit his body, his hot, aching cock.

"Oh, man, I can smell you. Fucking A." Brant shivered, a dull flush climbing his spine.

Lex moaned, his heart pounding. "That's good, right?"

"Fuck yes. You make me hard as a rock."

"I want that." He reached around, pushing up under Brant's dick.

Brant spread for him, hips pushing out at him, letting him rub and rock. He wanted in, but he needed to prep. He wasn't going to hurt Brant. After all, foreplay was a glorious thing, right?

He reached down and cupped Brant's balls, held them, weighing them in his palm.

Going up on tiptoes, Brant grunted. "Lex!"

There were benefits to knowing a man's body. He played with his prize, that fuzzy sac drawing up hard. He pressed on that tiny tight hole with his thumb.

"Lex.... Oh, God. Get me ready." Brant was pushing back hard, begging for it.

Damn, that was sweet. Perfect. His. Lex felt a surge of pride. He leaned forward, lips sucking up a mark on the nape of Brant's neck.

Keening, Brant leaned his chest on the couch, reaching back to spread his asscheeks.

"Oh, Jesus." Was this fucking real? He thought it was, but maybe he'd fallen and hit his head. Lex grabbed the lube, because they were cooking with oil and he needed to hurry.

He slicked two fingers up and pressed them in deep, moaning at the glorious tightness. Brant was just amazing, so hot and ready, and all he had to do was work his fingers back and forth, watching as he spread his lover.

Damn. Damn, he was so hard he hurt.

He got Brant slick, open, ready for him. Then he fumbled with the condom. He felt clumsy as hell, but his hands were shaking with pure need. Lex finally got it on, got the whole of it slicked up.

"Lex, honey. Please. Make love to me."

"I've got you, love." Lex was going to give Brant everything. He held Brant open with his fingers, spreading his lover wide and pushing in.

"Oh, fuck. Yeah. Lex. That's it, honey." Brant pressed against him, meeting him halfway.

Eager love. He leaned forward, covering Brant's back with his chest, shoving in deep.

Nodding, Brant drove him, hips gliding back and forth. Finally he grabbed Brant's hip, stilling him, driving a little bit harder. He could do this forever. But at the same time, he wasn't gonna last long.

"You're so fucking tight, babe."

"You forgot full. Full of you."

"So fucking amazing. So perfect." Lex couldn't believe how good it was, him and Brant. He felt guilty, knowing that he had this while Travis had lost it, but it was what it was. He loved his friend, but he wasn't giving up a good thing out of misplaced guilt. Especially not a good, naked thing that moaned like Brant.

He moved, sliding, slipping in deep. *Uhn.*

Jesus, his balls were heavy, swinging and bumping into Brant's. Lex closed his eyes, then forced them open, wanting to see every bit of this. Every single bit.

He reached out, hand wrapping around Brant's shoulder as he slammed in deep.

Brant arched up and back, clutching at the back of the couch. That was a gorgeous view—muscles working, skin flushed dark. Brant was like his high school wet dream, only so much better. So real and wondrous. And tight, Jesus Christ.

All he could do was moan and thrust, giving Brant all he had. He wasn't willing to go too hard and hurt that hip. Brant met him smack-dab in the middle, their bodies slapping together.

God, he could do this all night and only last a moment.

"Touch me, honey. I need."

"I will." He reached down, found that rigid cock, and stroked it. "Jesus, baby. You're dripping for me."

"I know." Brant panted out the words. "I can't stand it. I need to come so bad."

He pressed in deep, let his eyes close so he could focus. "Do it. Come on my cock, baby."

"Oh. Oh, fuck. Say that again."

Lex banged into Brant, putting his mouth to Brant's ear. "Come. On. My. Cock."

The world came to life in the muscles around his prick, the trembling and milking enough to make his toes curl. Lex moaned, the sound shocking, loud, and he jerked, dancing for Brant. Seed sprayed over his hand, hot and thick and wet.

Lex just lost it, sawing back and forth, thrusting half a dozen times before he came. He wanted Brant to feel every pulse of his orgasm.

Brant's answering moan made his eyes cross, made him cry out. Damn.

"Nothing has ever felt this way, baby." He barely got the words out, but he needed to say them. He kissed Brant's shoulder, licking the sweat.

Brant only nodded, back heaving against his chest.

They needed to move, maybe to shower, something, but right now this was perfect. Right now he breathed in his lover and hummed with absolute joy.

This was real.

16

For having "nothing," Lex sure had a lot of shit. Together they packed up two pickups, a U-Haul trailer, and his SUV, and that was after taking loads to the St. Vincent's.

Brant couldn't imagine trying to move now. He had a metric fuckton of shit. More than Lex for sure. The man had a good many movies and books, but his collection of sheets and towels was pretty pitiful. And that TV was already in his back seat.

Brant grinned a little at that. He was never going to turn down the idea of a bigger TV.

"Jesus, you think all this shit will fit in your house, man?" Lex's friend, Dusty, looked at him, a wicked grin on his face. "I mean, do you have a mansion?"

"I don't, but I can sell stuff that I need to."

"We'll see what fits and what doesn't," he answered. "It's going to be great."

Lex scowled at Dusty, who never dulled that bright smile.

"Right. I know you. You'll have posters hung every-where," Dusty shot back.

"Hey! Maybe I can have a tiny man cave…."

"You can have the third bedroom, honey." No posters. Those things were awful.

"I bet he only needs half of it, but it will smell like a gym."

Nate snorted, but when Dusty added, "And gun oil," they all cracked up.

That had never occurred to him, though. Having a cop in the house. Having a gun in the house. Did Lex have a gun safe?

"Do you have a gun safe, honey?"

"I do. It's not a big one, but it doesn't need to be. We can put it in a closet. Does that work for you?"

"Yeah, that's cool. I just didn't know if we needed one." He knew how to shoot a firearm, but that hadn't been his job in the service, and he hadn't shot one since.

"We'll see what the situation looks like. I have a regular sidearm and an ankle pistol. Do you have a firearm?"

"I don't, honey." Part of him was all *Christ, that's hot,* and part was freaking out a little bit.

Lex winked, then ran a hand up and down his back. "You ready?"

He shook himself mentally. He wanted this. "I am. We'll have our bring-Lex-home caravan."

"Good deal." Lex took a short kiss. "Holler if you need to stop."

"I will. It's an easy drive. We might stop in T or C for coffee and a pee."

"I love T or C. Guys? You good?" Lex asked Dusty and Nate.

"We're ready. We'll see you when we stop." Nate looked almost giddy.

"Got it." Lex winked broadly at everyone. "Let's do it."

Brant climbed into his car and started it up. This wasn't how he'd expected to head home. He'd expected to be down, to be grumpy, not loaded to the gills and bringing Lex home. He couldn't stop grinning, even as his nerves jittered.

Brant wished Matty was here, to share this with, to tell him that it was going to be amazing. To tease him.

He had a terrible little pang then, because every time he remembered Matty was gone, his chest hurt.

"You are supposed to be here, man. You're supposed to help me out, talk to me."

Matty never answered, which was good. Only crazy people in movies talked to ghosts. People who heard ghosts talk back were committed. He shook his head. This was a good thing. He wasn't going to have it any other way.

This was his good thing, dammit.

Still, he'd like a little…. His phone rang, Bridey's name popping up. Christ, Bridey was good at that.

He hit the hands-free. "Hey, Bubba."

"Hey, you. What up?"

"I—" How did he say this? How on earth did he admit that he was bringing a lover home?

"You okay? I know you miss Matty."

"I do. Bad. I-I got something to tell you, man." He opened his Coke, his head beginning to throb.

"So tell me." Bridey didn't have a lot of patience for bullshit.

"I met someone." Three little words. So many were so fucking important. *I met someone. I'm into him. He's moving in. I love him.*

"No shit? Will I like him?"

"Way to make it about you, Bri."

"Yeah, yeah. Tell me about him? Is he local? Is he a doctor?"

"He's a cop, and he was born and raised in Albuquerque, but he lives… lived… in Las Cruces."

"Lived?" Bridey's voice sharpened. "What does that mean?"

"It means I've got his TV and all his clothes in the back of my SUV."

"Holy shit. Do Mom and Dad know?"

"Nope." He hadn't not told them. He just hadn't told them.

"Huh. Well, thanks for the family trust," Bridey teased.

"I met him at Matty's funeral. He's Travis's best friend. Is that gross?" He didn't want to be gross.

"Uh…." Bridey paused, and he saw his brother in his mind, chewing that lower lip. "Nah. Maybe ironic?"

"Butthead."

"Uh-huh. Name?"

"Alex Espana. Lex. He worked up in Albuquerque for a long time, and then he moved to Las Cruces."

"No shit? How long has he been a cop?"

Brant paused. Did he know that? He wasn't sure he'd ever asked. "Ten years or so."

"Wow. So he's old, huh?"

"He's in his thirties, butthead, and he's stacked to the ceiling." Lex was so totally not old at all.

"Oh, nice." Bridey chuckled. "When do we meet him?"

"Let me get him moved in." God, meet them. Lex would explode. Boom.

"Yeah, okay." Bridey was rolling his eyes. He would bet money on it.

"Maybe you should come first." *Ease Lex into it.*

"Sure. I mean, if you take me to Santa Fe."

"Fair enough. Maybe come for Balloon Fiesta?" That would be fun as hell and would give them some time to settle into routine.

"Uh, bro? Your man's going to be scarce then, I bet. So many tourists and all."

Dammit. Right. Whoa.

"Uh. Well, come in late September, then. After Labor Day, not as hot. He ought to be settled in by then too."

"Uh-huh, and you'll have time to get shit organized. I'll

come then." His brother had a knack for reading his mind. *Creepy little fuck.*

"Sounds great. I'd love to see you, man. How's the ranch?"

"Busy. We had a bumper crop of calves." Bridey chuckled, so proud. "I'll bring you some beef when I come. It's about time I filled your freezer again."

"Y'all are too good to me." The ranch provided the best beef, better than he could afford on a daily basis.

"I know." Bridey hooted, the sound so home it made him ache. He'd left home to serve, and then he'd left home permanently to be with Matty. Did that make him stupid? He didn't think so. He had a life that was gaining new ground every day, one he couldn't have in Texas. He did miss his people, though. And flat Texas nachos, though Lex was good at those.

He had the mountains and his house, Ruidoso and Durango and Jemez right there. He loved Santa Fe and the Turquoise Trail and even the zoo in Albuquerque, which was like a retirement home for old zoo animals.

"How about Momma's llamas?" Momma changed what she was raising as often as she changed hair color.

"She got tired of blowing out their coats. Now she's raising mini donkeys."

"Oh, God. Are they cute as fuck?"

"I haven't sent pictures? Oh, God, bro, their ears!"

"Send them! Do they have names?" *Do they have a purpose?*

"They do. There are only six now. There might be more soon." Bridey huffed out another laugh.

"Oh Lord." A pregnant mini donkey. He could just imagine.

"Yeah. They're something else. Those little hooves are sharp."

"Do they kick your widdle ankles, Bubba?"

"Shut up," Bridey muttered. "Anyway, seriously, you should call the 'rents."

"I will. Let me get all this shit settled with Lex, and I'll call and confess all. I'll even send pictures." He heard Bridey open his mouth, and he hurried on. "And no. No dick pics. Don't even ask."

"Damn. It was worth a try." Bridey rumbled, this funny little sound so uniquely him. "Okay, I got to get back to work. Miss you, man."

"Miss you, Bubba. Talk at you later." He hung up, feeling a little bit lighter in his soul.

His brother was a great barometer, and while Bridey was surprised, he didn't seem worried. This was a good thing.

Now all he had to do was get them home and figure out how to get all this stuff in his house.

17

*L*ex grinned at Nate and Dusty, who were sitting on his couch, now ensconced in Brant's living room, albeit behind Brant's existing couch. "Anyone want another beer?"

"Not me. I'm the man charged with getting us safely to the hotel, since Dusty drove us all the way here."

"Y'all don't want to stay in the guest room?"

"No offense, Brant, but I intend to turn Nate inside out, and y'all don't need to hear that." Dusty looked like the cat that was all about getting the cream.

"Dusty is a stud," Brant said, his voice teasing.

"I am, and I will take another beer, thank you."

"You got it." Lex rose, moving to grab a beer for Dusty, more pizza for him. "You want anything, baby?"

Brantley was perched on a barstool, looking a little dazed and more than a little worn out. "A Coke, please?"

"Sure." He figured Brant needed sleep, but the guys needed to unwind and hang. He might have to send Brant off to bed at some point. After all, Brant had to be at work in the morning.

Lex checked his watch. Not even eight. Oops. And where

were the cats? "Honey, are the beasts still locked in the bathroom?"

"Yeah, I wasn't sure how the guys felt about them."

"Well, they're thinking of getting a pet. You guys want to wait until in the morning to meet them?"

"No. No, we want to see them. Are they friendly?"

Brant snorted. "They've been known to be."

"Well, Mouse is… interested." Lex chortled.

"And Peaches and Cream are going to panic. Just be patient." Brant opened the door and three hysterical cats hit the ground running.

Lex watched in awe as they made laps, making this amazing racket.

Then Mouse tackled him, claws out. *Oh, Jesus.* He knew better than to push or squeeze by now, so he supported that heavy body with one hand, rubbing ears with the other.

"Holy shit. Is that a baby tiger?"

Brant started howling with laughter, head thrown back.

Dusty just stared, eyes wide. Nate was chuckling too, but Lex had to grit his teeth and have a battle of wills with the Maine coon. "I told you I'd be back, beast. Relax."

Mouse yowled at him, expressing his extreme displeasure.

"Man, he's got your number," Nate murmured.

"He does," Brant agreed. "Mouse adores him."

"Ow." Dusty stared down at Peaches, who had climbed above the cowboy boot to grab his knee. "What is she doing?"

Lex stared too. *Wow.* "I have no idea. She usually hides."

"She's saying hi. Just be gentle. She gets scared." Brant was laughing at them.

"Okay. Hey, pretty girl. You're some fluffy stuff, huh?" Maybe Dusty sounded enough like Brant to put her at ease.

Cream was in Brant's arms, making herself tiny. That was more like what he knew and understood. He got Mouse up, head on his shoulder. "No biting, beast."

He began stroking Mouse's back, humming softly.

"He's pondering your ear." Nate jerked his chin at Mouse.

"I have no doubt. He's a biter."

"He's a love," Brant argued.

"He's amazing," Lex countered. A love? Maybe not, but he adored the monster cat anyway. Who wouldn't—smart, fierce, and utterly self-assured.

"Cats. I always kinda thought they just went in the barn." Dusty had Peaches, who'd scaled him like a tower, in his arms, and she was nuzzling his jaw and purring like a chainsaw. She'd warmed up to Lex pretty quick, but this was a minor miracle.

Brant watched with a grin that was half-surprised and half-pleased. "Look at that. She thinks you're a cat person, whether you do or not."

"I'm not not one," Dusty said. "I just never thought on it."

"Well, she's not up for adoption, but you can borrow her."

"I will." Dusty hummed, petting, and Nate chuckled.

"Damn," Nate said. "Now we will have to get a pet."

"Could be worse." Brant smiled wryly, Lex thought. "It could be a mini donkey."

"A what?" Nate's eyes went wide.

Dusty just cackled. "Oh, man. My mom wants one."

"I'll give her my momma's number," Brant said. "She's breeding them."

Dusty's lip curled, the look absolutely evil. "That sounds great, buddy. Thank you."

"No problem." Brant winked. "You have brothers?"

"How do you know?"

"Oh man. A guy knows."

Lex snorted. "A Texan, you mean."

"Of course." Brant waggled his eyebrows. "I mean, you have what? Thirty-eight brothers and sisters?"

"Shut up." Lex mock-scowled. "Cousins. I have two sisters."

"Forty?" Brant's grin was fond, warm, and so fucking happy.

"Maybe fifty." That was Nate.

"Get them, Mouse. They're being mean to me."

Mouse yowled, shocking the living shit out of him, and they all stared.

Lex hooted. "That's it, buddy. You get me."

"He totally does. You have seduced my cat." Brant didn't look the slightest bit put out.

He winked at Brant. "At the very least. I think I may have seduced more than the cat."

"Ew!" Nate waved a hand in front of his nose.

Dusty, though, he applauded, the bastard totally into being seduced. "Good for you!"

"Thank you. I would bow, but Mouse would dig in." He had pizza somewhere.

"I'll give them some cat chow, but you'd better put him down first. He'll tear you up when he jumps."

"Okay." He set Mouse on the floor, getting a grumpy look for his trouble.

"Come on, y'all. Kibbles." Brant whistled the kitties up, and sure as shit, they scrambled like they were starving.

Dusty actually looked hurt. "She deserted me."

"Kitty kibbles. All pets are food driven, you know?" Lex thought Dusty had to get that, given he grew up on a farm, but hey, who knew?

"I get it. Hell, I've been known to desert Nate for chips and guac...."

"He has." Nate winked. "Queso."

"Oh yeah. That's understandable." He got it.

"I heard that, butthead," Brant called.

"Yeah. But queso!" He found his pizza and was pleased to see no cat hair.

"Butt queso?" Nate said. "Kinky!"

"You are disgusting, man." He had to say it.

"That's what happens when you hang out with medical people, honey." Brant came in and sat with him this time, not on a barstool.

He wrapped an arm around Brant, happy as a bug in a rug. "Hey, babe."

"Hey. Welcome home."

Oh. Oh, that sounded…. So fucking good. Home. Not just to Burque, but to Brant's house. Where he could live.

"Thank you, baby. I'll get this sofa out of here tomorrow." This living room wasn't big enough for two couches.

"We can put it up in the man cave," Brant murmured. "The smaller one. The cats will love it."

"You just want to watch me pump weights."

"Well, duh."

Dusty and Nate watched them with fond grins.

"What?" Lex grinned back, knowing it was just a case of the old married couple going *awwwww*.

Dusty nudged Nate with an elbow, and Nate grunted and rolled his eyes. "Apparently I think we should get to the hotel, man. We both need showers and all. We'll come over and help unpack tomorrow."

"I really appreciate all the help." Lex and Brant stood, Lex holding out his hand. "Take that two-liter with you."

"Are you sure? There'll be a Smith's on the way," Dusty said, but Nate knew him and just grabbed the Coke.

"Thanks, buddy. Weck's for breakfast?"

"Sounds great." He could totally murder a papas bowl.

"I'll see y'all in the afternoon. I'm going to work half days tomorrow through Wednesday." Brant grinned and waved. "I'll bring tacos."

"Oh, now, a man who knows how to get things done." The guys hugged and waved, and Dusty had to push Peaches into Brant's hands.

Lord, Nate was totally going to have to get Dusty a cat.

"I'll get you in touch with her rescue." Brant winked at Dusty as Nate moaned.

Dusty nodded. "I'll need that number for your momma too. Night, guys."

"Night. Thank you." Lex closed the door behind the guys, leaving the light on for them.

"Nate is never going to let them visit again," Brant muttered, then came right to him, pushing into his arms.

"You think so?" He heard gnawing, so he glanced down to find Mouse chewing his leftover crust. "Huh."

Brant began to laugh, leaning against him, letting him feel the long body. "I need to give you back your key, huh?"

"You do. I need to be able to purchase groceries and go to my interviews."

"And know that you live here, huh?" Brant kissed the corner of his mouth and pushed away, going to the kitchen and the junk drawer.

"You mean I could have copped a key anytime?" He followed, grabbing the plate away from Mouse before he did.

"Like I didn't give you one early or I don't have spares. Oh, FYI. Steve next door has a key, if you get locked out, and there's a spare under the big pot on the front porch."

"Nope." Lex shook his head. "Steve I can see, if you trust him, but no pot keys. Not in any neighborhood." His cop self just denied that completely. "Tell me which pot."

"The one with the geranium...."

He marched right out to get it, because if Brant had no sense of self-preservation, he would fix it. He might put in some lights and a camera too. Just because he might be parking a cop car out front, and that could create a target. Silly man. Seriously, Mouse wasn't a guard dog.

He came back with the key, locking up behind him. "I'll put this one on my key ring. I can give the guys one too, just so we have a safe extra out there."

"Okay. No one ever uses it, honey. It's just there for emergencies."

"I know. A lot of people do that. Which is why we won't." He kissed Brant's nose. Brant was living with a cop now; the rules were a little different. He knew what people did. Especially in ABQ versus small-town Texas.

Brant looked a little confused, and Lex wondered how long it had been since someone took care of the man. So he stole another kiss, really wanting to let Brant know he was loved.

"You came home. I thought I would be sitting here moping."

"Yeah? I thought I would be jacking off until my dick was chapped just thinking about you." He winked when Brant burst out laughing.

"You're lucky. I packed all your porn, honey, that and your dildo."

His cheeks heated. *Caught. Oops.* Not that he was ashamed of liking ass play. "We can put it with yours, Brant."

It was his lover's turn to blush. "Yeah, yeah. You ready to go watch TV in bed? My hip is killing me."

"Shit. Let me put away the food, huh? Then we can have a hot shower and bed." They could snuggle and chat until Brant fell asleep.

"I'll help. I like how your dresser fits in the bedroom, by the way."

"Yeah? I love it. I'm glad you do too." He'd been worried, but he fit well.

Together, they got everything from his fridge put away, along with the leftover pizza. They headed to the back, his arm around Brant for fun and support.

Even with the mess, it felt amazing, having his things here.

They wandered into the bathroom, and Brant got the water going while Lex got out towels. He was going to have to unpack his ditty bag, put his toothbrush next to Brant's and his brush in the medicine cabinet.

For now, that hip needed some steam and some massage. His man had done a lot of driving over a very few days. Driving, lifting, carrying. Moving could be hard on a body.

"I love your bathroom, babe." He eased Brant's shirt up and off.

"Ours."

"What?"

"Our bathroom."

Lex beamed. "I guess so, huh? Wow."

"It's a little weird, huh? But cool." Brant worked his belt open, eased his zipper down.

"It is. I like it so much." He was trying not to get all het up, as Brant needed to rest.

"The water is going to feel so good."

Okay, this whole thing had happened fast, but it felt totally right. Lex shut out the cop questions in his head, just closing them down.

"You're all tense. This'll make it better, hmm? Some steam."

"Definitely." Lex helped Brant strip down too, wanting them in the shower together. He was actually a little nervous —this was a real thing. Not a date, not a booty call. This was him and his lover sharing a shower together.

He adjusted the water, wanting steam. For-real steam. Brant began to touch him, dragging those sure hands over his shoulders, fingertips digging in. He moaned, the massage so yummy, even though he thought he was supposed to be rubbing Brant's hip. Maybe he could anyway, as soon as he remembered how to move.

"God, you're built like a brick shithouse. I think I'll keep you."

"Okay." He rubbed his hands over Brant, tracing lean, sharp lines. "I like how you're put together, baby."

Brant murmured his thanks, but when Lex found that poor hip, the muscles hard as rocks, his lover groaned.

"I got you, Brant," Lex promised.

"Sorry. Just tender, you know?"

"I do. You worked hard." Poor baby. Brant was a stud, never bitching, but Lex hoped soon he would ask for what he needed.

"I'm glad we got your stuff in. We'll unpack over the week, huh?"

"We will. I promise to make breakfasts too." Well, after tomorrow.

"Hell, I'd be happy for cinnamon rolls on my day off, honey."

"Oh, I can definitely promise that. I'm a glutton for them." Lex was way more into those than doughnuts.

"I'm in." Brant rested his forehead on one of Lex's shoulders. "Did you want to meet for lunch tomorrow or just all go together?"

"We can just all go when you get here." Late lunch would be great if the guys wanted Weck's for breakfast.

"Good deal. I'll change h-here."

Oh, that must be sensitive. He held Brant up with one arm and massaged harder. "That's it," Lex murmured. "Let it go. Just like that."

"Lex." Brant leaned, muscles shaking as they relaxed, trusting him.

"Mmm. Yeah." That trust was a treasure, and Lex tucked it in deep, right against his heart. Lex wanted them both melted, both melted and easy in their skins. They swayed together, the water beating down, beginning to do its work on sore muscles.

"Damn, that's fine, man. Seriously. I've never felt so loose."

"Good. We'll work on it."

"That sounds like fabulous work."

"Yeah." Touching. Lots of touching.

His hands were addicted, fascinated, not even sexually, although that was a big part of it. Mostly it was Brant's skin, the texture of it, and the way his touch eased. He wanted to make things better for Brant, just by being there. Hell, that was what he felt like he was supposed to be doing, right? Make things better, all around. Not that Brant's life seemed bad at all. Just without him, and that was important.

"Where are you, honey?" Brant kissed the curve of his jaw, the touch featherlight.

"Arranging your life." He chuckled. "I was just thinking how miraculous this all is."

"It's overwhelming. Wonderful." Brant chuckled, the sound low and husky. "Miraculous."

"It is. I love it." He hugged Brant to him, just pressing them together.

"Come to bed?"

Lex's phone began to ring, and he frowned. "I wonder who that is?"

"I don't." Brant cackled.

"What, is Mouse calling from downstairs wanting tuna?" Lex didn't go answer. They were in the shower, and he was between jobs. He had the luxury of going to voicemail.

"God, can you imagine? If Mouse could text?" Brant stared at him, blue eyes dramatically wide, water drops on his pale eyelashes.

"We'd be running like servants all the time."

"Because that would be different than normal." Brant reached out the shower door and grabbed towels. "You know it's Travis."

"Oh." Oh, right. Trav would be burning with curiosity. Damn.

"We can pretend the phones were off."

"The...." Sure as shit, Brant's phone began to ring.

"Good idea, baby. I'll call him tomorrow." He would too.

Right now was about drops of water on Brant's eyelashes and the heat of wet skin. Right now was about their first night together in their bed.

Theirs.

He glanced out the shower curtain to see three cats sitting in a row, peering at the bathtub.

"Uh, babe? Are they going to eat us?" Lex asked.

"Nope. They're fascinated by the fact that we submerge ourselves in water. I get this every morning."

"Uh-huh." They were going to attack. He had no doubt. They were going to take them down and devour them for daring to disrupt the house.

"Trust me. They need opposable thumbs to work the can opener."

"Right." Mouse would feed on them for weeks. He knew it. Lex turned off the water, mourning the loss of the heat.

Brant wrapped him in one of the towels, rubbing him lazily.

Hello, warmth was back. Yum.

"I will protect you, honey. I promise."

"That works for me." Lex would trade off the cat protection for no hidden keys.

Sure enough, it only took a laugh and a shoo and the hunting posse separated in a flash of fur.

"My hero." Lex slipped into a pair of jammie pants emblazoned with Cookie Monster faces.

Brant flexed playfully and threw on a tissue-paper-thin pair of PT shorts. Oh, yum. That was both hot as hell and endearing.

"I'll clean out stuff for you over the week." Brant crawled into the bed and handed him the remotes.

"We have time. Hell, I'll be around a lot for a few days, at least." He wasn't sure when the department up here would want him to start.

See him be all confident that they would take him in at all.

There was no guarantee, even if his old boss seemed to think there was a place for him. Plus, he was at a deficit on detective again.

The Duke City was a tough fucking beat, even if you weren't starting at the bottom again.

He grinned when Brant poked his ribs. "You're thinking again."

"Occupational hazard."

"You want to share or should we just watch Joe Kenda?"

"Work worries. We should watch Kenda." He rubbed the small of Brant's back.

"Oh, don't stress. You got this."

"I hope so. That's my one worry with this, that they'll put me in traffic or something."

"Doesn't your seniority from before count for anything?"

"My retirement." His lips curled in a smile. "My PERA carries, but that's it, though I know they can use me in better ways."

"Well, don't let them sell you short, huh? You're worth a lot."

"Thank you, baby." Pride swelled in his chest. The way Brant believed in him, even though he'd never seen Lex at work, made Lex so damn happy. Hell, he'd only known Brant a handful of days and they were already moving in together. It seemed like an amazing dream.

Lex slid under the covers after he plugged in his phone and laid his watch on the nightstand. "God, this is nice." Was that super trite?

"Yeah. It's amazing, for this to be a thing." Brant reached for him, and he took Brant's hand, so they lay there watching TV and holding on. Wow.

He sat there, wide-eyed and smiling well after Brant fell asleep.

Lex finally slid his hand free so he could turn down the TV and shift Mouse, who was on him like a ton of bricks, to a better spot. He had to be up at a reasonable hour, at least. The guys wanted breakfast. He would provide.

When the light clicked off, Lex expected his brain to race, to just keep him up all night.

He was asleep in seconds.

18

*D*octor Nunez grinned at him in the hallway. "Leaving already?"

"Yeah, I have a ton of leave." *And a new lover.*

"Are you going to bring him up? Introduce him?"

"Uh, sure." He shook his head when he said it.

"Uh-huh." She pursed her lips and opened the calendar on her phone. "Maybe next Friday? After work?"

She would be relentless until he agreed to bring Lex in. "As long as he doesn't have an interview, yeah."

"Good. We'll all go to the Thai Tip, huh? I can call and make a reservation. What's he do?"

"He's a cop." He waited for her to raise her eyebrows or something.

"Is he? He'll get work, then. We need more good police-men, no?"

"We do. He's a good guy." Hot. Studly. Genuinely decent. Hell, the man loved his cats. Especially Mouse, who was a challenge.

"I'll look forward to meeting him, then."

"I'll make sure he eats Thai."

Dr. N. was addicted to Tom Kha Gai, so they spent a lot of

office meals at the Thai Tip. Who didn't want soup that came in a giant tureen with Sterno under it?

She nodded and disappeared into her office, and Brant took the opportunity to hit the road, not even bothering to change his Mickey Mouse scrubs before heading home. The drive was easy, the sun beating down. He sang along with the Eagles, then Garth. Life was good.

Brant had a second of panic when he turned down his street and there was a truck in his driveway. Lord, how long would that last?

He hoped it began to turn into a deep pleasure every time he saw Lex was home. He parked and sat there for a second and breathed. His hands were shaking, but that might be hunger. He grinned. He'd had cereal because he'd left Lex sleeping. Nate and Dusty were staying through to tomorrow morning, and they were all supposed to lunch, but he didn't see their truck. Huh.

Lex met him at the door, sliding both hands around his waist once they got the door shut. "Hey."

Oh. That was nice. Better than nice. His nerves settled like Lex had lidocaine in his hands. "Hey, honey. How's it going?"

"Well, no one came to breakfast, but that means I get you for lunch."

"Oh no! What happened?" He pushed in close and stole a kiss before he let Lex answer.

"Nonanswering of phones leads me to believe a hotel room with phones off happened. I bet they had wild monkey sex and decided to stay in and meet us for supper."

"That sucks for you." It worked out great for him, though. He was so ready to keep Lex company.

"Nah. They're both drivers. We'll see a lot of them. Do you need to change? A drink?" Lex drew him deeper into the house.

"Yes." They were sharing kisses as they walked, and it was dizzying, heady, and he found himself moaning. Lex hummed, that hand on his hip so warm, relaxing muscles he hadn't even noticed were tight. He leaned a little harder, the world going soft and easy.

"What do you want for lunch?" Lex asked softly. "We can order, or I can just make sanguiches."

"Oh, we can invent sandwiches. We'll go out tonight." *Kiss me more, love.*

"Good deal." Lex did just that, pushing him back against the counter in the kitchen to kiss him deeply.

It was surprisingly hot—the way the edge of the counter pressed into his back, the pressure of Lex's erection against his thigh. Damn.

He clutched Lex's shoulders, hanging on for dear life. Brant wasn't sure what else to do.

Lex broke from the kiss just long enough to strip his scrub top off and let it flutter to the floor. "Pretty baby." Those long fingers skated over his chest.

Brant's flush burned from his belly to his cheeks. "Pretty, huh?"

"Que lindo. I could just touch and look for days." Lex slid one hand up his torso, and it felt like Lex was counting his ribs, naming his muscles.

He shivered, his nipples hard, his cock pushing at his briefs. Then Lex found his nipple, squeezing it with a steady pressure that made his eyes cross. He went up on tiptoe, his body tingling all over. Lord, he could see why Dusty and Nate might have just stayed in.

"Been thinkin' about you, baby. All morning."

"Yeah? I was at work—" He was saying dumb shit, his brain so not firing on all cylinders.

"Mm-hmm, but you're not now." Lex rested their foreheads together, fingers still plucking at his nipples.

Every little pinch made him jump. "Nope. Now I'm with you."

Lex's grin was half-evil, half-pleased as fuck. The man was just so gorgeous and needing him bad. "You okay, baby?"

He answered by bringing their lips together. He was so much better than okay it wasn't funny. He wanted to scale Lex like a tower and ride him. He was on top of the damn world.

The rap on the front door made him jump. "No…."

"Damn it." Lex rested their foreheads together. "I'll get it."

"Do we have to?" They could pretend to be in another dimension.

"Well, they did pretend to not hear their phones."

Oh, right. Dusty and Nate. They had helped them move.

"Uh-huh. And stood you up for breakfast."

The knocking turned to banging. "Open up, you pervs!"

Lex kissed his nose, then left him to pull his shirt back on while going to get the door.

"At least growl at them a little!" he hollered.

"I will!" He heard the door open, heard a burst of laughter from Nate and Dusty.

He slipped down the hall and into the bedroom, needing to splash water on his face and find a pair of jeans. *God. Buttheads.*

Still, he was smiling, wasn't he? The laughter sounded good. He might have to kick their butts.

Brant headed back down, and the kitchen smelled like Mexican food.

"We got a shitload of El Pinto to make up for missing breakfast," Dusty told him. "Lady at the hotel said they had the best salsa."

"You two have shitty timing, do you know that?" He shook his head, but he had to laugh. Had to.

"Eh, you need help unpacking your house way more than you need to unpack your balls," Dusty said, and Nate groaned.

"Bad one, babe. Bad." Nate began unloading containers.

"Terrible, Doc." He rolled his eyes. "Y'all want tea, beer, or Coke?"

"I'd love some tea," Dusty said at the same time Nate said, "Coke."

"Sure, what kind, Nate? Lex, honey, what about you?"

"Dr Pepper?"

Lex chuckled. "Tea. I might have to drive yet today."

Oh, he hoped not. He was really wishing the guys had brought lupper. Lunch and supper. Or maybe they could order more... something, if not pizza.

He poured three iced teas and handed Nate a Dr Pepper.

"Thanks, man. Sorry we reworked the whole plan." Nate filled a plate. There was enough food to last him and Lex a week, maybe.

"It's okay." He rolled his eyes, then winked. "Turned your phones off, huh?"

Dusty grinned, and his cheeks turned bright red. "Uh-huh. We'll move furniture. I promise."

"No worries, guys." Lex handed Brant the tamales. "I have a plan."

"Yeah? What's the plan, honey?" He grabbed two and a taco.

"The little couch can go in bedroom three. Right?" Lex waited for his nod. "So can my weight bench. We'll trade out TVs too. The only other thing is getting the mirror on my dresser in place."

"No problem." Nate got all flexy. "Easy as pie."

Dusty hummed. "Mmm... pie."

"Yum. Did you guys want pie? I have a graham cracker crust...."

Lex gave him an amused glance. "Eat."

"Yes, boss." He settled at the pass-through and dug in. He was hungry. Work hadn't been awful, but super busy.

Lex chowed down too, the guys all chatting about whether to hang the TV or put it on a stand. They were going to have a place that was like a media room—that huge TV, the speakers. Damn.

"I have the stand, guys. No sense putting big holes in this old adobe. It's a bitch to drill." Lex smiled easily, then reached over to put a hand on his leg.

"I'm easy. Either way works. Just remember that Mouse is a jumper, so you'll have to brace anything."

"Okay. We can do a few safety straps." Nate tapped on the table. "The speakers we can mount, though. Since the walls are so thick it won't shake anything."

"That would rock! I love knowing we can turn it up." Lex was damn near bouncing.

"Yeah. And it will be opposite the bedrooms, so no one will worry about sleeping." Brant liked that. He had a feeling he would be sleeping when Lex was awake on occasion. Cop work.

His schedule was steady, sure, and he liked it that way. Monday through Friday, eight to five.

"You okay with all this?" Lex asked quietly.

"Hmm? Our company? They're solid." They were Lex's friends, and they came bearing enchiladas.

"No, all the moving around and stuff. If there's anything you don't want us to move…."

"If there is, I'll speak up." He wasn't shy. "I was thinking about putting that computer desk on the street. I gave my desktop to the daughter of a nurse at work. I use my laptop on the couch."

"Are you sure?"

"It's pressboard. No big." It was true. He'd been meaning to get rid of it.

"Someone will snatch it, I bet." Nate ate another taco in two bites.

"Oh yeah. Okay, I'll clean out that room and then start on the bedroom so you can settle."

"We'll all work on it," Dusty said. "I'll come with you, Brant. Let the beefy ones do the heavy lifting."

"Rock on. I haven't been in that room in forever."

"You tend to just see the rooms you use all the time, right?" Nate winked. "Like I never go in the sun room but to water."

"My plant!" Lex looked around. "Did you guys bring my plant?"

"It came in the front seat of my car, honey. I watered it deep and left it in the shade in the backyard."

"Yay!" Lex made yay hands with the sound, which made them all snort. "What? That is my very first living thing I lived with."

"Well, the care and feeding of Brant and cats might be more difficult."

Lex didn't look scared at all.

"I'm not worried. We'll figure it. After all, I've been managing alone. Together has to be easier." At least Brant hoped so.

That smile. Oh, it was worth every bit of cat pouting and sweat from moving.

"Come on, y'all. Let's get this thing done. I want to see this house put together." Dusty swatted Nate's butt.

"Hey! I was eating."

"Well, you can have thirds after we work." Dusty flexed his lean muscles.

"I'll get that desk out." Lex started directing. "Guys, start the TV move?"

"Man, I thought I was going to leave that to Lex and Nate," Dusty bitched, but went, so he followed Lex to clean out the desk and start cleaning out that closet.

There wasn't much more than weird stolen office supplies, dried-out sticky notes, and there was a picture of him and Matty from the day he left for Basic.

Oh, Lord. He couldn't wait to show this to Matty, see if he

remembered how drunk they'd gotten the night before, how they'd eaten Doritos and olives and pizza rolls and listened to Pearl Jam for hours. Matty would just....

Pain hit him like a sucker punch to the gut. *Motherfucker.* Matty wouldn't anything. Matt was fucking dead.

Matt had died with his brains blown out on a parking lot next to a goddamn gas pump.

"Brant?" He and Lex were alone suddenly, and Lex put both hands on his shoulders. They were hot, solid, and they anchored him, forcing him to breathe somehow.

"Yeah."

"You just got all pale." Lex kissed his cheek, then touched the photo. "Is this you?"

"Yeah. When I left for boot camp."

"Wow. Look at your baby face." Lex chuckled. "My mom has mine from high school and the academy."

"Yeah? Is she excited that you're closer now?" He would put this one away until it didn't hurt so bad. Hell, Lex didn't even recognize Matty, the damn picture was so old.

"I think so?" Now Lex looked uncomfortable, shoulders rounded. "I need to take her to lunch."

"Does she know about me?" He should probably have known that before, huh?

"She does. I want you to meet her, but I probably need to go see her alone first." Lex shrugged off whatever was eating him and grinned. "The sibs will come too, when you meet her."

"Yeah? Cool. One day soon my brother will come out. He's ready to meet you." Hell, he'd be lucky if Bridey didn't try to seduce Lex.

"I would love that." Lex didn't seem at all fazed by the prospect of brothers. Just moms.

"Okay. The desk is ready. I'm going to see what's in the closet." He just hadn't ever put this room together.

"Sure. I don't have a lot to store, but I would like a nook

for the gun safe somewhere. I need to run to Walmart or something to get a standing one for the office closet, I think." Lex didn't seem fussed by that either, so Brant was going to let it be. He trusted Lex, but who knew what could happen?

People broke in. Home invasions. Cop haters. God, he'd never worried like this before.

"You're thinking again." Lex was right behind him when he peered into the closet. He kinda wanted to tell Lex he needed a moment, but he wasn't sure if that was rude. They were still learning the rules.

"Am I? I have to stop that shit." He stood up and started pulling weird storage boxes out to stick in the garage.

"It's not healthy." Lex grabbed a box. "Nothing that will melt, right? You sort, I carry."

"Nothing that will melt. This is paperwork, for the most part."

"Gotcha." Lex trundled out of the room, whistling.

He looked at the near empty, soulless room and shook his head.

Look at me, Matty. I have a live-in.

19

_T_he house looked amazing.

His TV was all hooked up, and the couch was cleaned and in place with the cats already ensconced on it. The guys had left for the night….

And Lex was starting to worry that Brant was having second thoughts. He was so damn quiet. Too quiet.

"Are you going to miss them?" Brant walked out of the bedroom, hands landing on his shoulders.

"Nah. I mean, with our schedules I'll probably see them as much now as I did in Cruces." He let his head fall forward. Damn, that felt good.

"You worked your ass off today. The house looks great." Brant dug in harder, fingers moving in a lazy circle.

"Mmm. The guys were great. And man, you cleaned." Lex moaned a little, feeling each muscle loosen.

"I couldn't fucking believe how nasty things were when we moved them. I mean, the cat hair."

"It piles up. My mom has plants. Leaves fall off and get everywhere."

"Now we have plants and cats. The dust bunnies are going to feed."

"I know." Lex made a fake mournful noise. "I mean, the only reason I didn't have dust bunnies was I had so little furniture I could see them all the time."

"Yeah, you know, those posters were special. I can't believe we forgot them." Brant was beginning to cackle.

"Oh, hush. I saved the one. The Sandias? Mom got it framed for me. I can put it in the man cave or even the garage."

Brant started massaging his neck now, and Lex thought he'd keep the man. "Is it man cave or men cave?"

"Men. For sure. We have many couches and beds to cuddle on now."

"Mm-hmm. I can lounge and watch you lift weights. I'm all in." Brant sounded like it.

"Yeah? It wouldn't be weird to watch me work out?" That would be cool, to have someone to talk to. Lex hated the gym, but working out alone led to… laziness.

"It would be like soft-core porn…."

He flushed, his cheeks heating. "Good deal. I like the idea of showing off. For you."

Brant kissed his temple. "You think we'll stop being hot for each other anytime soon?"

"Nope." He reached back to stroke Brant's cheek. "I think we're gonna be like bunnies."

"Nothing wrong with that, honey." Brant leaned down onto him, forehead on his shoulder.

"Nope. What's your pleasure tonight, baby?" If Brant was ready for bed, he would go. Lex was kinda pooped.

"I was thinking about lounging on the couch like slugs and watching TV."

"Well, come on and sit with me." He held out a hand, so Brant came around to join him and Mouse. The girls were on the long lounge section. Brant sat close, arm to arm.

So Brant didn't look unhappy. Not at all. Maybe he was overthinking. Cops did that, or so Lex was told.

Brant found some goofy British show about chefs and castles, then started petting Mouse, who was still in his lap. That was weirdly intimate, but still so cool.

He was living with someone.

Him.

He was living with someone. Travis would be so….

Travis. His eyes flew open. "I haven't called Travis."

"Shit. You want me to go to the other room?"

"No." Lex tugged out his phone. "Let me just see if he can do lunch tomorrow." His fingers flew as he texted.

"I'll be home for lunch tomorrow and Wednesday. Maybe go for breakfast or lunch Thursday? Is that weird?"

"No. No, it's cool." Lex chewed his lower lip, hoping Travis wasn't pissed.

Brant pinked and chuckled. "No, it is weird. Y'all have lunch tomorrow. I can totally save my hours."

"Baby, Travis says Thursday is fine." He grinned, relieved on both counts.

"Are you sure? I don't want to be some freak boyfriend."

"Not even for a little while?" he teased. "I think you should push it."

"I just…. This is all so new, and we got interrupted this afternoon…."

"I know." He set his phone aside to wrap his arm around his man. "It feels pretty damn good, having you want me."

"I do. Want. You know."

"Yep." He hit On, bringing up the TV. Looked good. The sound had to come down…. There.

"Mmm… perfect." Brant settled in, a soft sigh sounding.

"Yeah? I think so too." So no second thoughts. Yay.

Maybe tomorrow he'd make cookies. Brant needed peanut butter cookies. Lex did love to stick things in the oven and pull them out and see something come from nothing. Yeah. That was a good idea.

It was sort of the way he dealt with his life, full stop.

He was grinning just thinking about it, which made Brant chuckle along, even though the man had no idea what he was smiling about.

And when Brant lifted his face for a kiss, it was perfect.

$\mathcal{T}$ravis looked tired.

Lex felt a pang of guilt for forgetting to call, but he'd been damn busy. Not just with Brant. Moving had been a drain, and the guys had taken up some time. He guessed it said something that he was seeing Travis before he saw his mom.

"Hey. How's it going? You're still on half days at the school?"

Travis nodded. "I am. I just get tired." He gave Lex a wan smile.

"Oh, hon, I'm sorry." He slid into the booth across from Travis. "How can I help?"

Because he did want to help. Travis was down. Like, lower than he'd expected.

"You can talk to me. Tell about the last few days. Are you settled? Are you moved? I need to know everything!"

"I am. Brant is talking about inviting you to come over for supper next weekend. Is that cool with you?" He grabbed a menu.

"He does? Are you sure?"

"I am." Lex grinned over the top of the laminated paper.

"He's worried you never want to see him again." Then he sobered. "He's missing Matt bad. It would be good for you two to see each other, but I don't want you to push too fast."

"I bet he does. They spent a lot of time together being buttheads." Travis winked at him. "And I feel terrible at how I treated him."

"Well, there you go." *Burger? Or breakfast all day?* "Do you need any help at the house, hon? Anything I can do before I get to work?"

"I don't know when it's okay to start moving some of his things. Do you?"

"No." He shook his head on that one, trying to give it some thought. "I mean, my grandma never has moved anything, but she was older when my abuelo passed. I know Dan Medina got rid of everything within six months when his wife died from cancer."

"Huh. I don't know, it hurts seeing all his clothes hanging in the closet. Maybe I can just move them into the garage." Travis offered him a quirky little grin. "This stuff is hard."

"It is. I wish I could do more, but this is about you, not me." Lex winked. "What are you having?"

"I'm thinking lemon chiffon pie and chocolate silk pie for dessert."

"Both, huh?" Lex looked at the menu again. "Maybe the chicken parm and linguine." There was nothing better than chicken parm in a casual dining place. Fried to a crisp with bright red sauce….

"Yes. I'm currently on an all-sugar diet."

"Ah. Well, I'll join you in a pie and take a piece home too." After salad and garlic bread he might take both pieces home. Huh. What was Brant's favorite pie? "Do you know what kind of pie Brant likes?"

"Apple. He always orders apple."

"What was Matt's?" He hoped that didn't hurt too much

to ask. "I know he liked lemon cake. I remember that from the wedding."

"Key lime. He loved key lime pie with a passion." Travis grinned over. "Brant would know that. He brought Matt one every year."

"Aw, that's too cool. I think he's been busy enough to not think about it too much, but he was kinda down a few nights ago."

"Yeah. I feel terrible about hurting him. I was an asshole."

"You were hurting. Coke, please," he added to the server. "He knows that, I think."

"Even if he doesn't, he'll be nice. He's a good guy."

"Yeah." Lex grimaced. "I've been worried this would be too weird for you. And me, which is why I was all texting. I should know better."

"Why? I get to see you more often. That's going to be amazing, right?"

"It is." They had to have things in common still. Movies. Music. Food. Something. He would look forward to finding out.

"When you get back on the force, will you come to my class and talk about your job? The kids are so worried about the police."

"I will. I can't blame them." That was a terrifying thing for the kids in New Mexico. Cops often meant family issues or problems with border agents.

"No, me either, but they need to know some of you are the good guys."

"Most of us."

"Right. Most of you."

He shook his head. "Encourage them, huh?"

"I do. I swear to you, I worry about them every day. They need to believe there are adults that care."

"There are. You do amazing things." He settled on the parm.

"So, back to you." Travis stopped as they ordered, and his crazy buddy did order a piece of pie for his main.

"Uh. Okay, shoot." He wasn't sure where they'd stopped.

"Housewarming present requests?"

"Well, Brant had a lot. Something arty that's not a poster to put in the man cave?"

"I've been in Brant's house. He's very into his Southwestern decor. It's adorable."

"Well, there you go. Something from Old Town." He loved Brant's house, because it never seemed overdecorated or contrived.

"Fair enough. I remember when he bought that house. You should have seen him waffle." Travis laughed, and God, it was good to see.

"Yeah? Like about what?" He grabbed his drink when it arrived, sipping it instead of gulping like he wanted to. Maybe he should get a water too.

"Oh Lord. Was this the right neighborhood? Did he want a new build or a vintage? The only thing he was sure about was that he wanted a big backyard. This was after the deal with that asshole."

"Asshole?" God, he did love getting details about Brant's life that his lover just didn't consider important.

"Oh, there was a shit breakup, apparently, and the guy stole most all of Brant's stuff, packed it in an SUV, and then got himself killed on the highway."

Lex blinked. Then he blinked again. "Jesus, Trav!"

"Right? Brant was livid. Just pissed." Travis took a long drink before starting again. "But Matt always said that was when he knew, all the way, that Brant was a Burqueño. He never once talked about going back to Texas. Instead he started house-hunting."

"I think maybe he made a good choice." He adored the house, and the yard was made of awesome.

"Oh, I think so. It's got great bones, and it's got the charm he wanted."

"Totally." Lex did love the way Brant loved his house.

"Matt wanted him to buy a condo. Something upscale and fancy."

"Yeah?" He couldn't see his Brant in a condo. "Whose idea was it to buy your house?"

"Oh, we had it built. We both wanted something brand-new, a blank slate." Travis winked at him. "No yard to speak of."

"Ah. No, I noticed that. I know you have a black thumb." Hell, Travis always had. The man had killed their mung bean sprouts in kindergarten.

"I do. Is your plant still alive?"

"It is. Dusty and Nate took good care." His cheeks went red-hot, because Lord, had he told the whole world about that plant?

"Hey, it's good. Good practice for the monster cats."

"Do they like you?"

Trav's eyes went comically wide. "God no. The Persians hide, and that evil monster just scratches everything."

His Mouse? No way. He just shrugged. "We have an agreement, I guess."

"You and Brant?"

"No, dork. Me and Mouse." He winked broadly.

Travis gave him a disbelieving stare. "You. And the cat. You have an agreement?"

"Yep. I do what he wants, and he doesn't hurt me." Much.

"Wow. You're being abused by your lover's cat."

"No. We have a relationship." That did sort of sound like he was being abused. Mouse was very dominating. If Mouse had opposable thumbs, man, Lex would have to worry about things like finding Brant cuffed to the refrigerator. He chuckled. Nah. Mouse would just order pizza. That cat was obsessed with a deluxe pie.

"What's funny? Are you fantasizing about a cat?"

"No, but I was thinking about one. Mouse likes pizza. Dusty and Nate found out the hard way."

"Oh. Oh, those are your friends from Cruces? Did Mouse the Bully steal their pizza?"

"He did. Next time they come up, we'll all go to supper." He felt a serious pang of guilt about not inviting Travis over to meet the guys.

"I'd like that. I... I think I'm going on a cruise this summer. Not a pick-up thing, but just something totally different." Travis sighed, took a sip of his drink. "Is that weird?"

"No. It's good for you." He thought it would be great for Trav to get away for a bit.

"Yeah? It's not too soon? I mean, I just.... The summer is too soon."

"Nah. I think it's great. I mean, that's why you're a teacher, right? So you have your summers."

"Yeah, and now I can travel." The tears welled up in Travis's eyes, and Lex braced himself for a storm, but Travis just blinked them back.

"You can." He reached a hand across the table, so Travis took it, holding on.

"Invite me to supper some evening? So I can make up with Brant and tell him how sorry I am."

"Absolutely. I'll get with Brant and see what all our schedules look like, but it should be soon." He wanted that, for real.

"Thanks. Now, when do you go talk to the guys at the precinct? You need to get that detective desk." Travis glanced over. "Did I say that right?"

"You did. I go see my old sergeant on Monday. He didn't want to deal with me this week." Lex was worried that meant no job, but he could go Rio Rancho or Los Lunas or even Santa Fe if he had to.

"You be careful, huh? I don't... no getting shot."

"I'll do my best, buddy." His salad came, so he let go of Trav's hand. "I know it's scary."

"Yeah. I don't know how Brantley copes. It took forever and years of therapy after he got shot."

"It did?" Brant seemed so… well, not post-traumatic, really. Lex got it. He'd done the mandatory therapy the force had required after the bomber and everything…. Now he just worked out when the demons came looking late at night. Coping mechanisms.

"Yeah. Yeah, I mean, this time he didn't get hit, but…." Travis shivered. "At least Matt didn't hurt. He would have hated living with a serious brain injury. He wouldn't have thanked anyone for that."

"No." No, that much he knew. Brant had signed the guys' wills as a witness and had been their medical power of attorney. Mental note, he needed to ask Travis about changing all that now.

"Okay. Happy things. Tell me your favorite thing about your new house."

"The yard. We've had dinner out there most nights. I love it." His mom would love it too.

"Yeah? So you're glad he didn't tear it out and put in a pool? That was my suggestion."

"You're kidding. I mean, water guilt." He loved the wisteria and cactus and hummingbirds. Brant had worked his butt off for this.

"I know. I thought it would be nice, though. I go to the aquatic center, you know that." Travis stuck out his tongue, just teasing away, which was so good to see.

"I do. I have a man cave gym room." That was still so damn cool.

"No shit? He gave up his office?"

"He did."

"Well, I'll be damned. It must be love." Travis winked. "Though I know the desktop was gone."

"He uses his laptop on the couch." The filing cabinet was still in the closet, just for ease of storage.

"Yeah, he still uses the treadmill at the gym?"

"I guess? I have room to put one in...." He did, in fact. Lex had thought about a Bowflex or something, but he could so put in a treadmill.

"Eh, ask him. He runs on his lunch hour in the hospital. He gets some sort of bonus."

"Oh! Right." That made sense. He wouldn't mess with that.

The food came and they started talking about random shit, easy stuff, and it felt good. Oddly like high school, where they were just two guys hanging out. It was nice to relax.

Travis teased the hell out of him for settling down, and he dared to tease Travis about how often he ordered takeout.

He felt like things might be all right.

That was a pretty damn good feeling.

21

*B*rant came home Friday shaken.

The detectives had come to the office to show him pictures of a dozen different men who were possible suspects in Matty's murder. A couple he could reject out of hand—the guy had been Hispanic, maybe Indios, but not black, not Anglo. There were two who were definite maybes, but it had been dark, and the guy had worn a hoodie. He'd seen a skinny, young dude with red shoes.

"Why can't I remember more, Matty? What the hell?" He was supposed to go to the grocery store, but he didn't want to. "I fucking feel like the world's biggest motherfucking loser."

He slipped out of his car and stretched, his back popping, his hip screaming at him. Stress always made that bitch wake up and drive him nuts. It didn't make sense, not a bit.

Brant let himself in, finding Lex there, sound asleep on the couch. A stack of paperwork sat next to him, all neatly filled out in Lex's block printing. Someone must have gotten himself a job.

Suddenly he couldn't breathe; he couldn't quite manage to move. Christ. Christ, if he didn't know better, he'd think he was having a heart attack. He stumbled to the bathroom, searched out his Ativan, and forced himself to take one before he sat down on the pot.

His hands shook, so he stared at them, clenching them to stop the tremors. *In. Out. Breathe.*

It was the detectives, he knew it. They'd come, and he hadn't been able to do it. He hadn't known. What if he had just let Matty's killer go?

"Baby? Is that you?" Lex called from just beyond the door.

"Yeah. I didn't mean to wake you. How's it going?" He washed his face off real quick. *Get it together, son. You got this.*

Then he opened the door, wearing a smile.

"Hey." Lex kissed his cheek. Those dark eyes took in every bit of him. "You okay? You're pale."

"Rough day at work. The detectives came by." He could order from DoorDash, right? Green chile burgers.

"Did they have any news?"

That knowing gaze was too much, making him duck past to head to the kitchen. "They had a bunch of photos. I couldn't recognize anyone."

"Baby, I saw the CCTV. There wasn't much to see."

He reached for a beer, then shook his head. *No. No beer with the antianxiety drugs.* "Want a Coke?"

"Sure." Lex followed him like a K-9 rather than a boyfriend. "You want me to follow up?"

"Whatever will find Matty's shooter, huh?" He felt the pill starting to work, the world going a little bit easier, a little less sharp around the edges.

"You know it." Lex put both hands on his arms, rubbing up and down.

He leaned back into Lex's strength, willing himself to be cool. Calm. Collected.

"I got a big package of information to fill out today. Looks like my interview Monday is just a formality." Lex kissed his neck.

"Yeah? Are you excited?" *Do you know what shift you're getting? Do you know what you're going to be doing? Do you know who you're going to be working with?*

"I have no idea. I know I won't start at detective. They have someone retiring in six months, and I'm one of three guys they'll consider, since I was working my way up so close in Cruces, but I'm not sure what division I'll be in until then."

Well, what did he say to that? He just reached up and took Lex's hand. It was the best he had. Especially right this second.

"You want to order in?" That little squeeze of his hand told him maybe Lex understood.

"Yeah. I really do. I'll grocery shop tomorrow."

"It's Saturday. We'll go together."

He sighed and nodded. "I'd like that."

"Cool. I want some Fritos for Frito pie." Lex rubbed at his back with the one free hand.

"Oh, I knew I chose you for a reason. We should grill some chicken over the weekend."

"I like it. Then we'll have protein all week if we get busy." Lex hummed and swayed with him.

God, he wanted to ask a thousand questions, but he didn't want to sound like a fluttering dick, so he let it go. Lex would tell him about schedules and shifts and all when he knew.

"Hey, come sit, huh? I'll grab your computer, and we can order supper." Lex drew him to the couch, letting him carry the Cokes.

"What are you thinking? We got options." He'd even get Annapurna's.

"Green chile cheeseburgers."

Man, they were in sync right now. Brant nodded. "I was just thinking about that."

"Excellent. I'm craving that and fries. Maybe a milk-shake." Lex grinned at him. "You want to run to Blake's? We could be daring and go see a movie."

Only if they didn't get gas afterward.

"Sure. I'm game." The pill was really working, so he could let Lex take him out. Right? "You willing to drive?"

"I am." Lex hopped back up. "I'll change real quick. You rest your head."

"Thank you. I think I will." He stretched out, his back popping. He thought Lex suspected he'd taken something, but it wasn't illegal. Hell, the script wasn't even out of date.

"Be right back." Lex was off, and he did close his eyes but jumped when Mouse landed on him.

"Hey, you big beast. How goes it?"

Mouse yowled dramatically.

"Oh, don't give me that. I saw you napping with Lex." Brant rubbed those big ears. Mouse blinked, and his eyes crossed. "Yeah, that's it, isn't it?"

"Are you giving cat scritches?" Lex was laughing. "Because the girls are feeling neglected."

"Are they? Peachie! Cream! Come on, baby girls!"

The Persians popped out from under the ottoman, purring and meowing. He held one arm open, and he was suddenly covered in kitties. They were telling him all about it too, loud and proud.

"You are owned," Lex accused, and he nodded. *God yes. Totally.*

Lex plopped back on the couch, not seeming to be in any huge hurry. That was probably good, because Mouse pounced, taking Lex down to groom him.

"Uh. Who's owned?"

"Me. He's got me." Lex laughed and rubbed as commanded. *Good man.*

"I love this—having you here." He meant it too. He adored having Lex around, sharing the stupid, normal, silly stuff.

"Me too." Lex rolled his head to look at Brant. "Let's stay in."

"You want me to order online? I'm all over that." He would love to sit and cuddle, stay in out of the Friday-night busyness.

"Yeah. I think that will work." Lex kissed his elbow, which was all Mouse was allowing.

"Green chile cheeseburgers and fries. I'm on it." Staying in was perfect.

Safe.

22

"*H*ey, Espana! Good to see you back." Leo Huerta clapped him on the back.

"Good to be here, man. When did you go from a uniform to a suit?"

"When I took Robbery instead of holding out for Homicide." Leo shook his hand. "You on patrol?"

"Until I can move up, yeah."

"It'll happen quick, man. You've got time in service. You want Vice? Narcotics?"

"No. Vice will want undercover." He sat, trying not to show how weird the new uniform felt. Starched. "No, I'd rather work under you, or with the guys at Homicide. I'm good at interviews and canvassing. First-on-scene stuff. I mean, I know I won't get a choice, but that's my jam."

"Uh-huh. Detective will come sooner that way too." Leo grinned at him. "Sucks getting old, huh? You start wanting to stay home a little more."

"I got a reason now."

"No shit? Well, good on you." Leo chuckled. "We want you assigned to a unit, then."

"Put in a good word for me, man. I'd appreciate it."

"You know I will. So, coffee?"

"Please. I've been off work for a week or two, and I feel lazy." He could get to being a laze, if it wasn't for the mind-numbing boredom.

"Yeah? How is it down in Cruces? Busy?" Leo led him to the break room.

"God, yes. It's crazy right now with all the extra political bull." He shook his head. People were scared.

"Yeah. You had that whole bomber thing. That was wild. You are the one that got him, huh?"

"I'm the one." He pressed away the cascade of memories that tried to push into his mind.

"That was good, no? He needed to be stopped." Leo clapped him on the back. "Hate to have to draw your piece, but it was a clean shot."

"It was." That was always such an asinine statement now that he'd had to shoot someone.

"Right. Coffee."

He would say Leo paid attention, and he appreciated it. Some guys didn't. He just nodded, ready to get to all the little meetings and such he had today.

God, he hated first days. At least this was a first day in a familiar place. He still knew a lot of the guys, and HR was already talking positively about his extra education and about him taking tests….

"Come on, man. Let me introduce you around. You've been gone awhile. Although you were up for your friend's homicide, no? So you met a few new guys?"

"I did. We had a few talks." God. His friend. He'd barely known Matt, but Brant and Travis deserved better from him.

"Cool. My condolences. I hope his family is okay."

"They're getting there." What else could someone say? No one was okay, and Leo knew that. "So, how's Denise?"

"She's good. Real good. We're talking about having one more baby."

He blinked. "Shit, man, good luck."

"Hey, if it doesn't work, it'll be fun to practice."

"I guess so!" Now that he could laugh about and clap Leo on the back. Suddenly he was surrounded by cops, and he was home. Really home all the way.

Dios. So many handshakes and names and offers to help him out.

He couldn't wait to tell Brant about everything. All of it.

Lex stopped cold for a moment, then grinned. He'd never, ever wanted to tell someone about his day like this, not even his mama when he was a kid.

This must be what it was like, being in love.

His heart kinda... pounded for a moment. Just a moment, though, because the guys allowed little more than that. Everyone had a question about the bombings, really.

Then it was time to get to work. He went to roll call, met his new partner, Jo, and then checked out his squad car.

Lex took a deep breath. This he knew. This he got.

This was just work.

BRANT WENT through work like a robot, his stress levels so high the only way he could cope was to shut down. His patients deserved better than this, but thankfully everyone was well-baby checkups and common colds and a couple of bad cactus attacks. Poor babies. Festering cholla sucked so hard. At least there were no fire ants.

Nan and Carol went to lunch with him, and he stopped by the Whole Foods to grab a fancy cake and a couple steaks to celebrate Lex's first day back to work. He was buzzing with tension about it, absolutely certain Lex was going to get injured somehow.

Would they even know to call him if something happened?

Oh.

Oh, Jesus.

The thought was harsh enough that he pulled off into a Smith's parking lot and just breathed.

His head pounded, the blood in his temples rushing so fast he thought he might pass out.

Fuck. Fuck, man. I can't do this. I got to get my shit together.

He reached for his phone, needing to call Matty, to just talk this out. Brant slammed his hand against the steering wheel. Matt was gone. He couldn't call.

His phone rang, and he dropped it, his gorge rising.

"I swear to God, if you're calling me from beyond the grave, Matty, we're not friends no more."

When it quit, then started to ring again, he knew he needed to get it. It had to be family. When he looked, he saw Bridey's name. Fucking brothers and their guts.

He swiped, slapping the tears from his cheeks. "What's up?"

"You tell me, bro." Bridey sounded downright worried.

"Another panic attack. Nothing big." He didn't bother to ask how Bridey knew. Bridey always knew.

"You gonna see someone about all this shit?" Bridey wasn't big on therapy, but he thought it had helped Brant, and he knew it.

"I…. This is stupid. I just need to get over it." He leaned his head back. "I'm worried that he'll get shot."

"Who?"

"Lex."

"Well, that's always a possibility, since I take it he's back at work?" Bridey was so helpful.

"Yeah, he started today."

"Gotcha. Well, you're gonna have to get used to it, man. I mean, that sounds callous, but if you want to be with him…."

"Why do you think I'm out here in a parking lot in my fucking car, asshole?" He wouldn't let Lex know. No way.

"Hey! Did I know you were?" Bridey sighed. "Look, I know a little about this, right?"

"Yeah. Yeah, I hear you. I don't want to stress him out."

"Sure, but you also have to tell him it wigs you out. He'll know something is wrong and think it's him and not your freaky ass."

"Yeah, and what if he leaves my freaky ass? I've been through that." He didn't even like to think about that.

"That doesn't even bear talking about." Bridey was very plain about his... ex.

"No. No, I never think about him." Except for right now.

"Well, don't. Think about Lex and about starting out right."

"Right. I got him a cake and I bought steaks." That was right, right?

He rolled his eyes at himself. *Right, right, right, right. Christ.*

"Oh, good deal. That will make him smile, I bet."

"Yeah. Yeah, it will. Mashed or baked potatoes?" He felt himself begin to relax.

"I would say baked. Did you get bread?"

"I got salad and a french bread."

"Wine?"

"Yeah." A nice merlot that he hoped Lex liked.

"Well, you're set." Bridey chuckled, the sound warm. "Just chill, bro. Breathe."

"I'm trying. I really... I'm into him, Bubba. Deep." He was more than into Lex. He thought it was real.

"Then be honest, huh? Don't let him think he's doing something wrong."

That was probably good advice. Lex had dealt with a bomber. He probably got post-traumatic stress and shit. He'd think about it. Later. Not tonight. "I'm going to go cook my man supper."

"Okay, bro. Go get 'em."

"Love you, Bubba. I'll call tomorrow." He could breathe. He could do this.

"Love you." The line clicked off.

Time to get home and celebrate Lex's first day on the job, dammit.

When he got back to the house, he did all the normal things. Feed the cats. Clean up all the shit Mouse had knocked over. Go through the mail. The routine calmed him even more, and by the time Lex pulled up, he had the grill going, the wine breathing.

Lex came into the kitchen to give him a kiss. "Hey, baby. Be right back. This uniform itches like crazy."

"I'll be in the backyard. Steaks for supper, okay?"

"That's amazing." Lex's smile went right to his toes.

Brant heard Mouse talking to Lex, yowling and bitching all the way down the hall. Oh, someone better put his boots in the closet. They would end up shredded if he wasn't careful. Or pooped in.

He chuckled and shook his head. It was hard, being the focus of all that fuzzy feline love, and Mouse was obsessed. Who was he kidding? So was he. Brant hauled the steaks and potatoes out to the grill. He'd parcooked the potatoes in the mic, but he wanted that baked flavor.

He turned on some music and grabbed the acrylic wineglasses.

Lex joined him a few minutes later. "What can I do?"

"Pour the wine? How was your day?" *I worried about you.*

"Mostly boring. I did a lot of meetings, paperwork, met Jo, who's my new partner. All routine." Lex poured out, then came to hand him a glass.

"Is he cool?"

"She." Lex grinned. "And she's a baby. Twenty-three, desperate to learn and make a difference. I like her a lot."

"Oh, wow." How did Lex get the rookie? To test him?

"Yeah, she's eager, been on the force for eighteen months

and has a reputation for being a great cop. You'll like her. Her wife's name is Denise. She's a teacher at Cibola."

"Oh, cool." At least she was family. That would make things easier.

"Yeah. I think they were throwing her a bone, letting her have someone that understands." Lex lifted his glass. "Thanks for the wine, baby."

"You're welcome as the flowers in May." He liked how relaxed Lex appeared, so he went to beg a kiss.

They stood there for a long moment, their mouths meeting, Lex pushing in to taste him. He wrapped one hand around Lex's hip, thumb drawing circles.

"Mmm." Lex licked his lower lip. "Much better. How was your day, baby?"

"Just another day in paradise. Two more cholla victims. I wish parents would check their yards better."

"Ouch. Poor kids. I had a spray paint and a yard art theft."

"Something cool?" He flipped the steaks.

"A giant chicken."

"That's pretty damn cool." He had a flying pig and a Godzilla stepping on a gnome.

"Yeah. The guys want to pool some funds and buy her another one. The lady is elderly."

"Aww. That sucks. Who the fuck does shit like that?" The same sort that shoot unarmed IT guys for nothing at a gas station.

"Kids, I bet. We might yet find it somewhere." Lex stroked his back with the hand not holding wine.

"I hope so. That's incredibly uncool."

"It is." Lex shook his head. "I see a lot of that."

"I'm sorry." He didn't know what to say.

"That's what makes it so awesome when we make things better. The captain has me doubling up. He wants me to do some training on interviewing and gathering evidence."

"Yeah? That's great, huh?" For a guy who had a brother who was a rural officer, he knew dick-all about cops.

"It is. It's the one thing I lack before I take the detective exam."

That he knew. That he got. "That's not bad at all, then. Do you know what division you want to work in? Hand me the plate."

"Well, I'd love Homicide, but I'd take Robbery slash Violent Crimes."

That was a sentence you didn't hear around the barbecue grill every day. "What's the difference? I mean, I know the definitions. I'm talking about for you."

"Well, Homicide is slightly better pay and way better hours, believe it or not. Especially here. I mean, out of over six thousand violent crimes a year, only sixty-one are murder cases."

"Wow. If you just brought the average down by a little, you'd only have one murder a week."

Lex blinked at him but decided to chuckle. "Right?"

Yeah, he didn't want to explore what he meant either. He didn't know.

"You want to eat in there or out here?"

"Out here, if you want. It's pretty in the shade." Lex set his wine on the table. "What do I need to get from inside?"

"The salad? It's in the fridge." He checked the potatoes, satisfied with those. "Are your folks tickled that you started back?"

"They are, though Mama wants me to bring you for supper and is now frustrated by my schedule." Lex headed inside, then reappeared moments later with salad and bread. "Oh, that reminds me. Travis wants to come over for supper too. We'll need to do that this week, I guess. I start my four-twos next week."

"Right. Sure. Just let me know." God, he was going to have to write down the schedule.

"You got it." Lex took another sip of wine. "Everything smells so good."

"Thank you. I think we're all ready. Let me grab the butter and salt and pepper." Why did everything feel so stiff? Lex was fine.

"Are you okay?" Lex asked, jolting him a little with how that echoed his thoughts.

"I don't know. I'm a little grumpy, I think." He could hear Bridey telling him to just confess the truth, but shit and Shinola, he didn't want to be a titty-baby. "I've never been a cop's lover."

"Ah." Lex's eyes went knowing, sympathetic. "It was a dull day, baby."

"Good." He drew Lex over for another kiss. "I got you a cake for dessert."

"Did you? What kind?" Lex danced him in a slow circle.

"Chocolate cherry."

"Steak, wine, and chocolate cake? You're so getting laid."

Brant laughed, delighted. "Am I? That's awesome! It's like having a live-in lover."

"Right. I even help feed the cats."

"I am a lucky son of a bitch." And he was going to get over this shit too, if it killed him.

$\mathcal{S}$adie's smelled great. The hostess showed Lex to the table where Travis and Brant waited for him, and he hated the fact that he was still in uniform. He'd already left them waiting almost a half hour, though, so he hadn't wanted to go home and change. He really needed to leave some street clothes in his locker at work.

"Hey. Sorry I'm late." He squeezed Brant's shoulder when he slid into his seat at the table.

"Hey, Officer. Fancy meeting you here." Brant grinned up at him, smile only a little bit strained. "Have a chip."

"Yum." He grabbed a chip from the basket so he could dip it in the salsa.

"We've been sitting and telling stories." Travis grinned at him over a margarita. "I was telling Brant about how you refused to take your cousin Brittany to the prom. How you went with Tomas and we all gawked."

Lex relaxed enough to laugh at that. "Well, I had to do something. You saw Brittany's dress. No way was I going to be in pictures with that."

"It was… intense," Trav agreed.

"It was yellow."

"Bright?" Travis countered, and Brant began to chuckle.

"Electrical banana, man. Yel. Low."

"You would have had to wear a lime green cummerbund and tie to make it go." Travis waggled his brows.

"Yeah. Tomas had way better taste." He ordered an iced tea and a stuffed sopapilla with Christmas. Brant got carne asada tacos; Travis got a bowl of green chile.

God, it was good to be here.

"How was work?" Brant asked, those blue eyes watching him a bit too closely.

"Uh. Long." He'd been late because of a robbery with a shooting. At a gas station. Not something he wanted to talk to either of them about. Both of them were wounded deeper than Brant for sure wanted to admit.

It took time, and he wasn't going to share and open fresh wounds.

"Bummer." Travis rolled his eyes. "I had a biting, screaming meltdown today. I mean, not me. A student."

Brant met Lex's gaze, and they both cracked up, just hooting like big stupid loons.

"Yeah, yeah, I know. With me, you never know." Travis waved a chip at them. "Shut up."

"I never once thought any different." Brant wasn't even managing a straight face.

"How was your day, baby?" Lex grabbed another chip. They needed salt, but Trav hated it when he salted the whole basket.

"Good. Today was good and normal. Dr. N. only worked half a day, so I spent a while doing paperwork." Brant offered him a quirky grin. "I got tomorrow off."

"Did you, now?" That had promise. Coincidentally, he also had off tomorrow.

"I did. It's like a miracle." Brant's pretty blue eyes just twinkled, so merry and lit up.

"Huh, well, we might have to do something special."

"Yeah? You have a thought?"

Travis groaned dramatically. "You two just need to go and fuck like bunnies."

"Trav!" He didn't need that kind of teasing.

"What? You need to. It'll make you both better people."

Brant nodded sagely. "It will. But right now we're at supper with you."

"You are, and I appreciate it." Trav sighed and grabbed his drink. "I apologized to Brantley, by the way. He accepted. We're friends again."

"Oh, good." Lex hoped that was true. They all needed their friends. "I love you both."

"Yeah, yeah, yeah. I was a crazy asshole." Travis winked over.

"You had your reasons." Brant nodded once, like that was that.

Lex nodded too, but he was damn glad this seemed settled. If nothing else, that sort of hurt would fester all up. It had to come out. Which was why he'd have to talk to Brant at some point about what was bothering him so much.

He knew Brant had a prescription for antianxiety meds, he knew Brant was taking them, and he knew his lover didn't think he knew.

This whole thing with Matt was giving Brant fits. It was going to tear him up…. Lex didn't know whether Brant needed to talk to him or Travis or a doctor, but he needed to let it out. Right?

They would totally work it out somehow.

This navel-gazing was all hard.

Lex dug into the stuffed sopapilla, the green chile bright and the red smoky. Food was way easier.

Way.

"So, how's the job? Are you glad to be back out here?" Travis stole a bite of his meat.

"It's good. It's coming home, for sure. Whole different set

of crimes, of people." There was a lot more going on down in the international district, for instance.

"I don't suppose anyone's made any progress with...." Travis trailed off with a sigh.

No, and no one's going to. They had nothing—it was one of a hundred thousand desperate men doing desperate things. A dark hoodie. A single gunshot. They had nothing.

"They're still really pushing." Which was true. No one had called it a cold case by any means. He still couldn't quite meet Trav's eyes.

"Have you talked to his mom, Brant? Matt's, I mean. I haven't... I ought to, huh?"

"His birthday is coming up. Maybe."

Travis looked a bit stricken, but he nodded. "It is. Oh, wow."

"Right?" Brant stared at his tacos for a second. "Okay, new topic. Something less drama-inducing."

Travis looked over with a raised eyebrow. "Anyone found any warming lube they like?"

"You guys need anything else?" The waitress was bright red, but she managed not to laugh, gag, or throw them out.

"Just some more tea, please?" Travis smiled at her, sweet as pie.

"You got it." She left their ticket and fled.

Lex stared at Trav. "You know I'm still in uniform, right?"

"Uh-huh."

Brant shook his head. "I swear, y'all are so much like brothers."

"Yeah. Old friends get that way, right?"

Travis snorted. "Not that old."

"We're old enough," Lex countered.

"It's not the age," Brant added.

"It's the mileage," they all finished together.

"Hell, if that's it, I'm in deep shit." Butter wouldn't melt in Brant's mouth.

"You know it." Lex winked, then took a sip of Coke. "Is it weird to have sopapillas if you had one for supper?"

"Uh, honey. You're eating one now…." Brant lifted one eyebrow. "I'm fixin' to have to take him home, Travis."

"He's had a long day. You can tell from the lines around his mouth. Just to let you in on his secret tell." Travis patted Lex's hand. The one not stuffing honeyed bread into his mouth, anyway.

"Good to know. Are you ready, Officer? It's time to go home, shower, and nap."

"I think that sounds amazing." He put his hand over Trav's a moment. "You good?"

"I am. I've got the bill too, as long as I can get the rest of the dessert basket to go."

"Are you sure, man?" he asked, pleased down to the bone. "That's damn kind of you."

"Don't tell anyone at the jail, okay?"

"I promise." He crossed his heart. Travis stood when they did, so Lex hugged him. "Thanks, man."

"I love you. Be careful with you, huh?"

"I will. I promise." He didn't lie, but he wanted to. He wanted to comfort both of them, but the simple fact was he was a cop. That wasn't going to change.

He'd grown up knowing that was what he was meant to be. Serve and protect. Hell, he imagined Brant got it, but the thing with Matty was bringing up all manner of stuff in him.

Lord, now he was comparing his lover to what? An unused pool? Damn.

He touched shoulders with Brant on the way to the parking lot. "You okay?"

"I am. Glad we have tomorrow off together."

"Me too." The world seemed to have sped up since they moved in together. They could so use some downtime to just be.

He'd never really understood how complicated meshing a

Monday through Friday, eight-to-five schedule with a four-two where you were called out to ghost the detectives on your twos.

They stopped at his truck, Brant grinning. "See you at home in a few, huh?"

"I would say race you, but you know, cop."

"If you stop me, do you promise to frisk me?"

"I do. Thoroughly." He loved teasing Brant.

"Fair enough. I want to be able to accuse you of drastically inappropriate behavior."

"Well, I can think of a dozen inappropriate things just off the top of my head." Lex reached out to touch that fine, flat belly. "Come on, lover. Home."

"Yes, sir. I'll meet you there. You be careful."

"Ditto." He got into his truck, feeling weirdly like they needed to go together. It wasn't but a few miles.

His gut was going a million miles a minute, and he knew it was the shooting that had set it off. He had a little trauma himself, he guessed. The bombings had just proven bad things piled on each other.

That whole situation had shaken a lot of foundations.

He followed Brant home, drumming his fingers on the wheel. The radio was a constant hum and buzz, and he only listened with half an ear. Instead, he focused on Brant's tail-lights, willing them to get home safe.

Lord, he was acting like they were in the middle of a motherfucking zombie apocalypse. Lex took a deep breath, forcing his shoulders down from around his ears. *Right. Almost there.*

Why the hell were all the lights in the house on? You could see right inside. His heart kicked into high gear, adrenaline flooding him.

Brant parked and got out of the SUV, heading to the front porch.

Lex screeched to a stop behind him, then hopped out.

"Brant, wait! Did you leave all the lights on?" He put his hand on his sidearm.

"Nope. I'm sure it was Steve."

"Steve?" *Who the hell—* "Your neighbor?"

"Yeah. He asked if he could borrow some chicken broth. He was in the midst of making enchilada sauce."

"Chicken…." He still pushed in front of Brant to unlock the door, checking all possible danger areas before proceeding.

"It's fine. He's got issues with the dark. It's no big deal."

"Yeah." Lex moved methodically, ignoring Mouse and not losing focus until he'd checked every room. Then, and only then, did he relax. Secure.

Brant fed the cats and closed the blinds, moving nice and slow, like there wasn't a damn thing wrong.

When he was done checking the house, Lex grabbed a beer out of the fridge, feeling… mad wasn't the right word. More freaked-out.

"It's just Steve. He's a dork."

"That scared the crap out of me, baby. I was all worked up anyway. Work."

"Did something happen at work? Are you okay?"

Lex sighed, not wanting to tell Brant but wanting to be honest. "There was a robbery shooting today. Gas station. The victim is stable at UNM, but it shook me."

He saw Brant pale, but that was the only reaction. "That had to have sucked. Seriously."

"It was harsh. The perpetrator got away. They have more on CCTV than yours, so I imagine we'll get him."

"Good. Good. This is crazy, all the assholes. People are desperate. I think they're also looking for the easy way out."

"Exactly. That's why you have to learn to be more careful, huh? They could see right into the house, no? Someone could case this place in a second." Lex wanted Brant to be cautious with the house.

"I didn't do it, man."

"The blinds were up when you weren't home, though."

Brant blinked at him. "You were still here when I left."

"I—was I?" Shit. He was getting soft. "Okay, well, I'll check when I leave."

"Good deal. We'll be home tomorrow. Together."

"We will." He moved to hug Brant, glad the man wasn't all mad and stiff. "Sorry. Sorry, I wigged out."

"It's hard to turn it off, I bet. Cop brain." Brant came right to him.

"It is." He held on, letting Brant's warmth soothe him. Brant touched him, petting him in long, slow strokes, and for a second he thought about accusing Brant of treating him like Mouse, but then the thought tickled him, making him laugh right out loud.

"What are you laughing about, butthead?" Brant asked, pinching his butt.

"How I'm like one of the cats."

"I feed you better." Brant shook his head. "And I never threaten to skin you."

"True. I would make a shit rug." He kissed Brant's neck. "Speaking of cats. I'll give out treats."

"Kiss me first."

"You got it." Kissing Brant never got old. Lex had a feeling it never would.

When he stepped back, Brant blinked, swayed a little. "Damn, honey."

"Cats. Treats. Then we'll go to bed and, uh, I can frisk you." Was it silly to keep that joke going?

"If I'm really, really bad, can we do a cavity check?"

Oh. Oh, good one.

"I think it might be mandatory. Just for my safety." They moved apart, one to deal with the cats, the other to turn off lights and fill water bowls.

"You looking forward to tomorrow?" Brant grabbed two bottles of water.

"I am." He wasn't sure they were even going to do anything. Maybe work in the yard.

Maybe they could go shop for a hot tub. He liked the inflatables. Easy to move, and they could get a two-man one, which would save on water.

"Good deal, honey. Me too."

"Come to bed with me, baby." He grabbed Brant's hand, ready to go get sexy.

If he tried real hard, he could wear them both out until damned near lunchtime.

24

"So how's the live-in situation?"

That was a question tons of people seemed to ask Brant over the last few weeks. Coworkers. Dr. N.... Bridey.

Now Travis.

His answer was always the same.

"I don't know."

"Uh-oh. Not exactly glowing praise, my friend."

He sighed and shrugged, although how was Travis going to see it over the phone? "He's just really busy."

As in every day off, Lex was called in to trail Detective Blah or learn from Detective Boring. It was a little like living alone, but with more food in the fridge and more security system shit.

Mouse saw Lex more than he did, and he was getting damn grumpy about it.

"He should take the test soon," Travis said gently.

"I know. I'm not bitching." He was... well, he hadn't known he was lonely until he'd not been for a few weeks.

"Bitch away. It used to drive me crazy when Matt's schedule didn't match with mine. He had this one assignment where he worked with some bank in Japan. He was up all night."

"I remember that. God, I thought you'd both lose your minds." But that was one assignment. Not forever.

"You have to tell him, sweetie. Do you want to go to coffee? Or cake or something? We could go to the Flying Star."

"Oh… I don't know. I've had a few beers. I'm just going to stay here and watch the TV."

"I can come get you."

Oh, that was a temptation. "I could so go for a big piece of cake."

Travis laughed, sounding delighted. "I'm on my way."

"I'll get dressed."

"Dude. It's six thirty. At night. You're not dressed?"

"Shut up. The cats wanted to snuggle, and I—" He was pouting. He knew it.

"Oh Jesus Christ. I lost my husband and I was less of a little bitch." Travis cackled.

"Fuck you. Come get me." He hung up, heading to the bedroom to get dressed. Good thing he hadn't taken a pill too.

His phone rang, and he grabbed it. "You can't be here already, man."

"Who?" Lex sounded utterly confused.

"Oh, sorry. Travis is coming to get me for cake. Is everything okay?"

"Yeah. Yeah, I was just calling. I'm on my break."

Brant put the phone on speaker so he could get dressed. "Having a good evening?"

Lex chuckled. "Yeah. Having a taco, so I thought I'd call."

"Cool. Beef or chicken?" He wasn't even sure if Lex was scheduled today or on call.

"Beef." Lex sighed. "Damn it. No tacos for me. Love you, baby." The line clicked off.

"Yeah. Bye, Lex." *Jesus.*

Mouse jumped on the bed, one of Lex's socks in his mouth.

"Seriously?" He grabbed it, narrowly avoiding getting bit. "One, you are not a dog. Two, you are mine. Remember who feeds you."

Mouse meowed plaintively.

"He's busy. He's saving the world and shit." He yanked on his shirt. "I wish Matty was here, kit. I'd ask him if he thought I was too boring to be with a police officer."

Mouse rolled to his back, batting the reacquired sock with both front feet.

"Yeah, yeah, is that your entire opinion?" He grabbed his boots and pulled them on. "Matty would tell me to suck it up, and I wouldn't know if that meant dump him or deal."

Mouse purred, coming to rub on him as if asking him to stay home.

"Spoiled beast. I'll be home later. In theory, Lex will too. Maybe." He petted that furry belly, then headed back to the front room, ready to make sure all the blinds were closed.

The temptation to leave them open was huge. Stupid, but huge. He didn't really want to freak Lex out, maybe annoy him a tiny bit. Maybe enough to fight him a little, remind him that they had fire. They did, didn't they?

It wasn't only because they'd lost Matty and he didn't want to be alone and Lex had needed a place to stay, right?

No. No, Lex was calling him on his truncated lunch break. Just because. Roommates didn't do that.

He was being ridiculous, and he had a couple of beers in him. He needed to put his head on right. Needy bitch was not a character trait he evinced well.

Brant saw Travis pull in, so he locked up and headed out, thinking carrot cake in a big way. He texted Lex, just a *Trav is here. I locked up and closed the blinds.*

It wasn't a huge declaration of undying love, but it wouldn't start shit, so it would work.

25

*L*ex knocked on his parents' door, feeling so frickin' weird he didn't know what to do. Mama had asked him to come for lunch, and he really had no way of saying no, even if he'd really wanted to spend the whole day with Brant. He had a lot of making up to do for missing his days off with his lover.

Christ, he was tired.

"*Mijo*! Why'd you knock?" She grabbed him and hugged him tight, the smell of spice and sugar so familiar he wanted to cry. "Come in. Come in. Did you bring your friend? I made tortillas and beans."

"Brant is at work, Mama. He wants to take you out for supper one night next week." He found himself smiling, the curtains more faded but the same, the sound of a Chihuahua barking in the back room a constant in his young life. "What puppy do you have now?"

"His name is Cucuy. He still tries to run out the front door, so I put him away when someone is coming."

"Papa needs to put the screen door back on."

"Ai. He says he's going to Lowe's to get a fancy one. A storm door." She rolled her eyes. "You know him, huh?"

"I do. He's working?"

She nodded. "At the garage. I think he plays dominoes all day and pretends he's fixing cars. You look tired. How's the new job? Come and eat."

Mama's answer to everything—come and eat.

Of course, he lived for her tortillas and refritos.

"I am tired. I'm pulling doubles, really. They have me on a regular shift, then training for detective. Leo really wants me to push up." He was grateful for that, but man, he hadn't expected to be putting in so many hours so soon after moving.

"Oh, that's nice, no? You been wanting that for a long time. I'll light a candle on Wednesday. I made a quilt for you, for your new house." She fixed him up a bowl of beans and handed him a pile of hot tortillas. Add butter and salsa and he was in heaven.

"Did you? What's on it?" He loved her soft but usable quilts. His one from when he was a kid was still here on the twin bed he'd slept in.

"You sent a picture of the living room, so I used the colors from that. It's stars and cowboy boots." She blushed and fluttered a little. "You want to see it?"

"Of course I do, Mama." Why had he put this off so long? He grabbed her to hug her when she moved past him. "I missed you."

"I miss you. So glad you're closer." She kissed the top of his head, smoothing his cowlick. "Eat, *mijo*. It's good for you."

"Gracias, Mama." Lex put salsa and cheese in his beans, then buttered a tortilla.

Oh God. Brant cooked like a dream, but there was nothing like his mama's beans. They tasted like... hope, faith, and love all mixed together.

And lard. The key was lard.

Mama came out with a Southwesty quilt—the fabrics were Kokopellis and Zia suns and chiles. Cowboy boots were interspersed with stars, and he surprised himself by getting a little misty.

"Mama. It's beautiful."

"You like it?" She reminded him of when he was younger and Papa would bring her a new dress—nervous and pleased and eager.

"I do. It's gorgeous." Brant was going to plotz. It was so damn cool. "Brant will love it. Hold it up. I'll text him a picture."

She beamed at him, and Lex knew he'd said exactly the right thing. Lord, she needed to know he cared, and he felt like a real asshole for not coming to see her.

It wasn't even that she was going to be ugly about Brant. For fuck's sake, she'd known he was gay for years, but living with someone, that was different.

Lex thought it was a matter of degree. Once he hadn't seen her for a certain amount of time, it was just too hard.

"Do you need anything else for a housewarming? Kitchen stuff?"

"Uh, I can't think of anything, Mama. I want to get Brant something, though. He likes to cook outside…."

"Yeah? Like a smoker?"

"He has a big gas grill. I've seen him smoke with a hotel pan and some woodchips…."

She nodded to him, but she wasn't listening. Grilling was Papa's job—chicken, steaks, brisket, carne asada, green chiles. The carnitas were Mama's job.

"Anyway, a smoker is a good idea." He rolled beans into another tortilla.

"Good deal. See? I'm not worthless, am I?"

"Of course not, Mama!" He was shocked to hear her say it.

She winked at him. "Maybe a little bit, hmm?"

"You make tortillas. You'll never be worthless. So, what all is everyone up to? Tell me everything."

Mama came to sit, taking a tortilla for herself. "Oh, everything is the same—Aunt Flora is on the hunt for another man, and Uncle Teddy is back on the wagon."

"How's mis hermanas?" His siblings only talked to him when they needed advice from the cop brother.

"Angela is trying to have a baby. Francesca is working too hard, still. Chicago. Can you believe it? Our little Franny in a big city?"

"She's liking it, huh?" He would have to call her, make sure she was eating.

"She's busy. She called the other day for my tamale recipe. She's cooking for friends."

"Good for her." He'd always known Franny would go far from New Mexico while the rest of them stayed. She had wandering eyes and a knack for PR. She made them proud.

Of course Angela was a nurse at Pres, was married to a radiologist, and was stupidly happy.

He reached for his mom's hand. "I love you."

"I love you, *mijo*. Why don't you come take a nap? Just half an hour, hmm? You can have your old bed, or even just here on the couch."

"Oh, Mama, I can't. I want to be home when Brant gets there. I owe him some of my time off." He grinned at her. "I would love to take some food to him."

"Are you sure? I would wake you up. And of course, you can have all the food you want. I'll make another batch of tortillas while you nap."

"Okay, okay." Brant wouldn't be home for ages. He could have a tiny nap. Without Mouse yowling at him.

"Good boy. Go lay down. I'll wake you. I swear."

"Thank you, Mama. I need to be out of here by three." It gave her such pleasure to do for people.

"I will do it. You sleep." She patted his shoulder. "Go on. Turn the TV on for noise if you need."

He was so tired he did just that. He set the alarm on his phone for two forty-five, putting it right next to the bed. Then he curled up under his quilt and fell asleep as soon as his head hit the pillow.

$\mathcal{B}$rant wasn't sure how to celebrate Matty's birthday. Travis was on his cruise, and there wasn't a cemetery to visit. Lex was at work. It felt weird to ask the people at work, and….

So he went to Rudy's off Carlisle, grabbed brisket and sausage and some of those good potatoes. Then he took it home and sat out in the backyard and made himself a sandwich with the white bread and pickles and onions they put in the sack.

"You remember how we'd buy these potatoes—three quarts of them between us—and we'd eat on them for a couple days. You hated the coleslaw, but the banana pudding? Damn."

No one answered but Mouse, who made a plaintive noise. He did love brisket.

"I know, I know." He fed Mouse a bite. "You'd tell me it wasn't as good as your momma's, and I would tell you it was as close as we could get here."

The girls jumped up on the bench, one on either side of him. They loved their little leashes, especially when they could access his food.

Mouse, on the other hand, knew he was being contained and hated it.

God, Matty thought there was precious little funnier than a big tall Texan taking his cats out to the backyard on leashes. Brant had a fine sense for the absurd too. He agreed.

"Christ, y'all. I'm sitting out in the backyard, feeding my leashed cats and talking to my dead best friend here. I'm losing my mind."

"I hope not."

Brant jumped about a mile, sure for a moment Matty had started talking back to him.

He spun around, his heart slamming against his rib cage. "Oh fuck. Lex. Damn, you startled the hell out of me."

"You left the door unlocked."

"Did I? My hands were full. You're home early." He didn't need to be started with.

"Interview ended early. Suspect started crying and confessing after ten minutes." Lex's grin was… cautious.

"Stud. There's enough for you. Have a seat." He could celebrate Matty with Lex, no problem.

"Thanks, baby. Mmm. Brisket." Lex plopped down, reaching out for Mouse, who went right to him, grumping away. "Why were you talking to Matt?"

"It's his birthday."

"Oh, right. You said it was coming up." Lex made a sympathy face. "I'm sorry, Brant."

What was he supposed to say? No big deal? It's okay? It wasn't okay. It was a big deal. He missed Matt. "Thank you."

"What can I do?" Lex grabbed a piece of bread and loaded it with brisket.

"It's good to see you." And in the daylight, no less. He was loving these longer days of summer.

"Yeah?" Lex beamed, shoulders relaxing as if he'd been unsure of his welcome. "I hear you. I feel so out of touch."

"You've been busy, huh? Working." *Staying in danger.*

"I've been pushing, yeah." Lex shrugged, then munched his sandwich. "I really want to take that test, and there are two openings coming up in the next month."

"I'll keep my fingers crossed for you." It would be easier than worrying about Lex getting shot every day, right? Detectives did a lot after the fact of the crime. Not as much danger. He'd been reading on the internet.

"Cool. Are we okay, baby?"

"Huh?" He caught himself picking at his sandwich, trapped in his own thoughts.

"You're super... formal." Lex was watching him. Like a cop.

"I'm just thinking. No big deal." He sighed, trying to find a smile. "Seriously."

"About Matt?" Lex sopped up some of the sauce on Brant's plate, an intimate action so at odds with the conversation that he wanted to laugh.

"About Matty. About you." He didn't know how to do this, and he didn't know who to ask. He hadn't been given a "how to be a gay cop's live-in" manual.

"Are you—I'm not getting kicked out, am I?" Lex was starting to look panicky, and Mouse jumped down from his lap.

"What? What are you talking about?"

"I just know I've been a disappointing lover lately. You look so serious." Lex hunched his shoulders some.

"Look so... I'm celebrating my dead best friend's birthday. Serious is the tone for that sort of thing."

"Oh. Right." Lex started to grin, then sobered. "Sorry. Sorry, I wasn't trying to make it about me. I just worry."

"Me too. All the damn time." It was becoming a hobby.

"About me?" Now Lex was leaning on the table, chin on his hands.

"Well, sure. Cops get shot here." And there wasn't anything he could do about it.

"They do. Nurses are more than fifty percent as likely to get assaulted on the job than other workers."

"I get bit a lot." He felt a little bit numb, like he didn't know what he was supposed to do next.

"Ow." Lex reached out for him. "I wish I knew what to say."

"I do too." He took Lex's hand for a second, squeezing, and then he let go. "You want some potatoes?"

"I think I need a plate. Be right back." Lex stood up, and his phone rang.

Christ, he hated that thing.

Matty, how am I going to do this?

Lex pulled out the phone. "Hello? Hey, man. No. Not tonight. Yeah, I get it, but I'm burned as hell. Oh, good. Thanks. Yeah." Lex hung up, then smiled. "Be right back."

"'Kay." Brant closed his eyes, trying desperately to figure out what the hell to do. Who was that on the phone?

Lex was back in a heartbeat, plate in hand. "You okay, baby? That was Leo at work. Wanted to know if I wanted to go on an arrest of another suspect from the confession today, but I told him I was beat."

"Well, you can eat and then rest? I know you've been working your ass off." And he was just working. Maybe he was boring. God, he needed to find something to do.

"That sounds like the best thing ever, baby. It really does." Lex loaded up that plate.

"Good deal." Maybe he'd go out after Lex went to sleep. Go to a bar or a movie.

"You're thinking hard. I'm not really that tired, huh? I just didn't want to go back in tonight." Lex made another sandwich.

He leaned over, kissed Lex on the cheek. "Maybe we can watch an episode of something we're saving on the DVR, then."

What he needed to do was quit talking to Matty all the

time and occupy himself. He knew how to do that. He was good friends with the people at the Denny's, for late-night coffee and eggs. He liked movies. He liked bookstores.

God knew he'd spent six nights a week on his own before, right? He just had to stop expecting Lex to occupy him. Lex had his job.

Brant would go back to living his own life.

"Sure." The way Lex beamed made him feel a little guilty. He wasn't sure why.

He fed Mouse another bite of brisket. "Good deal, honey. Sounds like a plan."

27

*L*ex whistled the last mile back to the house. He was feeling pretty good. A bag of Jack in the Box sat in the passenger seat, and his detective exam was scheduled for two weeks' time.

He couldn't wait to tell Brant.

He'd been really worried about his lover, but over the last few weeks, something in Brant seemed to ease. They didn't see each other much, but the lunchtime phone calls were cheerier and the antianxiety meds seemed to be at the same level.

One day they might actually be able to grill out or something. Maybe go to Abiquiú and swim.

Oh, that would be cool. Go to the lake…. Brant had said something a few weeks ago about how now it was hot he wished they could go tubing like in Texas….

Lex frowned. Brant's SUV wasn't in the driveway.

Weird. Brant hadn't said shit about being late.

He grabbed the bag of food, heading for the front door while he pulled out his phone with the other hand. He called Brant, hoping everything was okay.

The phone went to voicemail, so he went inside, turning on lights and checking on the cats.

They all came running, tails up, meowing for all they were worth.

"Hey, guys. Where's your dad?" He stroked backs for a moment, keeping an eye on the Jack in the Box, because Mouse was magical.

Mouse yowled and stretched, huge claws appearing and disappearing.

"I know. I didn't hide him." He tried calling Brant again, worried now.

It was well after dark, and Brant had to be at work Friday. Why wasn't he home?

The phone rang three times before Brant picked up. "Hey, honey."

"Hey. You okay?" Brant sounded fine, which was... good. Right?

"Yeah. I went to the movies. How's your night going?"

"Uh. Good? I'm feeding the cats right now." What did he say to that? Brant had every right to go to the movies, so why did it make him feel weird? "Did you go with Travis?"

"No. I saw the preview for this a couple of days ago and thought it looked fun."

"Cool. Well, I'm off for the night if you're heading home." He felt... really odd.

"Yeah? I'll be home in a few, then."

He heard someone say, "You coming with us tomorrow for the special showing of *Creepshow*, B.?"

"We'll see. Probably. See y'all."

How often was Brant going to the movies? Why didn't he know about it? Lex pondered that. "Cool. I got Jack in the Box. I'll put it in the mic."

"Good deal. See you soon, honey."

"Cool." He hung up, then immediately called Travis.

"What's wrong?" This was not the response he was used to getting.

"What? Nothing, hon. I mean, nothing dangerous or bad." He wasn't one hundred percent sure nothing was wrong.

"Oh. Oh, good. I'm just not used to you calling after nine. What's up? Are you ready to take your exam? I totally want to have you both over for supper to celebrate when you pass."

"Is it after nine?" He'd thought it was like eight forty-five. "I am. Two weeks."

"Just barely. You nervous?"

"Well, I wasn't…. Trav, I came home and Brant is at the movies. Is that… is that normal? I mean, for couples?"

"Did he know you were coming home?"

"No. No, I got off a little early because I pulled too much OT last week."

"Well, then… I mean, he's not supposed to just sit at home for his whole life, right? He used to go do something with Matt once a week, and he spent a lot of time at Denny's or the movies or the bookstore. If you two were supposed to have dinner together and he blew you off? Then that's weird and a little mean."

"No, I mean, I just didn't expect it since he has to work tomorrow." Now he felt totally unreasonable.

"Yeah, it's weird to come home alone, huh?"

"It is. I've never done this before." Everyone had always teased him about being a player, but he really had never been half of a full-time couple. He had no idea what to do.

"Neither has Brantley. I know he's missing Matt. He's not a guy with a ton of friends. He tends to make one at a time."

"Oh." Right. How many times had he caught Brant talking to Matt? "What do I do?"

"Honey, he's going to have to get used to being with a police officer. You're always on call; you're always busy. If spending his evenings and weekends at the movies is how he copes…. It's better than picking fights, I guess?"

"Of course." He just didn't want Brant to get so bored that he left. Well, asked Lex to leave.

"I'm proud of him, you know?"

"You are?" He felt like a fish out of water, gasping and flopping around.

"Sure. His best friend was shot and killed, and he turned around and hooked up with a police officer in Albuquerque just weeks later. He's running on faith, huh?" He could hear Travis's smile.

"He is." That kinda brought an answering smile to his lips. "I guess he's probably just as freaked as me."

"I think he's lonely, Lex. When you get time, love on him."

"I will. I swear." He would start tonight.

"Feel better?"

He opened his mouth to answer, but then Brant beeped in. "I have to go, man. Brant's calling." He hit the button without waiting for Trav to respond. "Hey, baby. What's up?"

"I ran out of gas."

"You what?" Lex didn't even know where Brant was.

"I don't like to stop at night. I was going in the morning."

"Shit, baby. Where are you? Stay with the car, and I'll come get you and get some gas." How could Brant run out of gas?

"I'm at the Smith's on Fourth. I got this. I can see the gas pumps. I just didn't want you to worry."

"Wait, you're walking?" Lex grabbed his keys and headed out, making sure no kitties tried to slip out. "Baby, you need to stay in the damn car."

He didn't want Brant out there, an Anglo with a limp carrying a gas can? Jesus, that was a mug-me-now scenario.

And someone was happy to shoot guys at the pump at fucking Smith's too.

God damn it.

He hopped in his truck, wishing he had a cruiser. Sirens would be nice right now. "Keep talking to me, Brant."

"I'm fine. I'm going to run into the Smith's and buy a gas can." Brant sighed. "I can't fucking believe this."

The Smith's store and the gas pumps were separate on Fourth, so that meant more walking. "I have one in my truck. Just stay in the store, okay?"

Please, just do what I'm asking.

"You don't have to come out. You just got home. Just a sec." Brant's voice went a little fuzzy. "Gas cans? Thanks, man."

Stubborn butthead. "I'm in the truck, baby. I'll be there in, like, ten." He was hanging on by a thread and not yelling.

"Love you."

Well, thank God for that. "I love you too, Brant. Just hang on and I'll be right there."

He hung up and gunned it toward Fourth Street. They were going to have a come-to-Jesus meeting about taking care of things, most specifically taking care of Brant.

Brant headed for the gas pumps, cussing himself like the idiot he was. He knew better than to run the car low, but he was so close to the house, and he had a gas can in the garage with five gallons in it.

The street wasn't deserted, but it was damn dark, and he knew he made a vision with his new spare gas can from the Smith's. Probably an attractive one, as far as the more criminal element went. To people's credit, at least two people had rolled down their windows and asked if he needed help. There just wasn't a lot of traffic this time of night, though, and Lex was on his way.

He made it to the lights around the pumps, and he had to stop, because for a second, he couldn't breathe.

Fuck.

Fuck.

This wasn't the station where the shooting had happened, but they all looked the same, didn't they? They all had the little center place where you could buy cigarettes during regular business hours and the trash cans with their little indentations for the squeegee deals.

There'd been brains on the hose. Matt's brains scattered like little meat nuggets. The ravens would eat them, if they hadn't all gone to Santa Fe for the summer.

Brant gagged, the smell of gas and copper blood so strong he swayed, closing his eyes for a moment.

A hand landed on his arm, and he jerked away, ready to beat the ever-loving fuck out of someone. "Back off!"

"Hey! Hey, it's just me." Lex stood less than a foot away. Jesus, what if he'd been someone else?

"Sorry. Sorry, I was—" What? Losing his fucking mind? Because that was sure what it felt like. "I got a gas can."

"I see that." Lex looked grim. "You should have just stayed at the store, baby. It's not safe out here."

"I'm a grown-up. I got this." Except he really hadn't. He couldn't stop looking around, eyes searching for a dark shadow, the muzzle of a gun, the flash when the trigger was pulled. God. God, he wanted to go home.

"Even grown-ups need help," Lex snapped. "Give me the gas can. I'll fill it and mine so you can wait to get a full tank until tomorrow."

"Look, I'm sorry, man. I thought the car would make it." He didn't need to be snapped at.

"I know." Lex took a deep breath. "I was worried. I went to the Smith's and you were gone."

I'm surprised you even noticed. The thought was ugly and mean and beneath him, so he didn't let it out, although the frustration and anger that drove it didn't leave. "I was trying to save us time."

"Well, you scared the shit out of me." Lex turned to the pump. "I mean, I'm a cop. I can think of a thousand ways this could go wrong." The set of those wide shoulders was super stiff.

"No shit." Brant didn't think he'd ever get gas again without his heart racing.

"What?" Lex glared at him over one shoulder. "Then why didn't you stay with the car? *Mierda*."

"Because I'm a grown fucking man. Because I can't live my entire life hiding in the house with my cats!" And God knew it was a temptation.

"I never said you should! But this is what couples do, damn it! They depend on each other."

Good thing it was late and no one was around. They'd be drawing stares, as his momma would say.

"I—" How was he supposed to? How the hell was he supposed to depend on this? "I didn't even know you were going to be home."

"No, I get that." Lex cut the air with his free hand. "I just mean—after we talked. It wouldn't have taken any longer for me to find you than not to at the store."

The temptation to just scream was vast. "Fine."

Jesus, he just wanted to go home and go to bed.

"I'm going to get you Triple A, for fuck's sake. You need to take care of yourself."

"Oh, fuck off. I do just fine. I managed just fine for a long time, man."

"Obviously not. Look what happened to Matt."

Brant stared at Lex, a jolt of pure pain slamming through him. They hadn't been reckless. They hadn't been stupid. They had stopped at a well-lit station for gas after a movie. "Fuck you and the horse you rode in on."

He took the full gas can and headed back to his car, leaving Lex to deal with the other can and paying. He was a cop; he could handle it.

"Brant!" He heard Lex cussing up a storm. "Will you wait?"

"No, motherfucker, I don't think I can," he muttered. Then out loud he yelled, "I'm sorry I caused you trouble, Officer. I didn't mean to be there during a shooting!"

"Oh, Jesus Christ! I'm sorry. That was a stupid thing to say!" Lex was slamming the nozzle back into the pump.

"It was." He just went to the car and popped the door to the gas cap. He was burning, he was so mad. Burning.

Lex caught up with him a few minutes later, handing over the other gas can without a word.

He took it, emptied it, and handed it back. Then he stowed the new can and got in the car.

Please start. Please start.

She turned over like a dream, gas gauge showing almost half a tank. *Okay. Okay. Right.* He rolled down the window. "I'll meet you at home."

Lex stared at him for a moment, then nodded. "Okay."

He took a deep breath before meeting Lex's eyes. "I love you."

Just in case. If something happened on the way home, he wanted Lex to know.

"Love you too." Lex nodded again before heading to his truck.

God, his head was the size of a friggin' watermelon.

Home. Shower. Bed.

LEX GOT HOME FIRST. Okay, so maybe he floored it, singing very loud to Evanescence. He let himself in, pushing Mouse out of the way with his foot.

"He'll be right here. Stop being a butthead."

He saw the lights from Brant's car in the front room

windows seconds later, so he turned right back around, going to meet Brant at the door. "Hey, baby."

"Hey, you." Brant tried to smile for him, then gave up. "I didn't expect to see you tonight."

"I know. I pulled too much OT last week, so they sent me home. Half shift tomorrow too." He grabbed Brant and hugged him tight, the worry lingering more than the snarl.

"Yeah? You won't know what to do with yourself."

"I know!" Lex took a kiss, pleased as fuck when Brant didn't pull away. "So, what did you see?"

"Huh?"

"At the movies."

Brant shrugged both shoulders. "One of those found-footage horror movies. It was marginal, but I had a few laughs."

"Cool. Look, I didn't mean…."

"I don't want to talk about it, man." Brant turned away and shook his head.

"We'll have to talk about it at some point." Lex rolled his shoulders. "I'm sorry. I shouldn't have said that about Matt."

"You should be. We weren't doing anything stupid. We weren't doing anything wrong. We were getting gas. Some asshole with a gun and an itchy trigger finger is the one that was in the wrong." Brant glared at him, those blue eyes furious. "Don't you dare blame me for this, for being 'unsafe.' It wasn't my fault."

"I know it wasn't." He spread his hands. "It scared me. I just—I know you're not made of glass, but I want you to be safe." He wasn't sure how else to put it.

"I'm fucking trying to not be scared!" Brant stared at him, pinning him to the wall. "I'm trying not to panic every time you don't fucking come home. I'm trying not to be scared to go outside at night. I'm trying not to have a panic attack when I get gas or when I hear a car backfire or when something random happens that I shouldn't even be worried about."

Lex's heart squeezed in his chest. God, he got that. He so got it. How did he get Brant to understand that? "I—I worry every time you go to work, because nurse. I mean, I don't think someone will bomb you, but who the fuck knows?"

"Nobody."

And that was it, wasn't it? No one could have expected Matt to die that night. No one could have known the bomber was going to hit the hospital. No one had any control over what other people did, only their own actions. "Right. So can we try not to be scared together a little more?"

Brant blinked at him, a soft chuckle escaping. "I—yeah. Yeah, I think we could try that."

"Good. Okay. You mind if I eat? I got you a sourdough thingy and fries too. I didn't know that you would be—" No. He wasn't going to rag Brant about not being home. Brant had a right to go to the damn movies. They just needed to talk more. Be not scared together.

Brant ignored the last part of his sentence. "Oh yeah? You know I love those. Thank you."

Boom. "You're welcome. Go sit and I'll be there in a few. What do you want to drink?" The cats were losing it, so Brant needed to go make nice with them before they destroyed the sofa.

"Just a Coke, thanks." Brant started talking to the cats, and they all started talking back like they understood.

He chuckled, heating up food, pouring the drinks while the microwave ran. Lex was super glad Brant seemed pleased with the food. Hell, maybe it was because he'd remembered. Who knew?

"Did you have a good day? I mean, before me," Brant called from the sofa.

"Stop it. It was good. I got my test scheduled." He held his breath. Would Brant be tickled?

"Yeah? Congratulations! Are you excited?"

"I am." His palms got sweaty when he thought about it. Still, it was time. While he knew the hours would still be full of suck, Albuquerque was actually a fairly large force. They had a rotation that was far better than Las Cruces's.

"Good deal, honey. We should put it on the calendar."

There was a calendar? "We have a calendar?" He tried for light, because this was gold. This was what he needed to know and do.

"Well, I have a calendar, so now, I guess you do too. I tried to keep track of your schedule, but damn."

"I know." He shook his head, setting food and drink down in front of Brant. "You show me what I need to do, though, and I'll try to keep it on the rails."

"Thank you." Brant smiled for him, then tucked in, letting Mouse steal a fry.

Lex fed one to each of the girls too, and they seemed ready to forgive him for hiding their dad.

Brant was quiet, and Lex found that he missed the way they had chatted about silly things. They hadn't been together that long that they didn't have anything more to say than "how was your day," right? He wanted to say something weird and shocking, just to break whatever awkward spell the relationship fairy had put on them.

"You okay?" Brant asked. "I mean, I know you're stressing your test, and I didn't help."

"I am. I mean, I know what I need to know, but it's pressure." He propped his head on his hand. "I'm a little lost here, though. I feel like, I dunno, I had no idea you were at the movies or what you had for lunch." That came out all wrong, and Lex shook his head. "No. That sounds like you did something wrong. I mean, I miss talking to you."

"Yeah. I hear you." Brant sighed softly. "You have a good family with the force, and a good partner."

"I do. I also have a lover." He reached out to touch Brant's hand. "Travis said you're missing Matt so much. I didn't real-ize, baby. I mean, I knew, but I forget your people aren't here."

"Yeah. I probably would have just stayed in Texas, but Land of Entrapment." Brant leaned back into the couch cush-ions. "Matty was a good guy."

"Tell me more about him?" Maybe Brant would talk to him about Matt instead of talking to Matt. Besides, he wanted to know what kind of man was Brant's best friend and Trav's husband.

"What?"

"Matt, baby. I never got to really know him. Tell me about him."

"Oh, man. I've known him since we were in kindergarten. I have a thousand stories."

"Then tell me your favorite." He would love that. And maybe he would tell Brant one about Franny, who he missed so bad and who still hadn't sent more than a text from Chicago....

"When I was in the hospital in Germany, he flew out with Bridey. He showed up wearing a gorilla suit. An honest-to-God gorilla suit. Nobody's really sure why. Nobody knows where he got the costume, but he sure made me laugh when nothing else could."

"That's awesome." It was too. And he sat there for an hour listening to Brant talk about Matt, which meant Lex couldn't stop smiling.

Brant leaned into him, resting hard. "I wish you could have known him better. He would have loved hearing all your stories."

"I would have liked him a lot, I can tell." God, Brant had a lifetime of stuff to talk about. He couldn't imagine losing a friend like that.

"Yeah. Yeah, I think so." Brant inhaled, then let it all out. "I bet you're tired, huh?"

"I'm okay, but you have to get up." He stood to take the trash to the lidded can, then came back to hold out a hand to Brant. "Want to take a shower with me before we head to bed?" He wanted to touch. Just gentle and sweet, nothing super sexy times.

"I do." Brant took his hand, twining their fingers together.

"Bueno." He squeezed, drawing Brant back to the master. He could do this. He could remember to take the time to talk.

"I miss you." The words were soft, and it would be easy to ignore them, miss them in the rush of the bathroom door opening.

No way, though. No way was he going to just let it go ever again. "I hear you, baby. I promise to listen, because I miss you too."

"I'm trying to get it. I'll figure this out, I swear."

He got the water going, watching Brant when he stripped down, those scars reminding him of all Brant had been through. "I believe you, Brant. I understand."

Lex got that they'd hooked up in a time of stress, that they both had shit to deal with, that his job was never—never—going to be easy.

He got that.

He always got that, even as hurt and mad as Brant had been, Brant's last words before he rolled the window up were "I love you."

That was the most important part. They would learn this other stuff one loving, one meal, one fight at a time.

"Come on, Officer. The cats are watching."

28

"*M*an, what a feast!" Brant stared at the array of Chinese takeout boxes lined up on Travis's fancy granite countertop. "Did you invite a lot of people?"

"No. Just us. I didn't know what you two wanted." Travis chewed his lower lip, looking nervy. "Matt always ordered."

"It looks amazing." Lex grabbed a plate and a fork and started dishing up. "I'm starving."

"He's been stress jogging," Brant explained, barely holding back his grin.

"Yeah, yeah. I can think of better stress-relieving exercises." Travis rolled his eyes and grabbed an egg roll. "Seriously, you two. You're supposed to be tearing each other up for at least another year."

"We've been doing that too." Lex gave them both an arch look. "I passed, didn't I?"

"You did. And you have two whole days off." Brant resisted the urge to go over and beg a kiss. "Mouse will be so pleased."

Oh, now. He got this sloe-eyed, heated glance from Lex. "Only Mouse?"

"Ew!" Travis waved his egg roll in the air. "No prenookie lookie in my kitchen."

"Does that mean no kissing too?"

"God yes!" Travis gagged dramatically.

Lex was going to hurt something laughing, and when Brant added, "What if we take it easy on the tongue?" it was all over for all of them.

Travis just howled, slapping his leg with his empty hand. "Oh, I can't breathe."

"No CPR. That could be misconstrued as tongue action." Brant was going to die a la the bad guys in the Roger Rabbit movie.

Lex hooted like a giant owl. "But I just got recertified!" He made kissy faces at Travis.

"Don't you even bring that nasty mouth over here." Travis grabbed a spoon and wielded it like a sword. "Eat your kung pao and leave me be."

"Well, better mouth-to-mouth before rather than after." Lex beamed at them both. "Thanks, guys. I needed to celebrate."

"You're welcome, Detective." Travis grinned back.

Brant clinked their beer bottles together. "You did it, honey."

"I had incentive." Lex winked, and Brant had to admit that Lex was working hard to be home more, to be there for him.

"So, Detective Espana, tell me, are you going to have to start driving a black Ford POS now?"

Brant ignored Travis's teasing and grabbed himself a plate. Mmm… moo goo gai pan. His favorite.

"Ha-ha. But yeah." Lex's expression was actually a little chagrined. "No sleek SUV for me since I'm the new guy." Lex put some fried rice on Brant's plate too.

"Thanks. It'll happen, honey."

"It will." Lex was happy. Like for real.

"You two are just silly with it." Travis grinned at them, the look bittersweet. "Matt would have loved this."

"I'm sure he knows." Brant reached over to pat Travis's hand.

"Yeah. Yeah, I hope so."

Brant didn't worry about that part. Even if he didn't have to talk to Matty as much as before, he knew his buddy was listening.

He had faith.

"Mmm." Lex licked his fork. "That sesame stuff is good."

"Yeah," he agreed. "You just can't make it taste like that at home."

"I don't try." Travis laughed when they both stared. "Guys. I don't cook. You know that."

"That's why you're so skinny, right?"

"Nah, that's the speed." Travis said it with a completely straight face, then wailed with laughter when Lex gave him an outraged glare. "Oh God, your face. Does that mean Brant has to give up his marijuana card?"

"No. He has a card. He just can't blow the smoke in my face. Besides, he's into the edibles." Lex rolled his eyes. "You're a butthead, Trav." Lex reached out, warm hand on Brant's hip.

"Yeah, but I'm your butthead, so…."

"I suppose we'll keep you."

Brant chuckled, stuffing food in his mouth to keep from teasing. Travis needed someplace to belong right now too.

Just because he had his with Lex didn't mean he got to be an ass. In fact, he just said a little silent prayer of thanks for today.

Lex had made detective, he had good friends, good food, and he and Lex both had the weekend off.

Life was pretty damn fine.

"…you listening, baby?"

Brant blinked over. "Nope. What's up?"

"I was asking if I made you cookies this weekend, would you make me enchiladas? I'm craving."

"I do have the skill. I can be persuaded." He leaned over for a kiss, managing to bring their mouths together for a second before Travis hit him with the spoon.

$\mathcal{I}$nterested in learning more about BA's cowboys? Want free fiction and news? Join my newsletter!

Spurs and Shifters

https://lp.constantcontact.com/su/A9CRUzp/baandjulia

ABOUT THE AUTHOR

Texan to the bone and an unrepentant Daddy's Girl, BA Tortuga spends her days with her basset hounds, getting tattooed, texting her grandbabies, and eating Mexican food. When she's not doing that, she's writing. She spends her days off watching rodeo, knitting and surfing Pinterest in the name of research. BA's personal saviors include her wife, Julia Talbot, her best friends, and coffee. Lots of coffee. Really good coffee.

Having written everything from fist-fighting rednecks to hard-core cowboys to werewolves, BA does her damnedest to tell the stories of her heart, which was raised in Northeast Texas, but has heard the call of the high desert and lives in the Sandias. With books ranging from hard-hitting GLBT romance, to fiery ménages, to the most traditional of love stories, BA refuses to be pigeon-holed by anyone but the voices in her head.

BA loves to talk to her readers and can be found at http://batortuga.com/.

Hey, y'all!

Thank you for giving Ammo and Enchiladas a try. I hope you enjoyed the story, and will consider leaving a review at the eBook retailer website where you made your purchase.

Don't forget to "like" my BA Tortuga page on Facebook to keep up with new releases, author news, special discount codes and sale announcements. And if you're interested in sneak peeks, rodeo pictures, and general fun, please come see the BA's Cowboys on Facebook. We'd love to have all y'all!

Yeehaw!

BA

ALSO AVAILABLE FROM BA

Just Like Cats and Dogs

What the Cat Dragged In

Southern Cats Series

By Design

Tiger by the Tail

The Spirit Quest Series

Crossing the River

Chasing the Moon

Breaking the Ice

The Stormy Weather Series

Rain and Whiskey

Tropical Depression

Hurricane

Two is Never Enough Series

Claiming Their Mate

Needing to Breathe

Wildcatters Series

Oil and Water

Eye of the Dragon

Standalones

Adding to the Collection

Back Forty

Best New Artist

Boots, Chaps, and Cowboy Hats

Boys in the Band

Calling His Bluff

With Julia Talbot

www.ingramcontent.com/pod-product-compliance
Lightning Source LLC
Chambersburg PA
CBHW052038240626
47153CB00006B/2140